The Gilded Shackle

Book 1: Gifted

C.T. Griffith

ISBN: 978-0-692570-40-1

Edited by Elaine Roughton and Sylvia Griffith
Cover Art by Karyn Lewis Bonfiglio
Cover Design by Angelique Mroczka
Typeset by Angelique Mroczka

Printed in the United States of America

For my mom, Sylvia.

Contents

Prologue

The *S.S. Henrietta Lacks* was the sole vessel that bore humanity to their new home system. The Human colonists christened their star *Eos*, meaning "dawn," and their new planet *Ersa*.

Ersa was a stunningly, *improbably* Earth-like planet, with a single moon they called *Theia*. *Ersa* had slightly heavier gravity than Earth, abundant surface water, and a flourishing ecosystem including several unique species of pre-industrial, sentient humanoids. Their new home also held another surprise. The beautiful, rugged planet was located on a convergence—a fault line, or rift—in the framework of the multiverse.

The first wave of rift energy presented as powerful electrical storms, with a secondary effect of spawning strange and improbable events. The baffled colonists had to deal with wildly malfunctioning technology, strange mutations of both native and Terran lifeforms, and a full complement of phenomena that could only be described as supernatural. On top of those difficulties, conflict with the native sentients was an ongoing possibility. Although not technologically advanced, many of the native races had the ability to manipulate and wield these *eldritch* forces, often to disastrous effect.

In these dark times, people prayed to the old gods of Earth for guidance and aid. And, for the first time, they got *answers*. Shortly after the rift phenomenon began, the devout began manifesting "divine" abilities, including precognitive visions and healing powers. And, as if in answer to their prayers, another starship crash-landed on Ersa. Although most of the travelers died in the crash, the survivors found Ersa to be too harsh an environment for permanent survival as well. Immortal on their homeworld, the Sidthe knew they were doomed from the moment they first drew breath on Ersa. But in the decades before they died, they befriended the Human settlers and shared freely of all that they were. The Sidthe travelers had naturally-occurring psi abilities that gave them an affinity for working with arcane energies, and with this trait, they helped the Humans understand and harness what could only be called "magic."

In the few short decades they had before extinction, the Sidthe left a profound legacy. Their partnership with the Humans changed the world. Together, they bred Terran animals to be more resilient, altered native Ersan animals to be useful, and changed the planet's ecosystem in subtle ways to make it more habitable for future generations.

As the Sidthe died out, the Aoife took their place. A long-lived race, they stepped naturally into the cooperative role held by their predecessors. Their joint studies, be they magic or technology, were usually successful. Later generations improved upon their work. As time passed, magic dominated. The energy was abundant and easily harnessed by anyone with the will and ability to shape it. For a long golden era, Ersa's population, native and colonial alike, co-existed in a harmony of abundance and balance.

Although this equilibrium lasted for centuries, nothing is forever. Eventually, the ambitions of a few people with power led to political strife over the usual flashpoints—religion, resources, imagined slights, and influence.

The convergence bathed Ersa in ready energy for magic, but there had always been periodic lulls. During one of the more serious energy droughts, the most powerful made wild accusations of hoarding, and in their greed attempted to force the trickle of convergence energy to resume flow. In time, a magic-fueled war of epic proportions nearly swept the world clean. No one remembers exactly what happened because in the aftermath, there were no victors to write history. In the end, the battered survivors picked themselves up and began again. They started counting their years once more, beginning at zero to mark the birth of the new era.

In the fertile lands originally colonized by Humans, a new nation was born. The Empyrean, a joint venture between the remaining Humans and their faithful Aoife advisors, was determined to be a nation of learning, justice, and prosperity. With the Aoife talent for long-term planning, and the raw vigor and ambition of the Humans, they built a strong wall around the borders of their infant nation, and it began to flourish.

The young Human and Aoife society grew and the Empyrean became both wealthy and powerful. But as time passed, the Aoife began to take advantage of their longer lifespans and greater ability to create change. What began as a true and equitable partnership slowly morphed into something else...

Chapter 1: Making the Cut

April 9th, 3131. Spring Equinox, Eaoster

The main hospital ward at the Solmurry Demesne had many windows facing the site of most of the Eaoster Day festivities, but Teine was in no position to enjoy the view. Instead, the Human boy listened to the fabal game playing on the radio, and the cheers and catcalls of the other boys from his cohort while he lay in his hospital bed, eyes tightly closed. Trying hard to postpone the time that he'd be officially "awake" as long as he could, Teine could feel the bag of ice melting on his groin and the slight nausea from what Clinician Nocdoramis had called "general anesthesia." Whatever it was, it had kept him blissfully unaware during the Cut. Although Teine wasn't in any real pain, he was acutely aware that the moment he opened his eyes his life would change forever.

Not that I'm not ready, he told himself. *After all, I'm not a baby.*

It sounded to Teine like most of the other boys were awake and alert. Having met their Cut in alphabetical order meant most of them had been finished for hours. "T" for Teine had always left him toward the end, but he didn't mind—especially today. He hadn't been in any hurry to have his privates carved on, anesthesia or not.

Teine could hear the voices of the other boys in his cohort and in his mind's eye he could picture them clearly. Seymour would be plastered to the window, eagerly watching everything he could see. The others—sixteen in all—either slept, lounged in their beds, or were grouped around the solitary radio listening to the fabal match with breathless enthusiasm. The reception popped, hissed, and then cleared up in time for a batch of commercials.

"I can't believe we're having a storm during the last game of the season!" one of the boys grumbled. "Just our luck."

From the window, Seymour interrupted him, "Hey, everyone, look at this!" There were several groans as boys got up out of bed or off their seats. They sounded like they were all moving slowly towards the bank of windows to get a better view, and Teine could hear the amused chuckles and catcalls as the others saw what Seymour had pointed out. Teine debated getting up to see for himself, but successfully thwarted his own curiosity and lay still to listen to what the others had to say.

"Look! Even the master is going to get some. Look at him close in on those pretty Aoife ladies," Seymour observed. "I'm telling you boys, we could be scoring big out there if we hadn't just gotten Cut!"

"Why couldn't they have done it a month ago? Then we'd be healed up, and ready for *action*!"

"Yeah!"

The general murmurs of assent continued, until the announcements were over and the game was back on.

To quiet the fluttering in his stomach, Teine continued to feign unconsciousness, and turned his attention back to Seymour's whining about the inequities of their situation. "If we'd been out, this weather would have been our best friend," Seymour was ranting. "Almost every one of those prissy masters' wives has a hot Human handmaiden or two. We could have been giving them all a *big* welcome to Solmurry!"

Raucous laughter filled the room, and even with his eyes shut tight, Teine couldn't help but join in. Seymour had always been the cohort clown. Teine could practically see the gesture that must have come along with the "big welcome." Having grown up on one of the most famous Human stud farms, Teine thought he would have gotten over the jokes at their reputation, but he hadn't. They were always funny.

"Hey, Teine's up! I just saw him laughing!" one of the boys yelled.

Teine steeled himself and opened his eyes. Before he greeted any of the others, or even moved to a more comfortable position, he looked at the back of his left hand. It was clean, unblemished. No tattoo. *So, circumcision only,* he thought. Between the ice pack and the numbing agent, he was profoundly grateful he couldn't feel much down there.

"Congratulations, Teine!" howled Seymour from his vantage point by the window. He pointed jovially to the green diamond on the back of his own left hand. "*You're* going to be a stud!" There were more hoots and cheers and ribald commentary from the rest of the boys as Seymour danced around, shaking his pelvis.

"Bully for me," Teine grumbled, not sure if he was happy to have been selected for such an honor or annoyed that his eventual sex life would be dictated by duty and not pleasure. The others who had received vasectomies and the green diamond tattoos that proclaimed their sterility—*they* were the ones who had it easy.

Down at the other end of the room, one of the other boys was waking up from his anesthesia as well. Teine could hear him retching into the basin provided. The very sound made him a bit queasy, and he grabbed his own basin as a precautionary measure.

Once the nausea passed, Teine pulled himself into an upright position and reached for a pen and the journal he shared with his favorite sibling, Leis. The pair of them had entertained themselves for a couple of years by passing a notebook back and forth, working jointly to tell each other whatever story captured their imagination at the moment. Leis had given the journal back to him that morning before his surgery, and made him promise to save it until he was recovering.

The other boys in the room cheered as their favorite team placed the fabal egg for a two-point goal. Although the radio reception was dreadful, it didn't seem to dim their enthusiasm. After all, it *was* the bowl game!

Teine tuned them all out and eagerly began reading the story where he'd left off and Leis had begun.

"Miriam knew better than to venture into a cave by herself..." Leis had written in her neat, feminine hand. It began a response to Teine's cliffhanger about Miriam finding the cave while she was running away from a party of evil foreign horsemen that were terrorizing her village. Miriam was a half-breed, born to be the personal guard of her Aoife sire when she grew up. She was bright and resourceful, even though she was a girl and half Human. Usually her best friend Davy was with her, but since he was an Aoife and rather bookish, he'd been captured by the raiders earlier. It was up to Miriam to either find help, or save him herself.

Teine turned the page just as Seymour clambered unceremoniously onto the foot of his bed. "What in the world are you reading, man?" Seymour demanded. "It can't be schoolwork."

With a sigh, Teine closed the book reluctantly. Any of the other boys would leave him alone if he asked, but not Seymour.

"I thought you had money on this game, man?" Seymour prodded, trying to get a response out of the bigger, auburn-haired boy. "For someone who claims to like fabal as much as you do, you sure seem disinterested." In the room full of tanned blondes and freckled redheads, Seymour stood out like a raven in a flock of pigeons. The dark-haired youth, with his fair complexion and blue eyes, had a level of tenacity and fire that Teine admired but didn't emulate.

It was common knowledge that Seymour had been purchased from Cartierscross as a potential stud prospect. His stock was said to possess incredible concentration and ambition. But his health certificate never arrived, and by the time they got the child back to Solmurry, it was evident why. Seymour suffered from hemophilia, a rare blood disorder that made him bleed profusely with the slightest scratch and also made him more prone to internal injuries. Due to his condition, Seymour not only ended up with a green diamond tattooed on his left hand, signifying his status as an AM, or "altered male," but he'd also required having a healer from the Church come and oversee the surgery that effectively removed him from the gene pool and marked him as an adult. The sweet nun had even held Seymour's other hand while he was receiving his green diamond tattoo, healing him with divine magics. Then, in an act of compassion and mercy, she'd stayed to heal the other boys, as well.

"I love *playing* fabal," Teine reminded his friend, for perhaps the thousandth time. "Listening to it isn't nearly as interesting. *Especially* when you can't hear what's going on!" Realizing the futility of trying to read with Seymour latched on, Teine tossed his journal aside to save for a time when he could enjoy it in peace and quiet. Instead, he pulled out his sketch book and had Seymour trade out his pen for a charcoal pencil and a blending stub out of his book bag. He'd be able to draw and still keep Seymour entertained. He considered it a community service, because if Seymour wasn't entertained, he'd flit from bed to bed, engaging anyone who seemed conscious in exhausting, rapid-fire conversation. Teine supposed that Seymour was feeling so chipper because he'd had the benefit of magical healing. As an "intact male," Teine's own procedure had been very minor—circumcision only—and the affected area was nowhere near as painful as he'd feared it would be. He and the other IM's in his cohort—Marcus, Victor and Robin—would only be kept in the infirmary for a short time, for observation.

It seemed to Teine that the newest batch of AM's were moving far more slowly and gingerly than their comrades who'd remained reproductively intact. *Perhaps, because they'd expected to be?*

"What are you going to draw?" asked Seymour. The dark-haired boy scooted up closer to Teine so he could see. "A still life? Some fabal players? A landscape?"

Teine opened his sketchbook, moving past some of his finished pieces with a deliberate and somewhat grand slowness, taking a secret delight in his friend's fascination. Ever since the spring before, when Teine's best friend Vosh had been taken to Capital City to play fabal for the Solmurry team in the minor leagues, Seymour had instantly stepped up and attempted to fill the role. While Seymour was a poor substitute for Vosh in the roughhousing and sports, and had no artistic or poetic talent himself, he was capable of discerning good work. Teine had come to appreciate his active mind and was finding him to be an excellent sounding board for some of his creative attempts.

Although Seymour could drive him completely insane, Teine showed his appreciation of their friendship whenever the opportunity presented itself. "What would you like me to draw?" Teine asked. "You can pick, and I'll draw whatever you want."

"Naked women!" Teine and Seymour looked at the three cheering boys a few beds over who had suddenly responded. After a moment of blank stares, the entire room erupted in hysterical laughter.

Once Seymour stopped giggling, he gave the matter some serious thought. "Can I see the rest of your sketches before I decide?" As the game had been interrupted again by a commercial break, a couple of the other boys had wandered over to have a look, as well.

Teine nodded, handing over the book with what he hoped was a show of confident nonchalance. In actuality, his heart was suddenly pounding and his mouth felt like it had been stuffed with cotton. He'd actually be less nervous if he were showing his works to a teacher or some other professional critic.

Seymour held the book and flipped the pages while the others boys looked on. Teine flushed pink with both embarrassment and pride as Seymour paged slowly through the book, giving himself and the others time to truly study the work. Then they got to the section from the figure drawing class he'd gotten to take. Usually Human students were excluded from figure works classes unless they were sixteen or more years old, on mere principle. But Teine had been an exception, as he'd managed to wrangle a note from the instructor, and was backed up by his excellent marks in two other artistic disciplines. When he'd gotten word he'd been accepted into the class, Teine had hoped for naked women as models.

He'd really been disappointed when the whole class spent the first month drawing some strange, Outland Human contortionist with a bald head and a beard down to his belly. Of course, he was naked—and in a wide variety of impossible and downright horrifying poses.

The boys all laughed when they turned the page to the start of his figure studies. "Hey, Teine," Seymour said, elbowing him playfully. "I was so jealous you were getting to take figure drawing! Looks like the joke was on me!"

"Believe me," Teine said, extracting his sketchbook from his friend's hands. His ears burned as if they'd been held to the steam radiator. "The joke was on both of us." Fortunately the announcements had just ended, and the knot of art critics broke up and drifted back toward the radio to hear the last of the game.

On the other end of the room, Clinician Nocdoramis entered the infirmary and began making her rounds with the patients nearest the door. Her musical Aoife voice was soft and feminine in the background of all the rowdy boys and their cheering. To Teine's way of thinking, the delicate Aoife woman in the infirmary with a bunch of Human boys was as out of place as a beautiful flower growing in the middle of a vegetable garden. Her eyes were larger, proportionately, than those of a Human woman, set wide and slanted slightly upward at the corners. The planes of her face, like all of her kind, were drawn more sharply, with visible cheekbones and jawline under ageless, creamy skin. Her hair was a deep, rich gold, a shade Human blondes never seemed to match, and it waved gently as she tucked it behind her delicately pointed ears. He'd always longed to draw some of the Aoife, to catalog and sketch out the myriad differences between them and the Human models he'd seen, but the opportunity had never materialized. Teine hoped he'd eventually be brave enough to ask the Clinician if she'd mind if he took a couple of quick sketches. But any day which included an ice bag on his privates was not a day that inspired courage.

Teine sighed, lamenting his cowardice. He was about to tuck his artist's journal away when he realized that Seymour hadn't left yet. Good old tenacious Seymour. "What, you still want a picture?"

Seymour nodded eagerly, reaching out for Teine's book. He turned the page to a hunting scene that Teine was particularly proud of: Horses and hounds, leaping across the countryside on a cold winter's morning. The fields were turned under and snow lay thick as the horses' delicate legs churned it up beneath their hooves. Teine hadn't been completely satisfied with the horses, but overall, he thought it was one of his better pieces.

"I want one kind of like this," Seymour gestured to the sketch. "But can you show what they're hunting? I'd like to have one where they are hunting a dragon!"

Teine thought about it, mentally blocking out the scene in his mind. "What kind of dragon?" he asked.

"Just a brown. I want it to be believable."

Flipping the book open to a blank page, Teine started by sketching out the roughs where the main elements would be.

"Is that going to be the dragon?" Seymour asked, pointing at one of the shapes Teine had blocked out.

Teine nodded wordlessly. His charcoal pencil danced over the thick, creamy sketch paper, while Seymour got comfortable, tucking his legs under him and resting his elbows on his knees. With a wicked playful grin, Teine flipped the page and started sketching in a quick doodle of a silly looking, brooding gargoyle, sitting in the same position as Seymour.

It took the other boy a second to figure out what Teine was doing. Then Seymour groaned at the parody and cheerfully socked Teine with one of his own pillows. "Stop playing around! I want my picture!"

Chuckling to himself, Teine obediently flipped the page and went back to work on his commission.

Time seemed to have no meaning as Teine began filling in the details of the landscape. He wondered if God felt that way as She created. This time, he vowed he'd do a better job with the hunter's ponars. That breed of horse was difficult to draw, even for an experienced artist. They were long bodied, leggy and elegant, yet somehow managed to look sinewy and strong instead of fragile.

As Teine sketched, he found himself smiling as he considered the horses. Horses had been at the very beginning of his art career, though he'd come at it backwards and tried being a critic first. It all started with a ride on a merry-go-round. He'd chosen to ride an elephant, which gave him a fine view of four carved horses directly in front of him. He thought the sculptures were exquisite, with their arched necks, fancy barding, and perpetually flowing wooden manes. But something about them didn't seem right to his unpracticed eye. It had bothered him the whole ride, and he'd sat silently on his wooden elephant as the other children from his cohort had laughed and played. Finally, he'd decided. The sculptures, while excellently rendered and colorfully painted, lacked substance and realism. They weren't accurate, but were instead caricatures of what horses really were.

Later that day, when the Aoife teacher asked him how he'd liked the merry-go-round, he'd shared his feelings on the horses. She'd marched him right to the superintendent as soon as they'd gotten off the train. Teine was terrified, thinking he'd be in trouble. As it turned out, the teacher only wanted to be sure he was signed up for an art credit the next semester. As Teine had never drawn anything before then, he was very grateful for that tutor's watchful eye. Over the years as she'd returned to teach other classes, Teine had made a point of staying in touch and showing her his work. After all, she was the reason behind it.

As his mind wandered, his hands worked by themselves, and by the time he really looked back down at what he was doing, Teine's sketch for Seymour had begun filling out nicely.

Clinician Nocdoramus was standing over him with a fresh ice bag, a pitcher of tea with real ice in it, and some funny-looking liquid in a vessel resembling a shot glass. "Good afternoon, Teine," she said, moving his possessions from the table to a chair. She then set her tray down to check his chart.

Teine reluctantly closed his sketchpad and waited for instructions. He liked Solmurry's resident Clinician a lot, but he didn't know what to expect and was a little bit worried. "And a pleasant afternoon to you, Clinician," he replied.

She gave Seymour a stern look, and the other boy decided that he'd better find something else to do. With a smile, Nocdoramus wrapped a strange device around Teine's arm and began inflating it using a rubber bulb attached with a hose. "Are you feeling any pain?"

"Not really, no," Teine replied, a bit distracted by the strange thing on his arm. It pinched slightly, and pulled the hairs on his skin. When it had taken all the air it possibly could, she slid her stethoscope into the crook of his elbow and held up a finger for him to be quiet. As he watched, Nocdoramus turned the valve to let the air slowly escape while staring at the attached dial.

Then, she nodded to herself. Apparently whatever that was, the result was satisfactory. Without explaining, she took the shot glass off the tray and handed it to Teine. "Drink up. It tastes awful but it will keep you comfortable and prevent infection. How is your Amagorra? "

"She's doing quite well, thank you," Teine answered, then threw back the shot. Immediately, he made a face. "'Awful' is a bit of an understatement, don't you think?" he remarked, holding up the empty glass. "Rather like vanilla-flavored paint thinner."

Pouring and handing him a glass of sweet tea, she nudged him playfully in the shoulder with her elbow. "If I told you it tasted like dragon piss, would you drink it so quickly?" she chided. "Come now, do you need a lollipop like a nursling?"

"Yes," Teine said solemnly, making sure his eyes betrayed none of his mischief. "Yes, I do. And my comrades need some, too. We've all had a rough day."

Leaning forward to pinch his cheek, the Clinician laughed. "Now, there's the sweet talker I remember. I'll make you a deal, how about that?"

"What's the deal, oh Mistress of the Medicines?" Teine countered.

"The deal is, you go down there..." she tossed her head, indicating the other side of the room where one of their number lay in bed with his back to the group. "...and have a go at cheering up Marcus. He really took this hard."

Teine was momentarily alarmed, doing his best not to think about the kind of accidents that could happen during the surgeries like they'd all had. "What happened?"

"Oh, nothing so drastic as you're imagining, I'm sure," Nocdoramus replied airily. "He wanted to be an AM and was disappointed to not have gotten his green diamond."

Nodding sagely, Teine glanced around her at the figure lying in bed. "He's got a girl, you know. If he'd been Cut, they could have..."

"Yes, yes," she scolded him. "I understand how it works, and really I do sympathize. I know you IMs lead a much more disciplined life, but it's not without rewards. He needs a little help in seeing the silver lining of this particular cloud."

"Speaking of clouds?" Teine interjected. "Will we all be out of here tonight, before this light show rolls in?" He gestured to the window, where storm clouds loomed ominous and threatening. Teine could see the coachmen hurrying to ready several carriages. "I bet it's going to be quite a howler, since it's already disrupting the radio broadcasts."

Nocdoramus turned to look and froze in place, completely transfixed by the incoming weather. Teine wasn't surprised. He'd noticed long ago that the Aoife reacted differently to these magic storms than the Humans did. It awed and stilled them, and made them flush with… what? Energy? Passion? He didn't know, but he was sure there was an amazing poem or song in it somewhere. Teine spent a good two years pondering that mystery, before bringing it up to Vosh to ask his opinion. "It's just a storm." Vosh had replied. "Who knows why the Aoife do what they do." Teine hadn't brought it up to anyone since.

"Clinician?" he asked politely, trying to break into her reverie in the least intrusive way possible. "Can I stay and watch it from here? Or will you be discharging us?"

Shaking herself to break her concentration, she pulled her attention away from the window and turned to face Teine. It was a second before the faraway look in her eyes was replaced with her usual genteel amusement. "If the Church provides healers from now on out, we may reconsider this policy. But for now we'll be keeping all the AMs overnight as a precaution. Yes, you too, Seymour," she added, waving the other boy away as one might shoo a pesky fly. "You IMs are on a case by case basis." She gestured to Teine's pajamas. "Drop those trousers, young man, and let's have a look."

Chapter 2: In Our Defense

Lord Ebric Hilliard lounged on a bench with a good view of the main auction stage, and waited for bidding to begin on the next batch of young Solmurry-bred Humans. It felt good to rest his tired feet. Next to him, his least favorite cousin prattled on about "the excesses of noble society." Cousin Sonjay Hilliard, a shirttail relative from outside the walls of the Empyrean, was enjoying his first trip home in over a hundred fifty years. As one of Cousin Sonjay's chief hobbies was complaining, Lord Hilliard suspected that his guest was probably enjoying himself—a lot.

"The spectacle is rather appalling..." Sonjay whispered under his breath. "Gaudy and wasteful." Sonjay had the nervous habit of fiddling with his cravat, fondling the point of his left ear, and brushing back his hair repeatedly. "Resources like this could be put to much better use than the care and coddling of Titans."

He sniffled, pulling out a handkerchief to blot at his sharp nose. Tucking the cloth away, he predictably went for his cravat, ear, and hair again before continuing. "Humans are hardy creatures, and this kind of wasteful, indulgent frippery is *not* constructive or utilitarian..."

"Oh, I beg to differ. But what did you call them?" Lord Hilliard had finally grown irritated enough to speak, not in defense of his neighbors at Solmurry, but out of a desire to set the record straight.

Many of the Aoife that left the secure walls of the Empyrean to settle and grow businesses in the wilds of the Human lands ended up returning to the mother country with some very odd notions. Lord Hilliard, like most Aoife, truly loved his Humans. But he'd never seen an ounce of proof that humanity, as a whole, had what it took to effectively self-govern, much less do so with wisdom and justice.

Hilliard suspected self-governing Humans were possible, at least in theory, but his cousin's tirade had crossed the border of 'idle commentaries,' and was starting to sound like a personal attack on the Empyrean way of life. He couldn't, in good conscience, let it stand. He was about to explain, when, out of nowhere, his youngest daughter pounced on him and squeezed him about the ribs. He made a little wheeze that sounded like "H... oof."

"Eloquent, Cousin." Sonjay raised an eyebrow, turning his disapproving eye on the youngster. "And you must be little Nirilema. Almost a young lady now!"

Oblivious to the subtle criticism of her exuberance, Niri nodded. "Indeed." The girl turned her father loose, advancing toward her distant relative as though he were a long-lost soulmate. "And you must be Cousin Sonjay!" she squealed, spreading her arms wide, as if to embrace him. "How good of you to come and visit us! I expect you'll have many tales of the wide world beyond our carefully groomed portion of it. What *did* you call the Humans, a second ago?"

Lord Hilliard hid an indulgent smile behind his hand, enjoying Cousin Sonjay's obvious discomfiture. He managed to get in one last circuit of cravat-ear-hair before Niri wrapped herself around him as though he were a brother.

Lord Hilliard knew his own daughter well enough to know what she was up to. Little Niri was known for her fascination for all things foreign. Every time a relative traveled anywhere they could count on Niri shaking them down for information, stories, or perhaps even a map or other souvenir. The girl asked for books—weighty tomes on magic, distant lands and long-ago civilizations—on any special occasion.

A real, live, blood relative who actually *lived* outside the wall would be impossible for her to resist. Although part of him would delight to see his cousin squirm under Niri's voracious questioning, he decided to be merciful.

"Nirilema, my darling," Lord Hilliard intoned, ordering his features into a serious expression. "Did you *deliberately* leave poor Silpa behind somewhere, or are you lost?"

Nirilema turned to look up at her father, her cornflower blue eyes wide with feigned innocence. "I... er, Father..." she began, obviously fishing for either time, or a really good excuse.

"You left her behind," Lord Hilliard answered for her.

The girl looked away, digging the toe of her patent leather shoe into the rich sod of the lawn. "Yes, m'Lord."

He shook his head, feigning a level of disapproval he didn't actually feel. Spirited children were a fact of life. It never sat right with him that he was expected to scold his daughters harshly for transgressions his sons could freely commit. He admired Niri for her formidable intellect and curiosity, but society had a different set of standards for her.

"Were you just tired of Silpa fussing over you or are you up to something more devious? Hmm... I suspect you were planning to sneak a visit to see your friend, but noticed Cousin Sonjay and couldn't resist the opportunity to speak with him." Lord Hilliard tried to keep his expression stern, struggled against the smile that threatened to show itself. "Am I close?"

Niri's mouth shaped an "O" of guilty astonishment, then bit her lip. Finally, she nodded. "Marne's sick, and I know he's disappointed to miss this. He was so excited about the races! I... I thought I could slip in to see him, without..."

"Without getting caught? Without getting *him* in trouble?" he probed. "That's a dangerous game you play, and the risk is all on him. If the Lord of Solmurry thought for one instant that you and his son were friends, he would be *furious*."

"Is he *still* on about that?" Cousin Sonjay sighed. "Honestly, is he still holding that ridiculous grudge? It's childish!" At Lord Hilliard's warning stare, Sonjay modified his volume back to a loud stage whisper. "For heaven's sake! That was at least two hundred years ago. A sensible person would be over it by now."

"Sensible or not," Lord Hilliard chided him. "It's the way of things. Lord Solmurrian is a sensitive and easily offended man. His son, Marne, is a fine boy. Wild as a young deer, but a kind and thoughtful companion for Niri, when he can get away."

"Marne's health is fragile. He gets sick a lot," Niri added, glancing up at her foreign relative. "I wanted to bring him these." She reached into a pocket in her outer skirt, withdrawing several pamphlets advertising exotic travel destinations. "I thought it might cheer him up."

Her father sighed, "My dear one, if you *must* chase after any of the Solmurrians, I'd almost rather you follow the magician around." Leaning down, he gave her a half-hearted swat on the backside, and propelled her toward a shaded area with pavilions set up among the stately oaks.

"Now, go directly and find your mother and sisters, and do not leave them unless Silpa is with you."

Niri nodded, her eyes large and tragic, lashes heavy with unfallen tears. "Yes, m'Lord." And with that, she whirled and ran in the direction he indicated.

"She's a saucy little thing," Cousin Sonjay cracked. "Better rein that in early or you'll have your hands full in about fifteen years."

Lord Hilliard nodded silently. It was the only thing that his cousin had said all day that he agreed with. But that wasn't a topic on the table for discussion. "So... where were we?"

"You were asking me about Titans. That's the name Humans call these Empyrean-bred specimens. You were about to explain to me why all this..." Sonjay held his arms wide, as if to encompass the whole of Solmurry's grounds *and* their philosophy. "... isn't indulgent and wasteful, and how pouring resources into Humans you created on purpose actually *furthers* our civilization." Sonjay looked at his cousin expectantly before straightening his cravat, rubbing his ear, and brushing back his hair.

"Ah, yes. That." Hilliard nodded absently, gazing out over the gaily colored throng of spectators, slavers, Humans, and performers. "Every argument I can make comes down to one thing, and one thing only. Our people do not reproduce quickly enough, nor are we physically strong enough, to do all the things our economy depends on to stay vital and healthy. We don't *use* these Humans. The relationship is mutually beneficial and therefore symbiotic. Even you can't deny that Empyrean-bred Humans are healthier, better educated, and have far more fulfilling and meaningful lives than the Humans you're familiar with."

"Hmmm," Cousin Sonjay muttered, obviously unconvinced. "These Titans are nothing like the Humans on the outside, I'll give you that." He watched with interest as a string of statuesque, scantily-clad Human women passed by. Lord Hilliard could see him returning all the smiles, taking in the shiny white teeth, healthful curves and sleek, flowing hair with appreciation. "And I'll admit, your slave market is nothing like the ones on the outside, as well."

Hilliard made a noise of disgust. "Humans, preying on the misery of other Humans. Without our people to guide them, control their breeding, and educate them, they easily succumb to their own baser instincts. Then, they're little better than animals with thumbs." Cutting off his cousin's laugh with a curt gesture, he continued. "Come on, Sonjay! I want to hear you admit it. Any one of our "slaves," as you call them, has better education and healthcare than nearly *all* of the so-called "free men" outside the Empyrean."

Part of him knew he should end his lecture there, but he couldn't help himself. "The business of raising Humans is a very serious one. There's no money to be made in breeding low-end specimens. None whatsoever. These are the most expensive of expensive livestock, a commodity that every household craves, and custodianship of even one well-bred, properly trained Human can turn a mere household into a manor."

Sonjay chuckled at his cousin's zeal, but nodded, encouraging him to continue.

"Humans turn a generation so quickly that selective breeding can shape a population significantly in a short amount of time. You've seen what's on the outside—the bad teeth, the foul tempers, premature balding, physical unsoundness, and heritable mental illnesses. Our Humans have almost *none* of those traits. The average lifespan of a Human in the Wiydon Isles is a paltry fifty-eight years, and they are widely considered to be the epitome of self-governing Human civilization."

"What's yours, then?"

"Lifespan?" Lord Hilliard thought for a moment. "I suppose that depends on the bloodline. At Hilliard, ours are averaging seventy-seven years, as of our last census."

Sonjay made an appreciative noise and seemed to be about to say something else, before Hilliard held up a hand to still him. "If you're impressed by that statistic, the Solmurry varieties usually live well into their eighties, and many don't even retire from their duties until their late seventies."

"That is truly amazing," Sonjay grudgingly admitted. "When you explain it that way, having a good Human or two actually sounds like a worthwhile investment. If nothing else, it would be a fine way for a gentleman merchant to buy himself a few hours of leisure to pursue a hobby."

Glancing from side to side, to be sure they weren't being observed, Hilliard leaned in. "I have no love of my neighbor, but he has probably the best Human stock in the Empyrean."

"Well, at the prices they're bringing today, they'd better be," Sonjay agreed.

"There have been rumors, murmurings, for years that Solmurry isn't doing well financially."

"How can that be, with the prices their young stock bring?"

"Easily enough," Hilliard sighed. "I know all too well what it costs to bring a youngster from conception to sale date. Medical care, like regular vaccinations, routine dental care, not to mention the daily needs of a growing young Human. Expenses at every turn. And of course, prime quality Humans demand a good educational foundation so they are capable of learning and performing their eventual craft. Add the cost of leasing tutors from the Capital..."

His cousin made a strangled noise, as if he were looking at a balance sheet with all these expenses. He reached for his cravat to straighten it, then rubbed his ear before smoothing his hair back down, as proof against the unruly breeze.

"Don't forget the taxes," Hilliard reminded him. "There's a ten binna fee to register an infant and list his pedigree, plus the fifteen binna you'll pay the Sigolier for his registration mark. Then, another ten binna each time his records are updated, whether he's adding a new skill to his file, or being altered if he's not breeding quality. Sigoliers charge three to five binna for alterations to his identity sigil."

Grinning wolfishly at his less affluent relative, Hilliard continued, "And have you considered how much a growing Human eats?"

Cousin Sonjay paled visibly. Lord Hilliard continued without missing a beat. "They're so much larger than us when they're full grown, and all that bulk has to come from somewhere. It's no accident that most manors that breed any significant number of Humans also have enough land to farm and grow crops, raise animals for meat and milk, and have a side business or two to keep the income flowing and provide jobs for their permanent breeding stock."

"Like Solmurry's shipyards," Cousin Sonjay chimed in. "And all this time, whenever I thought of Solmurry, I thought of their ships…"

"Not that their ship building is insignificant, by any means," Lord Hilliard agreed, once again lowering his voice to where only his companion could hear. "But, Solmurry's real wealth and claim to fame lies in their heritage Human bloodlines. It would be a shame to let a dynasty of careful planning and selection go to waste because of bad management."

His expression a mix of surprise and wicked delight, Sonjay whispered, "Do you think Solmurry will eventually go under?" His eyes darted all around, taking in the gaudy, vibrant spectacle, as if acutely aware that it might just end, someday.

"It's not a matter of if." Lord Hilliard mouthed. "It all comes down to 'when.'"

As if in agreement, the wind picked up, accompanied by a rumble of distant thunder.

Chapter 3: Special Reserve

Leis sat inside the shade of a richly decorated canvas booth, running her brush slowly and carefully through Samia's thick, wavy, rose-gold hair. Taking the time to be sure that every little tangle was unwound carefully, she wove each lock into the braided coronet hairstyle she was assembling for her impatient younger sister. Samia squirmed incessantly, fiddling with the chart that displayed her accomplishments and pedigree, and rearranging the basket that held the envelopes for bids. The brightly colored canvas of their booth flapped in the brisk spring wind, with intermittent gusts making conversation impossible at any level softer than a shout. When she could hear them, Leis tapped her foot to the music from the lively brass band playing just a few booths away. She paused every few moments to braid in a flower she took from a nearby table. While Leis attended to her hair, Samia watched the throng of gaily dressed auction goers, vendors, and performers.

"How does it look?" Samia asked, chewing her lip and looking upward as if to see how her hairdo was shaping up.

"The same as it did the last time you asked me," Leis replied, her expression serene and a little amused. "Nice. Very nice. It will look just like mine, except the back of your hair will hang down, and you'll have flowers. A good choice for today, with all this wind."

"I'm sorry, sis," Samia murmured, her eyes darting to a juggler wearing a silly mask, following in the wake of a man dancing on very tall stilts. "I'm just nervous."

"Understandable." Leis reached for a flower. "Perfectly understandable."

Across the way, Leis noticed a batch of Human youngsters being led to the auction stage. They were waiting nervously in a staging area, where potential bidders could examine them up close. Aoife men and women stared at their knees, looked in their mouths, and squeezed their muscles, all while referring to the sale bill and taking notes of their numbers. These children were all selected from Samia's age cohort, but unlike Samia, they were being sold at regular auction, by a crier, to the highest bidder.

Samia, however, was special. Every year, the best breeders would select one from their crop of young stock that they felt represented the best of their breeding program. This Human was called the "Special Reserve." The master was allowed to set any reserve price he wished, and refuse to entertain any offers below that number. Bids were made only by sealed envelope, and the highest bidder above the reserve price would take her—but only if they could settle right then or if they had already applied for a letter of credit from the bank.

Special Reserve Humans were usually younger children from an especially successful breeding, and not needed within their house for furthering their bloodline. Samia was for sale because of her overall high quality, but also because Solmurry still had Leis. They didn't need Samia. Their oldest sibling had been sold because Master Solmurrian had compared Adina to Leis, and found he preferred Leis' rose-gold hair to Adina's vibrant flame red. But red hair and freckles sold very well, and Adina's finish price had set a record they hoped to beat with Samia.

Two Aoife men stopped by to have a leisurely look at the clipboard at their booth. The pair of elegantly-attired gentlemen eyed the chart detailing Samia's full four-generation pedigree displayed proudly on a piece of poster board clipped to a decorative brass easel.

"May I help you sirs with anything?" Leis asked, her voice polite and soft-spoken.

The two Aoife didn't answer, as absorbed as they were in the display. Turning their attention to the Human sisters, they watched for a moment as Leis continued work on Samia's elaborate hairstyle. The Aoife men glanced back at the pedigree again. Leis ignored them, giving Samia's hair a subtle tug when she squirmed under their scrutiny.

Eventually, one of the Aoife men cleared his throat. "So, are the two of you *full* sisters, then?"

Samia tried to nod, but Leis kept a firm hold on the nearly completed braid. "Yes, sirs," she answered, "My sister Leis here is two years older."

"Good, good," they responded. As they took a step back to confer, Leis suspected that she and Samia weren't the only "full siblings" at the booth. The Aoife men had similar features, yet very different from the Humans they were there to bid on. Even though both Leis and Samia were adolescent girls, they were broader and taller than either of the adult Aoife men. Instead of the strength and stature Humans possessed, the Aoife had a spare, willowy grace and slender hands that were far more flexible than the Humans' hands.

Aoife of all stations usually dressed well, but these two were exceptional. Both were stylishly turned out in matching surcoats of dark green watered silk, with details of hand embroidery at the sleeves and throat. Their fair complexions were bronzed to almost the same golden shade as their hair from exposure to the healthy outdoors, and their long, oblique-set eyes were the same startling shade of green. Their gaze danced back and forth between the two Human sisters.

"I wish they'd either ask more questions, or move along," Samia breathed softly to Leis, hoping to be heard over the windblown canvas. "They're making me feel nervous, just standing there and staring."

"*You* are making you feel nervous," Leis responded gently. "Why don't you take some deep breaths, but try not to be obvious about it?"

Samia did what she was told, her eyes dancing over the impromptu market square that had sprung up around the Solmurry auction grounds. Little canvas booths of every color and description had popped up overnight to sell locally produced wares and sundries to the throng of wealthy auction-goers. Jugglers, food vendors, dancers, art dealers and performers all sought their share of potential revenue, calling out to passers-by to hawk their goods.

When the last flower was tucked into place and the last hairpin set, Samia wore an elaborate crown of her own hair and flowers, with the back of her hair hanging loose past her waist to show off its enviable rose-golden sheen and length.

"Very lovely," commented one of the Aoife. "Now, could you give us a bit of a grin?"

Samia rose gracefully to her feet, the very picture of youthful Human obedience. Towering above the Aoife lords by nearly half a foot, the girl smiled a natural smile at first, then bared her teeth in such a way as to invite examination. When the two cast a questioning glance at her sister, Leis also stepped up to do the same.

"How many full siblings do you have? Oh, you both have such striking amber eyes."

"Thank you, sir," Samia replied automatically. She was used to compliments on her appearance. "To answer your question, there are four of us that are full siblings, and we have another eight that are from the same dam. Our eldest full sister was the Special Reserve from two years ago. I'm proud to follow in her footsteps to represent our line. All of us have full dentition, no cavities, and are some shade of redhead."

"And the other sibling, beyond you two and the one that was already sold?"

"We have a full brother, Teine. He's a year older than Leis, but he's not on display today because…" She made a 'snipping' gesture with her fingers, as if they were scissors.

One of the Aoife went nearly white with alarm. "I do hope he was left intact," he gushed. "If he's half as lovely as you girls, I might want him to service some of my brood wenches." His companion, clearly scandalized by such plain speaking, blushed deeply under his tan. Leis turned away to hide a smile behind her hand.

"Thank you, sir," Samia stepped in smoothly. "His name is Teine, if you care to inquire after him. I'm pretty sure he's been left intact. The rumor is that Lord Solmurrian's son will be training him for Display."

The Aoife gentleman nodded. "Lovely, lovely. Teine, you say? He'd be fifteen now?" He pointed at Leis. "Then you'd be fourteen, and you, Samia… that would make you twelve?"

"Yes, sir." Samia fixed him with her practiced smile, all the better to remind him of her pearly, straight teeth. "My birthday was just last month."

The Aoife reached into his pocket, drawing out a small, flat silver case, about the size of his palm. He thumbed a catch on it to expose many ornately engraved and hand-colored calling cards. "Please pass this along to your master. Tell him that Lord Erthwhyte of Anchester was inquiring about using one of his junior studs. Perhaps we can come to an arrangement if he'd like to use some of my wenches as breeders for the 'Sire and Get' class." He passed the card to Leis, who nodded politely and placed it in her pocket. While he was there, the lord also took one of the envelopes out from under a rock in a basket. He produced a pen from his wallet and filled out the enclosed card, sealed it, and dropped it into the bid box. Then, without further ado, the two Aoife tipped their hats, striding away like a matched set of handsome carriage horses.

"Best of luck!" Samia called out after them, waving gleefully. Leis put her hand on the younger girl's arm to prevent a further outburst just as Samia's pedigree display chart and brass stand went tumbling over. The windblown chart flapped away toward the merchants' booths.

"Cursed wind!" Leis said, laughing. Samia's good mood was contagious. Hiking up her skirts past her ankles, the elder sister turned sideways to get through the narrow opening to their booth. "I'll fetch it," she told Samia. "Stay here, and be charming!" Bounding after the sign, Leis dodged the festively dressed guests, each carrying their auction programs.

Leis could see she wasn't the only one inconvenienced. The fickle, gusty wind was doing quite the job on nearly every booth. Decorative cloth banners whipped and snapped in the breeze. Anything that wasn't secured could go sailing across the auction grounds at any moment. Wind chimes on some of the lower boughs of the oak trees created a melodious din, and the air smelled fresh, clean, and almost alive, heralding the storm that was to come.

Leis pounded after the escaping chart, hoping she could catch it before it got too dirty and banged up to be used. Just as she was reaching out, the chart almost in her grasp, a sandaled foot gently pinned it to the ground. "Oh, thank you!" Leis gathered up the errant sign, examining it for wear and tear. Fortunately, it was still usable.

"It was nothing," her grandmother answered. "Looks like you were getting your exercise for the day. How goes it?" She gestured to Leis, indicating that she was also going to Samia's booth.

Leis fell into step automatically, taking in her grandmother's sharp appearance. Amagorra was wearing an outfit that looked to be brand new, and sported some intricate beadwork she'd likely done herself. Like Leis, Samia, and their dam, Amagorra also was a shade of redhead. She'd started out as a rose-gold, like Leis, but now had thick cables of silver winding through her long, unadorned braid.

"We've had about fifteen bidders, Amagorra," Leis told her elder. "Most of them are breeders, though, and I know Samia would be unhappy with no trade beyond popping out a baby every year. She was hoping she'd go to a family, or to a business that needed another set of hands at a craft."

Amagorra nodded. "That's the curse of good bloodlines. The buyer who pays top dollar is usually looking for a measurable return on their investment—and *sooner* rather than *later*. Profit-oriented people have a hard time seeing past the quick return of breeding. A craftsman or family is hard-pressed to come up with the extra funds to purchase a well-bred Human over a lesser specimen. Yet the advantages outweigh the extra investment. Less downtime due to illness or injury, higher productivity and ability to work unsupervised, more versatility if trained in skills—all these things matter greatly over the course of a Human's useful life, but are harder to measure than the quick return of an infant."

Leis sighed and nodded. "Yes, yes, I see your point. It's sad, though." She whirled out of the way as a throng of giggling Aoife children and their pets passed in front of her. The colorful, gleeful mob wove in and out of the booths and other pedestrians, having the time of their lives. Most were waving ribbons tied to sticks, and some had noisemaker horns sounding a variety of tones ranging from shrill whistle to buzzing hum. Their high-spirited antics couldn't help but make Amagorra and Leis smile.

Amagorra patted Leis on the shoulder, then pulled her in close. Her wizened features creased into a conspirator's wink. "Samia's predicament would be sad if we couldn't stack the deck in her favor." She nudged Leis' leg as they walked, giving the girl a quick glimpse of silver and cut glass hidden in her hand.

Leis' eyes automatically widened. "You *have* it?" she asked, and then asked again. "*You* have it?" she breathed, "I thought it was only a legend, a fairy tale."

"This is no tale for a fairy," Amagorra quipped. "We paid good money to have this made and smuggled in. We are fortunate to be so well funded." She passed the item over to Leis, who longed to inspect it, but wisely waited until they were back at the booth.

Leis replaced Samia's pedigree board, eyeing it to see if there was any way to weight it down to keep it from flapping away again, while Amagorra entered the booth and greeted Samia. "Good morning, my child. Happy Eaoster." Amagorra embraced her granddaughter, kissing her on both cheeks. "I brought you a gift. I hope you enjoy it." From a pocket in her apron, Amagorra pulled out a silver filigree necklace. The pendant was the shape of an egg, with a green stone inside.

"Oh, Ama! It's lovely!" Samia trilled. "Beautiful! Leis, can you help me try it on?"

Leis passed the secret handful back to Amagorra, and then held out her hand for Samia's necklace. She admired the intricate silverwork before opening the clasp and starting to affix it around Samia's slender neck. "This is a nice piece, Amagorra. Where did you get it?"

"Edgar, the silversmith. He mentioned that he'd seen Samia admiring some silver and jade earrings, and thought she might like this as a going-away present. He sure saw me coming, that one," she finished, a playful cant to her voice. "I'm glad you like it." The old woman groaned as Samia stood and hugged her tight. "Careful, girl. Don't break me."

The three settled back into the booth to watch the foot traffic. Once Samia was engaged in a conversation with a passerby, Amagorra pulled the surprise item from her pocket and showed it to Leis.

It was a beautifully made silver monocular, with a cut glass lens on a chain. Leis made as if to hold it up to her eye, but hesitated, looking to her grandmother for permission. Amagorra nodded crisply, and Leis held the eyepiece to one eye, closed the other, and looked through.

"It doesn't work," she said, disappointment evident in her voice. "Are you sure..."

Amagorra said nothing, just draped the monocular's dangling silver chain around Leis' neck and gestured for her to try again. Leis repeated the motion and looked again.

The landscape exploded into rich vibrant colors and then settled into a golden halo around each living person. Some were so bright she could barely look at them, and some hardly radiated at all. She gasped in surprise and looked to Amagorra for guidance. Her grandmother, when viewed through the lens, was nearly invisible behind the powerful golden aura surrounding her. "What exactly does it show?" Leis asked.

"Goodness," Amagorra replied, leaning in to whisper, "And strength of character. It came from a chanter who specializes in detection magics. We should be able to use this to Samia's benefit today."

"How?"

"If we can find the right people for her, let's just say that money won't be an object. They will find all the funding they need to take her home."

Leis stared at her grandmother with open-mouthed surprise. "We're bankrolling this?" she whispered under her breath, astonished by the notion that Human slaves like themselves had access to such a princely sum. "We *can* bankroll this?"

"Indeed we will, if we need to interfere. Now, give it back to me, and we'll get to work."

Chapter 4: Elemental Forces

Across the main drive, under the shade of trees, a few canopies had been set up and benches had been brought from the Commons and placed in groups to encourage conversation. Human volunteers were serving refreshments to the weary and footsore. Directly across from the Special Reserve booth, two Aoife gentlemen lounged under a tree and compared notes. One of them had a battered green leather-bound tome, with many dog-eared pages—a book he waved vigorously at his companion as he was trying to make his point.

"… And *that's* why we've had such high turnout, even with all the talk of war. I was hoping the prices would be flat this year, but I can never seem to get that kind of lucky."

His friend nodded, a sympathetic expression on his angular Aoife face. "It's not just the breeding stock going high this season. Did you see some of the prices the *altered* males were bringing? It must be driven by demand. I hear the military did some buying earlier this year. What does the *Greenline Guide* say?"

Consulting the book, the first Aoife's reply was completely drowned out as a large family with many children passed between them. Both parents and all three children yammered at once, making it impossible for the businessmen to hear their own conversation.

"What?" asked the first Aoife. His friend replied with "Eh?" and they both laughed.

"So, what does it say?"

"The trend for Display is starting to swing the other way. See, here." He folded a page back, then tossed the guidebook to his companion, who opened right up to where he'd indicated. "That type is just not doing as well in this season's Displays. I think the trend is swinging away from those monstrously huge fellows and going back to a neater look."

"If that's the case, we're in the right place to be ahead of this trend, instead of behind it," his companion agreed thoughtfully. "We should skip the girls and look for a stud prospect, after their wizard's demonstration. I hear he's going to dig a well."

"With magic?" his compatriot blinked with incredulity. "That's *some* parlor trick. If that's the case, I'd definitely like to see it."

His friend nodded earnestly. "Indeed. One of my younger cousins just surrendered himself to the Monastery in Port Chandler. Now he's studying under an Imperial wizard." His brow wrinkled, and he lapsed into silence, twisting a blade of grass around in his fingers before tossing it aside. "Who knows? Perchance he'll be able to do useful tricks like that, once he's had some instruction."

"If so, you'll have to talk him into paying me a visit. He can dig all the wells he wants at my farm," his friend joked, noticing the other man's unusually somber mood. "Come on then, let's go on and see this wizard and his show."

The friends made their way through the crowd, pausing here and there at a couple of interesting booths to eye the local wares. Soon, they found themselves at the old well where both Human and Aoife people were starting to gather.

Madric Solmurrian, eldest of the Solmurrian sons, stood on a makeshift stage, striking a pose with one foot on the upturned bucket that was still chained to the well. Dressed in festive green robes for the occasion, he carried an artfully carved wooden staff. The carvings were both subtle and beautiful, with winding vines and leaves that also formed arcane symbols if one were to examine it closely. In honor of the holiday, the handsome, well-built Aoife wore a woven crown of twined green vines, which offset his rich golden hair. There were a disproportionate number of eligible young Aoife women in the audience, and the magician had a smile for each of them.

The two merchants looked around for a seat, but all of the benches, chairs, and even the hay bales brought in for extra seating were full. Two of the Solmurry Humans noticed the merchants and rose to offer them their bench. Clapping the Humans on the arm in gratitude, the Aoife men took their seats. The displaced Humans knelt on the bare ground to listen, rapt curiosity on their upturned faces.

"There are many different branches of magic," Madric began. "And new kinds of magic are being recognized every day. Today, the focus of our demonstration is on Elemental magic." The magician's voice carried effortlessly to the onlookers at the back of the crowd, and he had the dramatic gestures and expressive delivery of a natural-born showman. "Now, can anyone name any of the different kinds of Elemental magic?"

On a bench in the front row one Aoife girl sat with her Human nanny. Her hand shot up, waving excitedly. As she was the only volunteer in the rather large audience, Madric gestured to her. "My! Here's a bright young lady! What would your name be, my dear?"

"Nirilema Hilliard," the girl chirped, returning Madric's welcoming smile with a blushing grin of her own. Then, her awkwardness evaporated and was instantly replaced with intense eye contact as she sat up tall and leaned slightly forward. "The recognized kinds of Elementals so far are Solar or Air, Water, Fire, Teutonic or Ersan, and Chemical."

Madric laughed, stepping forward to greet the young miss. "My, my, there are students entering the monastery who don't know so much! Who thinks Nirilema deserves a prize for being so well-studied? Put your hands together for the little girl!"

The audience, already in the spirit of the demonstration, clapped on cue, and some of the Humans even cheered and whistled. Nirilema leaned far enough forward to tug on Madric's sleeve and motion him to come closer. "I don't need a prize," she told him. Her blue eyes were serious in her rounded child's face, and she raised her voice slightly so Madric could hear her over the crowd. "But I would like to speak with you, after your demonstration."

"Certainly, my dear," he agreed. "But for now, enjoy the moment." Turning away from the girl, he held up his hands to quell the applause. "Well, young Nirilema Hilliard, most well-read child I know…" The crowd laughed, as if on cue. "I bestow upon you my crown, as Master of the Festivities."

He removed his woven circlet of vines and placed it gently on the Aoife girl's head. At first, it looked as though it would fall over her face and end up around her neck, but then something amazing happened. The circlet of vines moved of its own accord, the vines sprouting new growth that entangled existing branches then tightened to pull the circle closer, and make it smaller. An instant after the crown had sized itself to fit her girl-sized head, the vines broke out in buds that immediately bloomed into pale blue and yellow flowers—a perfect match for Nirilema's dress.

"Thank you!" Nirilema exclaimed. Then, as if she'd been trying to hold herself in check, and failed, she blurted out "That's fascinating! How did you do it?" Her enthusiasm was anything but reserved and ladylike, and the crowd chuckled again.

Madric tweaked her nose, playfully. "My dear, if I gave away all my secrets, I'd be out of a job. Now, why don't you assist me?"

Nirilema's eyes widened at this unexpected honor, but her nanny huffed and clucked like an offended hen. "You may call me Niri," she told the wizard. "And *you*, Silpa…" she rounded on the Human woman like an angry cat. "Be still. I'm sure it's perfectly safe."

"Indeed." Madric gave the nanny a sympathetic glance. "Now, Niri, please throw that bucket into the well."

Niri stepped forward, seized the bucket to do as she was told. Lifting it was a strain for the delicate Aoife girl, as the bucket was made of wood and steel, and the affixed chain was solid. When she heaved it over the lip of the well there was a satisfying splat when it hit the water at the bottom.

Meanwhile, Madric worked the crowd, "Every so often, even a good well will need refreshing," he told them. "The last time this one was seen to, I was in school and my younger brother was still in knee pants." Striding over to stand next to Niri, Madric towered over her, with a protective hand between her back and the well. Although he'd been about to send her back to sit with the audience, he thought better of it.

"Thank you, my dear. Now, would you hold my staff until I motion for it?" Niri, quite beside herself, nodded wordlessly. Madric passed the intricately carved staff into her soft, childish hands. With both hands free, the Aoife wizard began working the crank to draw a bucket of water out of the failing well. It was hard work, and he mugged a little, drawing titters and guffaws from his audience. "If it's that much work to draw up a bucket, think how hard it would be to dig another thirty feet and hit the deep aquifer!" he quipped.

"I'm trying *not* to," answered one of the Solmurry Humans, a big strapping lad probably a foot taller and a hundred pounds heavier than Madric. The crowd, already primed for interaction, laughed as if on cue.

Once the bucket reached the top of its chain, Madric lifted it out by its handle, then poured the inch or two of slimy, murky, sediment-filled water onto the ground so everyone could see its quality. Niri leaned over to look, wrinkling her nose at the unappealing liquid.

"Clearly, this well is done for," Madric commented. Heads nodded in agreement. "Well, the work crew is in luck! Magic can do in minutes what it would take muscle all day to accomplish. Now" he intoned, turning back to the onlookers, raising his hands dramatically. "Watch and wonder at the mysterious power of an Elemental of Ersa!"

Madric began casting his spell, chanting in an arcane tongue that left the bystanders whispering among themselves. The crowd swelled as all the people nearby drifted in closer to watch.

The magician gestured to the unseen workings of the universe, coaxing them, bending them to his will. There was a shout of sheer astonishment as a lump of dirt in front of Madric began pushing up, as if there were a gigantic mole underneath. The soil piled higher and higher as Madric cantellated, until the dirt mound was about a foot high and began to take on vaguely humanoid features.

Niri's nanny squawked like a frightened bird as she rose and swiftly went to her charge, just in case the pile of dirt was inclined to harm little girls. The onlookers were all rising to their feet as well, trying to get a better look. The assemblage began to spread out to each side, each person seeking a better view. Soon, Madric gestured for his staff, which Niri obediently placed into his open hand. He tapped the butt of the staff on the ground in front of the squat, burly little figure, and said, "I have summoned you from Ersa's bones, and you will obey my commands until you return to your home."

The strange creature bowed once, and then seemed to look up with its rudimentary face, as if waiting for the inevitable commands. With a flourish that caused the audience to gasp in unison, Madric gestured to the well, "Dig! Dig, my servant of Ersa!" The elemental took two steps toward the well and seemed to almost dive into the soil, disappearing below the ground level as completely and smoothly as a swimmer could disappear into water. Speculation ran rampant, as all the onlookers muttered amongst themselves.

"You might want to stand back," Madric told the nearest people, his eyes dancing with mischief. Silpa, her patience stretched to the limit, gracelessly grabbed Niri and, over the girl's protests, fled with her back to where the other bystanders were breathlessly watching. As if on cue, sprays of mud and dirt came flying haphazardly out of the well. Minutes passed, while the energetic creature toiled at the bottom of the well. The elemental slung wagon loads of muck, which partially coated Madric and the closest observers. But no one seemed to mind.

Soon, there was silence from the well. People began muttering to themselves, wondering what would happen next. Then the elemental began piling itself up in front of Madric, as if reporting back on its mission. Without a word, Madric reached down and slung the bucket into the well. It landed with a vibrant splash, and soon he was hauling up a bucket of fresh, clear water. Taking the ladle that hung by the well, Madric began distributing the water to the people closest to him. Everyone who drank pronounced the water to be sweet and palatable. The applause started, and some of the Humans even whistled and stomped the ground with their enthusiasm.

"This afternoon, after tea, my Elemental and I shall be digging a completely new well by the stable. You are all welcome to come and observe the process if you wish." Madric stood, beaming, waiting for the crowd to filter away. Then he noticed the Doyen Prince and his retinue, including Prior Vihah, heading his way from the fringes of the demonstration.

His good cheer instantly vanished. He glanced down at the elemental and said "Be ready when I call, but you can go for now." The elemental bowed once, then crumbled away.

Niri approached, cautiously, taking in the sudden change in the wizard's demeanor. "May we speak?" she ventured.

Madric nodded, crouching down to her level to make eye contact and putting an arm around her shoulders to turn her back to the approaching Prince and his people. "Certainly, child."

"Can… can I learn to do what you do, someday?" Niri asked, the words tumbling out of her.

Madric could feel the Prince's shadow falling on his skin, darkening his mood even more.

"No, my sweet Niri," he answered, urgency making the sentence sound unnecessarily harsh, even to his own ears. "You cannot. The law won't allow pretty little girls like you into the Imperial Army, and to learn the ways of magic, you must be in either the military or the priesthood."

"But, aren't any women Gifted?" she persisted. "Surely, there are *some*."

"And surely as there are some, there are reasons to keep them from that study," Madric returned. "Either you discover your own gift and come to the institutions of your own accord, or keep your abilities hidden and be…" he glanced over his shoulder, fixing Prior Vihah in a brief but baleful stare. "…forcefully revealed."

Niri frowned, undaunted, and opened her mouth to speak again, but Madric cut her off. "Magic," he continued, "like all power, has at its roots the temptation of corruption. To truly study and learn, one must submit to the institutions, to protect the soul and prevent its defilement."

The words he'd been taught rolled glibly off his tongue, and he longed to replace them with descriptions of his own experiences. However, he knew too much graphic description would likely give the girl nightmares, and he was certain Prior Vihah would not be pleased with such candor. Instead, Madric gave the girl a sad, conspirator's smile. "I am sorry," he finished.

Niri turned and looked over her shoulder to see the Doyen Prince and Prior Vihah waiting to speak with Madric. "Good day, your Excellency, Prior." Then she turned her attention back to Madric. The wizard had the unsettling feeling that the child could read him like a book, but was wise enough to be silent.

"Thank you for the information," she told him, reaching out to squeeze his hand. Once she had him trapped, she pulled out a handkerchief, and wiped several flecks of mud off his face as though he were the child and she were the adult. Surprised, Madric could only submit to her ministrations.

"I suppose I'll return now," the girl told him, "to my tea set and dolls. Then I can dream of the day when I can have many, many babies, and no real interests in my vapid little brain beyond their care and feeding." With that, she dropped his hand like it was something revolting and stomped off, her nose in the air and her embarrassed nanny in her wake.

"Ouch," volunteered the Doyen. Madric rose from his crouch, keeping his expression carefully neutral. Unable to get a rise from Madric, the Prince tried again. "'Dig, dig, my servant of Ersa?' A bit much, don't you think?"

"It worked," Madric answered. "They stayed. They listened."

"It's not my place to criticize your style, my son," Prior Vihah interjected. "But it would seem to me that a demonstration of that... magnitude... would be better performed in an audience free of Humans?"

"Perhaps," Madric admitted. "But a people can only tolerate so much fear without lashing out to destroy what they fear. I believe that the Humans should fear magic, and rightly so, but fear it reasonably, as a horse fears its master. They need to be prepared, not frightened."

"You should also try to avoid recruiting little girls," the Prince added.

"That was her idea, not mine."

The Doyen breathed a deep sigh, and hooked his thumbs into his elaborate chain belt. "Ah, the Hilliard pride and the Solmurry temper. It's amazing that you and your neighbors aren't still slaughtering each other. If you *really* want to vex your younger brother, you should marry one of those Hilliard daughters, when they come of age." He beamed a satisfied grin at the magician, and jutted his chin purposefully at the retreating girl.

Madric raised an eyebrow, "That *would* vex him. I'll have to keep that in mind some year, for his birthday."

The Prince roared with laughter, clapping Madric on the shoulder. "Ah, your wit is ever sharp. Promise me that if you do decide to play that hand, you'll invite me to the party? I would approve your marriage license immediately, if I could only see the look on your brother's face!"

The Prior came around to Madric's other side. "On a related note to your performance..." he began, clearing his throat. His eyes darted to the Doyen. "If I might?"

"Be my guest," the Prince agreed amicably. "He's all yours."

"It seems that your skills continue to grow and grow," the Prior said, placing his bejeweled hand on Madric's arm. "Although I questioned the wisdom in allowing you to abandon your Brotherhood within the Church, your solitude and self-study over the last few years seem to be paying off. You are truly honing your summoning skills, as well as branching out into other areas. I've heard your enchantments are first rate."

"They are my favorite," Madric admitted, stepping out of the Prior's grasp. "Although I find they are exceptionally tiring. My concentration requires the strictest of solitude to be able to complete even the most rudimentary binding. I doubt I ever would have uncovered that ability, had I remained within the cloister."

"Then, we shall thank Our Lord that we saw the wisdom of your request," the Prior agreed. "It also bestows a little extra protection to your position. As long as you can enchant items, there is no need to send you directly into battle with the barbaric Islanders, if it comes to war. You can stay home, in your comfortable tower with your servants to tend you."

Suddenly, the wind picked up, carrying with it the vague scent of ozone and salty ocean. The oak tree overhead began to creak and groan, sounding eerily alive.

"Speaking of magic," the Doyen said, ruffling his pet hound's ears with a languid hand. "There's going to be a storm later."

"If that's the case, I might need to postpone the second part of my demonstration. That wind could be the least of my problems," Madric muttered. "I should get myself back to the tower. I have experiments working that should be interrupted, rather than expose them to the wild storm surges."

Prior Vihah looked positively delighted. "Perhaps I will stay overnight and avail myself of Solmurry's legendary hospitality. I could play a game of cards with your lovely nephew while the storm rages outside."

Madric, without looking at the Prior, shook off the suggestion. "You'd be welcome to stay, of that I'm sure, but haven't you heard? My nephew took ill yesterday. He's in the infirmary, and not strong enough for visitors."

"That is a shame. The poor child is always ill at the most inopportune occasions, and I never get to spend as much time with him as I would like." The priest turned to his Prince. "Have you met Lord Solmurrian's son?"

"Yes, yes," the Doyen answered impatiently, watching the Western sky. "He's too young to be interesting. When he's old enough to drink and gamble, perhaps then he'll hold my attention."

Chapter 5: Embarrassment and Frustration

"Oh, sheesh…" Teine complained, reaching for the drawstring of his pajamas so Clinician Nocdoramus could check his surgical site. Teine knew she'd been there to cut his umbilical cord and wrap him in blankets when Amagi had given birth to him. She'd cared for him when he was six years old and had shoved a bean up his nose on a dare and couldn't figure out how to remove it. She'd tended him during every childhood scuffle and sniffle, and he trusted her and loved her as if she were his own mother. She'd even saved his Amagorra's life when she'd had a minor heart attack the year before. Everyone agreed that Nocdoramus was the best Clinician anywhere in the Empyrean. But Teine was suddenly embarrassed about taking his pants off in front of her. It was ironic.

"I suppose you're of the age now when you could see Clinician McIlroy," she said, as if reading his mind. Since Teine was standing, she crouched to manipulate and examine his wound, putting the top of her head about level with his belly button. The other boys, watching the scene out of her field of vision, were trying not to laugh. Seymour went so far as to make a gesture suggestive enough that even the fragile hemophiliac could have earned some stripes across his back if anyone who wasn't one of their Cohort saw.

"Whatever you think is best, ma'am," Teine answered, giving his friend the sternest look he could muster. The next thing he knew, the Clinician was standing up and putting a tube of ointment into his hand.

"That healing spell really did the trick! But apply that cream for pain and itching whenever you need it until it runs out. We'll probably release you tonight. Now..." she said, reaching into her pocket.

Teine couldn't help but wince, dreading the newest pinnacle of embarrassment to come.

"Don't forget our bargain, you cheeky boy." Nocdoramus swatted him playfully on his bare rear with her examination gloves and tossed him two barley lollipops shaped like animals. "Go talk to Marcus." She turned to face the other boys and began handing out candy while Teine pulled up his drawers. By the time he was decent again, the Clinician was selecting a new victim. They'd all get a turn with their pants down around their ankles in front of everyone. Teine just wished he could have gone last instead of first.

While the others were distracted by the candy and the spectacle, Teine padded barefoot down the aisle between the two rows of beds until he got to where Marcus was lying.

"Hey, Marcus," he said, trying to be casual as he crawled up onto the next bed over. "I got you a barley pop. Which do you want? A lime deer or a strawberry pig?"

Marcus was silent, and for a moment Teine was sure the other boy wasn't going to speak. Although Marcus was one of the most introspective of the cohort, he was never *ever* rude. Finally, after what seemed like an eternity, Marcus found his voice. Rolling over onto his back to stare at the ceiling, he answered, "I know the strawberry's your favorite." His face looked puffy and his eyes were red, but he was still Marcus and still behaved with his usual consideration for others. "I'll take the lime one, then."

Teine handed it over, wondering what else he could do. He had no magic spell to break the silence and broach the subject. He supposed if he'd been in Marcus's shoes, with a girl waiting for him, he'd probably be crying as well. "Um... I see you're staying an IM too," he mumbled artlessly. To hide some of his embarrassment, he crinkled the wax paper wrapper off the candy and popped the clear pink pig into his mouth, leaving the sucker's stick to poke out between his lips.

"I was supposed to get Cut," Marcus sighed, unwrapping his own lime deer. Candy was a rare treat, and even teen heartbreak wasn't enough for him to miss out. "I just knew I was going to."

"Whatever gave you that idea?" Teine asked, trying not to slurp around the confection. It was an odd notion for a boy like Marcus to have. He was probably the most handsome boy of their agemates—bigger, more solidly built, and more muscular than all the rest. Ones like Marcus, with training, education, bloodlines, and manners went for big money at production sales or private treaty— if they were sold at all. In fact, the current rumor was that the young master would be choosing some Solmurry stock to show at his first Exhibition. Teine had heard from Leis that the smart money was on Marcus as the boy's top pick, but at the time, Teine had been so consumed with shoveling food in his face and trying to finish an extra credit assignment in his geometry class that he didn't hear much beyond that.

Marcus turned to face Teine, then sat up. Unlike Teine, Marcus did not leave the lime deer stuffed in his mouth while he tried to talk. "I don't know," he said, with a shrug. "Maybe it was all just wishful thinking. But I'm not really outgoing or charismatic enough. All I really want to do is work with the horses and be with..." Marcus's face contorted and he put his head in his hands. He sniffled once, then composed himself. "I don't suppose it matters," he added, his voice somewhat muffled by his hands. "She got sold today, anyway."

"Oh," Teine said, feeling the color rise in his cheeks. He'd really made a mess of things with this "cheering up" business. Trying to come up with something witty that could take all of Marcus's pain away was futile. He knew it. It didn't mean that he didn't care. "That's rough, Marcus."

"I bet you're happy, though," Marcus said, obviously trying as hard to make conversation as Teine was. "Now you've got a better chance of landing on the fabal team with Vosh."

Teine shrugged, wondering for the thousandth time why people always assumed his primary goal was fabal. Sure, he was good at sports and enjoyed the game, but he liked his brain and enjoyed using that more. Marcus did have a point, though. Most, if not all, fabal players were IMs, because the good visibility and marketing of the sporting events led to fame and increased both the number of requests and the sum of the stud fees involved. Teine wouldn't mind fabal; it was a fun job, after all. But why couldn't anyone appreciate him for his art, or writing, or something he actually cared about?

Teine was still fishing around for something else to say to keep the conversation going when Wallace walked in. He was one of Teine's relatives, a great-uncle or something. Though he was stooped and age spotted, Wallace was still sprightly enough to pull down a decent half day's work carrying the mail around Solmurry. At seventy-four years old he had a full head of white, wiry hair, and a rowdy sense of humor. Teine hoped he was doing half as well when he was Wallace's age.

Spotting him, most of the boys either got out of their beds to greet the old codger, or if they were fabal fanatics, merely waved as they clung desperately to the failing reception on the radio. It sounded to Teine like the teams were tied again, but it was getting next to impossible to discern anything through the static.

"I'm just paying a visit to the poor, the invalid, and the impotent," Wallace chuckled. Most of the boys groaned; good-natured teasing was expected from adults at this time. It was kind of a rite of passage and a sign of their acceptance into adult roles. "So who wants their mail?" Wallace held up a hefty sack. It seemed that nearly everyone in the infirmary had a piece of mail or two. That was a little unusual, even more so that they'd receive a mail drop in person. Each boy had a box in the Commons SPED where mail was dropped, and most of the boys didn't receive outside mail with any kind of regularity. Although a pen-pal or relative wasn't out of the question, they were all too young to be staying in touch with any long-distance lovers, and most of the boys their age avoided correspondence studies as if extra schooling bore the plague. As Wallace handed Marcus his two envelopes and Teine his four, Teine noticed that even Wallace had a green diamond on the back of his gnarled and veined old claw.

"What did you get?" he asked Marcus, mostly to make conversation.

Marcus tore open an envelope and smiled suddenly. "My dam ordered me the Dunner and Hotch book on steam engines!" he exclaimed. "It's not in yet, but she sent me a nice little note, too. I'll have to thank her when I see her."

Teine was instantly jealous. Dunner and Hotch's series, titled, "How Everything Works," was a raging success. He had a couple of their books himself, and every volume was packed with diagrams and detailed information.

Marcus's other piece of mail turned out to be an advertisement for the haberdashery in town—with a coupon attached for new customers. It was pretty smart marketing, in Teine's opinion. Once the boys got through the Cut and settled into their permanent jobs, they could count on an allowance commensurate with their value to

Solmurry. Although basic work clothes and underwear were provided, most young men were inclined to spend some coin on dressing well during their leisure hours. Teine checked his mail and found an identical envelope.

"What did *you* get?" Marcus asked. Teine was pleased to see that the letter and gift from his mother had perked up his friend's mood somewhat.

Teine set aside the advertisement for later and surveyed his three remaining pieces of correspondence. He felt like he was the richest man in the world. One had postage tickets attached and obviously was not a piece of correspondence from inside Solmurry. It looked fat and newsy, and had dreadful handwriting on the front. "That's from Vosh," Teine said.

The remaining two pieces of mail were from within Solmurry. He tore open the envelope on one and pulled out a hand decorated fold-over card. *"Snip Snip—Your Infirmary Trip..."* the front said, with a crude drawing of a pair of scissors which had been embellished by a little silver glitter pasted on.

He sighed with feigned exasperation. "Probably from Leis." He opened the card to read the rest of the poem.

> *"Snip snip—your infirmary trip*
>
> *I love my brother, so here's a tip!*
>
> *The other men can, but you can't...*
>
> *Till someday you can make me an aunt!"*

"She sure has a way of rubbing it in," Marcus noted.

"Yeah, mandatory celibacy never sounded so good."

Marcus chuckled at Teine's sarcasm. "Aww... look at that! She crossed out 'boys' to put 'men.' It was nice of her to remember. Bless her heart." Marcus had that silly grin he was known for plastered across his face again. Sometimes Teine had to remember that Marcus wasn't any kind of dumb, he was just *nice*. Teine didn't think he'd ever seen Marcus angry, and the boy was always thoughtful and had a kind word for everyone.

Teine, however, was free to snort in mock derision, "Bless her heart, indeed. Leis is a pain in the rear." But he couldn't help but smile a little. "She's no kind of poet, but it was cute."

"I wish I had sibs that wanted to talk all the time," Marcus mused. As Teine went to put the card back into its envelope, a small slip of paper fell out. "What's that?" Marcus asked, pointing to it.

"Probably trash, left over from making the card." Teine started to crumple it up, but there was Leis' handwriting on it. He looked closer. "What in the world?"

* * *

As angry as a wet hen, Niri stomped down the bricked pathway. Silpa followed at a respectful distance. The pair wove their way back toward the Pavilion where many of the wives and older daughters of the auction attendees were resting. "Marne was right," Niri muttered. "Madric wouldn't teach me."

"Thank goodness."

Niri ignored Silpa's clucking. "I know he has some *common* wench as an apprentice, so it can't be that I'm a girl, no matter what load of rubbish excuses he tried to sell me," she growled in impotent frustration. "Maybe he refused because I'm Lord Hilliard's daughter. Maybe I haven't studied enough to impress him."

"Well, it certainly can't be that. You study far too much." If Niri had turned back and seen the indulgent and loving smile on Silpa's face, she probably would have been even madder.

"Aaargh!" Niri fumed. "What can it be?"

"Good common sense?"

Niri shot a withering scowl over her shoulder. "Thank you for your boundless support."

As they were passing close to the Demesne, Niri glanced up to the second story, hoping to catch a glimpse of her friend. Marne was there, looking out the infirmary window at her. He was wrapped in a blanket, and clutching a basin close to his stomach as if he were afraid he'd need it soon. Even from this distance, she could see how pale and drawn he looked. While she watched, the frail Aoife boy waved weakly to acknowledge her, despite the heavy, ornate golden bracelet weighing down his left arm. She could see the shadows under Marne's grey eyes, the knowing expression on his youthful, angular face. His wave turned into a gesture inviting her up.

"I can't." Niri sighed, remembering her father's scolding. She shook her head, wishing she could tell him why. She hated that their fathers were enemies, and that he definitely had the worst end of it. She also hated that Marne was sick all the time. He was her very best friend, like a little brother, and she loved him with a ferocity that sometimes caught in her chest and came out as tears. She was helpless against his illness, like everyone else in his life. Part of her passion to learn magic stemmed from a burning desire to uncover the mystery behind Marne's infirmity, so he could get better, once and for all.

She blinked away the tears in her eyes, and a feeling of hopelessness overwhelmed her. Her quest to find a magic teacher was no secret. She'd been exploring every single possibility she could think of for the last couple decades, and had still come up drier than that old well. Because of her privilege and youth—she was only 84—she'd spent her entire life being indulged and cosseted in every whim, except this one. Madric's rejection really upset Niri, partially because he was *the* ranking wizard in the area and the uncle of her best friend, but also because she was fresh out of ideas on who to approach about learning the forbidden arts.

There was something else, too, something she hated to admit to herself. From the moment she laid eyes on Madric, or "Uncle Madric," as Marne would say, she was enamored of him. It was something about his facial expressions, and the way he'd spoken to her. Unlike other adults, Madric had looked right at her, as though he were really seeing *her* and not just the youngest daughter of a wealthy landholder. If she were to describe this feeling of butterflies in her stomach, and the hopeless certainty that she'd never see the magician up close again, it would probably make her older sister squeal with delight and try to probe her for details on this, her first crush.

She took a second and rubbed her stinging eyes with her sleeve, then looked up. Marne was still watching her, his head tilted quizzically. He looked for all the world like a faithful pet waiting for its master to return. Even though he was a story up, she could tell he was worrying about her and wondering what had happened. By way of a reply, Niri pantomimed sawing off her own head and drop kicking it.

"Young Miss!" Silpa gasped. "That is *not* ladylike. Young ladies do not ape street performers."

"*This* one does," Niri grumbled.

Up above, she could see Marne's answering grin at her theatrics. Then, he shrugged artlessly and held up his hands, as if to say, "What could I do?" or worse, "I told you so."

"You children really should take a proper class in sign languages, if you must do this."

"I hate that we just can't *talk*." Niri complained, bitterly. It's ridiculous! His birthday was a week ago, and I can't even give him his present or find out if he got the manservant he wanted." Her delicate hands balled into fists at her sides as her frustration increased in intensity. "He's *sick* and I can't even visit him!"

Silpa had perked up at the mention of another Human. "Do you remember the name of the one he asked for?"

"Hush, Silpa. I must think." Niri closed her eyes and pinched the bridge of her nose with her fingers, a gesture she'd seen her mother make when she was getting a migraine. Imitating her made Niri feel like she was thinking extra hard. "Teine," she said, snapping her fingers. "Yes, definitely Teine."

"I can't help you with a visit," Silpa told her. "But I may be able to get you information. Stay here, please. I'll be right back."

Niri sighed, watching her nanny walk away to flag down the first Solmurry Human she could find. Silpa of Cartierscross was in her early fifties and, to Niri's mind, an elegant old thing. Her raven-colored hair with streaks of grey and her pale porcelain complexion were then envy of many women half her age. Niri was proud to show her off because she was so lovely but, most importantly, because she loved her.

When Silpa returned she told her charge, "According to the rumor mill, young Marne got the one he wanted."

Niri raised a skeptical eyebrow. "How reliable can Human rumors be?"

Her nanny chuckled, "Oh, you'd be surprised." Silpa crouched beside her suddenly, looking Niri firmly in the eye. "Now, dear one, I hope you'll allow me to make a humble suggestion. It seems this has been a long day. You barely touched your breakfast, and we completely skipped lunch. I suggest that the world might look a little brighter, and you can tackle your problems with renewed vigor, after a quick bit of refreshment."

Suddenly Niri realized that she was starving. "That sounds sensible to me. Shall we go to the Pavilion and sit with my mother and sister?"

Silpa looked Niri up and down. "Not unless you'd like me to catch a beating. Look." She pulled a flat metal mirror out of her carry basket and showed Niri.

"I understand freckles are in this year," Niri snickered, raising an eyebrow at her mud-spattered appearance.

"Only if you're Human," Silpa countered. "Come on, let's duck in somewhere out of the way and get you cleaned up a bit before we take you to your mother."

Niri nodded, absently, looking up at her friend in the window. Suddenly, he grabbed his basin and darted from sight. "Oh, poor Marne," she sighed, as her stomach knotted in sympathy. But, when Silpa placed a hand on her shoulder to guide her away, she allowed herself to be turned off the path and steered toward the refreshment tent.

Chapter 6: Easy Marks

Leis and Amagorra set to watching the crowd, keenly combing the traffic for likely candidates. The day's festivities had brought out all manner of local characters and plenty of out of town visitors as well. Like every event, the personalities of note and power were Aoife, with Human servants and attendants. Leis noted Prior Vihah, the royal family's personal priest, strolling the grounds with two of his young acolytes, one Human and one Aoife.

Prior Vihah was no stranger to Solmurry. He was enamored of their choir and visited frequently. Leis had heard the kitchen staff complaining to her mother that the priest expected pampering far beyond what was normally offered a guest, even though Solmurry had a reputation for hospitality. According to the kitchen staff, the wispy old Aoife could put away enough edibles and drink to satisfy two hardworking Human shipbuilders. Leis noted with amusement that the priest, living up to his gluttonous reputation, strolled with a tumbler of beverage in one hand while nibbling on a kebab of meat and vegetables held in his other hand. Prior Vihah seemed to be enjoying himself, a mild amused expression on his face as he watched all the goings-on.

Leis longed to snatch the monocular from Amagorra and give the priest an inspection. Rumor had it that he did terrible things to those who were accused of practicing magic in secret. Such savagery seemed out of place compared to the amiable character he displayed. Yet, Vihah had been the one who uncovered and attended to Master Solmurrian's older brother, Uncle Madric, when his talent for magic had been disclosed.

Madric, Leis corrected herself, harshly. Since beginning to take over for her dam, who was retiring from her post in the nursery, Leis had come to think of Madric as "Uncle Madric," the way Lord Solmurrian's son referred to him. Calling the formidable Aoife magician "Uncle" would possibly earn Leis a sound thrashing, depending on who witnessed her mistake.

The Solmurry rumor mill was always abuzz with Madric Solmurrian's supposed hatred of Prior Vihah. The gossips said Madric harbored a silent, seething hatred for the priest that always bubbled near the surface. Leis found herself hoping the festival would be large enough that the two wouldn't run into each other.

Leis allowed her wandering eyes to rest on the most colorful patch of celebrants, and her gaze was automatically drawn to the Doyen Prince himself. The Aoife Prince, only son of Emperor Vondahasha, was young for a ruler, but had been manning the helm of their great Empire for the last decade. To Leis' eye, the Prince was a study in haughty confidence, like a strutting peacock. A pearly white coursing hound, exotic and breathtakingly graceful, followed at the Doyen's heels. The jeweled collar on his favored pet could have bought and sold a small village. In addition to his hound, the Prince was attended by several of his most notorious courtiers, all rakes and scoundrels, if the rumors could be believed. Their garish costumes jarred Leis' sense of decorum, but she couldn't help but watch. They, like their Prince, were all uniformly overdressed to the point of, to her practical Human eye, ridiculousness.

The peahens strode a few paces behind the peacocks. A gaggle of noisy, giggling Aoife women followed the courtiers. They were referred to as "actresses" in polite society, but Leis knew what they really were: courtesans and "fancy ladies" who entertained men for money. As they passed by, the 'actresses' drew some contemptuous stares from the more respectable women—wives, sisters, and mothers of many of the Aoife gentlemen who were attending the auctions or trading tales with their companions.

Nearby, a bunch of Solmurry Humans stood chatting in a casual group. Like the higher-caste Aoife, the Human men and women alike all wore their best clothes and were neatly turned out. Eaoster, or spring equinox, was traditionally a fertility ceremony, and the festivities were presided over not by Prior Vihah and his ilk, but by the local priestess of Alemis, the All-Mother. When Humans and common-folk embraced *all* the Eaoster traditions with enthusiasm, festivities often became rowdy and indecent.

In celebration of the holiday, all breeding restrictions were lifted, and the Aoife and Humans alike could bed with whomever they wished with no fear of reprisal or consequence. There were Humans from other households visiting Solmurry, and from what Leis could see, they were all doing their level best to secure themselves some horizontal companionship for the evening.

Any children accidentally "caught" at Eaoster were considered blessed, no matter how unlikely the union that produced them. Leis had also heard of the occasional surprise half-Aoife children born to Human women, but she wasn't sure if she believed such an outrageous thing occurred with any regularity. The only reason to beget half-breeds was on purpose, when the Aoife nobles needed bodyguards whose loyalty was assured.

Leis remembered her younger days and the Eaoster festivals she'd attended as a child. The adult Humans encouraged Leis and the other children to seek out the Aoife visitors, especially ones that looked nervous, and bring them a flower, a feather or an egg, and engage them in conversation. While any servant could look good in a highly controlled environment, only Solmurry Humans shone with the lack of any structure whatsoever.

Those charming and friendly children with their refreshments and baskets of flowers had made a lot of money for Solmurry over the years. While other manors produced everything from finished cloth to agricultural products, only a handful of Demesnes produced Humans in any great quantity specifically for resale. Although Solmurry was well known throughout the Empyrean for its shipyards, Solmurry Humans were considered some of the finest to be had anywhere.

Leis' musings were cut short by Amagorra's gentle elbow nudge to her ribs. The old woman jutted her chin toward an Aoife man and his lady strolling up the path. The lady was heavy with child and looked delicate, frail, and as though she was due any minute.

"What do you think?" Leis asked. Amagorra raised the monocular to view the prospective buyers. Leis held her breath as the lady noticed their booth, tugged her husband's sleeve, and beamed at him, pointing in their direction.

"Yes," Amagorra removed the monocle from her eye, allowing it to dangle around her neck by its chain. "I like them. They're both very kind."

Leis feigned disinterest and tried not to watch as the couple carried on a brief conversation that she could barely hear. It seemed the man was urging his wife to take her time, and look at all her available choices before making up her mind. She produced the catalog of the sale bill, and opened it wide to show him the centerfold dedicated to the Special Reserve.

He nodded, glumly following her lead to their booth.

Leis had to remember to breathe.

"Good day, fair lady and gentle sir," Samia greeted them as the pair approached. "I hope this day finds you both well. Do you have any questions I may assist you with?"

The Aoife woman fairly beamed, her rather plain, angular features lighting up with a genuine and kind-looking smile. Leis found herself liking her immediately without the benefit of a glance through the magic monocular.

Her poor husband seemed very nervous, and now that they were at hand Leis had a good idea why. She could see that they were not cut from the same cloth as most of the other Aoife bidders in attendance. They weren't nobility and they probably only had the resources of a reasonably well-off tradesman or smallholder. While they might be able to scrape together the price of a Special Reserve, a purchase from the regular auction would be far more reasonable for their budget.

Meanwhile, Samia had already drawn them in, artfully asking just the right questions to get the Aoife woman talking about the child she was carrying, and the first child she'd lost to Syndrome a few years previously. Her deft questioning soon uncovered their business at the auction that day. When they had married, the husband had promised his new bride a handmaiden from Solmurry as soon as they could afford the purchase. With a kind, earnest expression on her narrow face, and her hands folded almost as if in prayer, the Aoife woman was gravely asking Samia about her lineage.

"Do you have any Rudia in your pedigree? Rudia of Solmurry?"

Samia considered for a second, and then shrugged. That gesture would have earned her a sharp rap, if any of the comportment instructors had seen it. "What year? I've memorized back five generations…"

"Oh no, no, this would be *much* further back than five generations… Rudia was my grandmother's handmaiden, back when I was a girl. Perhaps seven Human generations?"

Reaching under her counter, Samia grabbed an old, hand-bound ledger and placed it reverently in front of the Aoife lady. "I believe this will be a good place to start our research. Do you want to come back here and sit with me?" The girl grabbed the chair Leis had been sitting on earlier and moved it next to her. With a smile at her new Aoife friend, Samia patted the seat and invited her into the booth.

Her husband held the curtain back and offered his hand to help his lady get settled in. He gave Leis a playful nudge as he passed, a gesture that would have felt overly casual and familiar, were it to have come from any of the Aoife Leis already knew. Strangely, though, she didn't mind. Then he winked at her over his glasses.

"I have a feeling I'm in trouble," he chuckled, nervously loosening his cravat and feeling for his purse. "I feel like I should be walking hunched over to protect my wallet." He shot an affectionate glance at his mate, who was already lost in reviewing the ancestry register with Samia. Leis couldn't help but like him, despite his lack of refinement.

"It's probably too late for that, sir," Leis teased in mock-sincerity. "Your best bet would be to either run away as fast as you can, plan on selling your carriage, or get comfortable sleeping in the guest bedroom." She was rewarded by his rueful chuckle as she poured tumblers of water for both Aoife from a pitcher they kept. Her duty complete, Leis stepped back and stayed out of the way while Samia worked the bidders.

Glancing over his wife's shoulder, the Aoife man chimed in, "You realize that if we place a bid for… Samia, is it?" Samia nodded eagerly. "We won't be able to bid on any of the others."

"Yes, my dear one," his wife agreed, as she patted Samia's arm. "She's the one that I want. If it's meant to be, it will happen. I'd rather chance it all on the possibility of bringing her home than settle for one of the others."

Leis noticed the sudden mistiness in her sister's eyes. She'd seen it many times before when other Humans of their number were leaving. There was a moment when they suddenly realized one chapter in their life was coming to an end and a new one was beginning. On Samia's face, Leis could see that familiar combination of relief that she was wanted that badly, and the sorrow of leaving behind everything she knew. Leis may have seen it all before, but it never failed to touch her. In a way, if everything about the transaction was right, it was far more like being adopted than being sold.

Leis wasn't the only one who noticed. The Aoife woman smiled with warm, almost maternal concern, as she rested her hand on the girl's arm. "Don't cry, little one. We're a happy family, and we've been waiting for someone like you for a long time."

Her husband shifted nervously, stirred into action like a horse smelling an impending storm. "I must go. There's business to attend to. Would you see she's made comfortable after she leaves your booth?"

"Yes, sir," Samia replied.

Amagorra also nodded. "We'll escort her to the Pavilion and get her off her feet for a bit."

"Excellent." He bent down and kissed his wife's smooth cheek. "Please, don't hold out for hope. I promise I'll do my best, though."

She smiled up at him, radiant and serene. "I know. Thank you, my darling."

He left them, calm and deliberate until he was clear of their booth. Then, he broke into a run, holding his hat fast to his head. Samia and her new friend giggled as they watched him go, then went back to the lighthearted business of getting to know each other.

As if on cue, Amagorra rose from her chair. "I, too, have business this day. I will return shortly." She tucked the monocular pendant into her shirt, leaving the chain around her neck. As she passed by, she gave Leis a knowing nod.

"I hope it works out!" Samia squeaked. She crossed her fingers on both hands.

Leis hoped to give Samia the same reassurance. "I believe it will."

The lady with them, Mrs. Aylmer, suddenly gasped in surprise. "What is it?" Samia asked, alarmed. "Are you all right?"

"Yes, oh yes! Is that the Doyen Prince, over there?" Her eyes were as wide as an excited child's.

"Oh, yes," Leis replied. She was not nearly so impressed. "We entertain him regularly. Our master is part of his Court. And," she added, trying not to let her lack of enthusiasm show in her voice, "It looks like they're coming this way."

Like a peacock in full strut, the Doyen Prince, acknowledged heir to their frail and fading Emperor, strode boldly toward them. His flowing golden hair was tucked behind his pointed ears and held in place by a jeweled circlet. As usual, the Prince was flanked by his muster of overdressed court fops and rakes. Leis noticed that several of them were already well into their cups, yet it was barely past midday meal. Suppressing her annoyance, she automatically checked her hair to be sure it was still tidy and attempted a welcoming smile. She hoped it didn't look as artificial as it felt.

"They are positively resplendent," Mrs. Aylmer breathed, taking in the jewelry and yards of sumptuous fabrics adorning her liege and his people. *An impressive sum of currency is tied up in those clothes*, Leis acknowledged silently. *Only the wealthy could afford to dress with such extravagance.*

Mrs. Aylmer was still entranced. "Beautiful, like butterflies."

"Butterflies with sharp teeth and heavy purses," Leis muttered under her breath.

"Special Reserve, Special Reserve," the Doyen said, sauntering toward them. "Must be special, indeed. Tell me, girls, how goes the bidding this day?" He spared a fleeting glance for Mrs. Aylmer, who was staring at him as rapt as if he'd just fallen from the heavens.

"V... very well, Your Excellency," Samia stuttered. She'd never been face to face with anyone ranked higher than her own master, unless you counted the gluttonous Prior who occasionally held services at Solmurry.

Leis chimed in, mostly to get the Doyen's attention away from her sister. She'd seen enough of him to know that he could smell fear like a shark could smell blood in the water. "We've had at least fifteen bids here, Your Excellency, and probably at least that many at the office. A good start to the day."

The Prince glanced briefly at Leis, then leaned forward over the table, placing one hand on either side of the ancestry register, clearly savoring the younger girl's discomfort. "Maybe I'll put in a bid myself." He winked playfully, but Leis recoiled from the cruelty she also saw in his gaze.

"Oh, surely she's special." one courtier proclaimed, leaning in with the Doyen and grabbing Samia's chin in his uncalloused, delicate Aoife hand. Leis bristled inwardly as her sister's eyes widened in surprise. "But what I want to know is, is she *reserved?*"

"Faugh! Dorian, you're positively lecherous. She's what, fourteen?"

"Twelve," answered Leis, firmly, unable to keep the disapproval from her voice. Of course they meant Samia no real harm. They were just looking for entertainment, and always found their fun at the expense of others.

"Twelve?" the Doyen laughed out loud, leaning back and pointing at his compatriot. "Twelve?" He roared with laughter, smacking the other man's hand away from Samia's face. "Twelve years old, and Human to boot! We need to find you a *woman*, Dorian." He clapped him hard on his velvet-clad shoulder. "A woman, meaning no younger than a hundred. Or a hundred twenty-five if her father's the protective type." The courtiers all roared, and Dorian laughed right along with them.

Samia looked a little shaken, but managed a faint smile.

"Now, there's a good sport," the Doyen said, returning her smile with an unreadable one of his own. "We'll take our leave." With that, he made one gesture to his retinue, and they followed him away, presumably in search of more interesting prey. He left the two Human girls and the Aoife woman to themselves to whisper about the encounter.

Chapter 7: Future Perfect

Teine found himself squinting to read his sister's petite handwriting.

"I know something you don't know. —L"

She'd even drawn a tiny little flower by her initial.

"I could fill a book with things I know that she doesn't," Teine said, hoping he came across with the right kind of cool indifference. The other boys teased him about Leis sometimes.

Marcus seemed to be less morose than he was when Teine started trying to cheer him up, but Teine decided to sit with his friend a bit longer just to be sure. It also got him a little further away from the knot of other boys still huddled around the radio. He could use a break from that crowd, and Marcus was congenial company. "So," he asked, by way of making conversation. "What assignments did you put in for? Horses, right?"

Marcus nodded, removing the candy from his mouth so he could talk. The features of the lime deer had melted away, and all that was left was a translucent green blob on a stick. "I also put in for ships and volunteered for more schooling at Tech," he replied. "My grades are good enough. I'd love to learn how the trains work, or maybe go to work at the power station in town."

Agreeably, Teine nodded. Any of those jobs would be good. They'd be interesting, which, if he knew Marcus at all, would probably be more important to him than the allowance. That was one thing they had in common. "Hey, I just remembered," he blurted out. "I heard a rumor about you."

"What, that I'm an IM and I've lost my girlfriend?" Marcus replied, sounding glum all over again. Teine winced inwardly, wondering if he ought to just cut his losses, shut up, and go draw something.

"No, no. Much more interesting," Teine countered. "You might have a bigger score coming up than a cushy power station job."

Looking a bit intrigued, Marcus leaned in. "Well, out with it," he urged, "I could use a bit of good news."

Teine leaned in too. "I heard from Leis that the young master is going to be entering stock in the Display. Rumor has it that you're his top pick."

Marcus blinked stupidly, and then grinned, "Really?" he asked, "You're not putting me on?"

"Not at all," Teine said. "Leis said so about a week ago. I forgot till just now. I figure since she's doing a half-day at the house spelling our Amagi, she'd be the one to know."

"That would be…" Marcus seemed to think about it for a second, and Teine could see his enthusiasm for the idea gaining steam. "That would be great! I'd be able to study anything I wanted, as long as it was challenging. And I wouldn't have to do any more half-shifts at the dairy."

Teine nodded. "You'd be too busy studying, and…" He paused, trying to figure out what a Display Human would actually do with their time. "…working out. And probably fending off all sorts of women," he added lamely.

"I'd get to be with young Master Marne," Marcus added. "Do you remember him at all? From when we were nurslings?"

"Remember him?" Teine sighed, picturing the frail Aoife boy. "My Amagi is his nanny and my sib is taking over her job. He's been in some of my art classes, and choir, too. I've never had a chance to forget him." Truthfully, Teine really didn't remember much about nursery school or Marne, only that Marne was a regular visitor there before he and his Cohort had started their formal schooling. He vaguely recalled that Marne read them an awful lot of story books. In fact, it was those books that had gotten him interested in writing stories himself.

"Story time was my favorite part of nursery school, and it was even better when he read to us. Remember how he used to do the voices?" Marcus said, a faraway expression on his face. "Do you remember the one about the giant, Paol Bunyard, and...."

"Didn't he have some monstrously huge blue cow or something?" Teine frowned, trying to remember the story.

Marcus laughed. "An ox. They call them oxes or oxen."

"What would anyone want with a pet cow?"

Marcus looked mystified. "I can't think of a single thing, and I work in the dairy. I guess people who can't afford good horses or a mule or anything else might use them for pulling."

Just then, there was a timid knock on the door. "Come in!" Teine yelled. But no-one entered, they just knocked again, but louder.

"You get it! You're closest," Seymour called to him. He'd joined the other boys who were huddled around the radio, the whole group staring at it as if eye contact could improve its reception.

With a groan, Teine got up off the bed. He opened the door to the infirmary and found himself face to face with a young man about his age. Towheaded, with a ruddy complexion and hair flopping in front of his eyes, the boy dragged along a big, monogrammed trunk with wheels on one end. He also had a carrying bag slung over his shoulder, which made him look more like he was moving in than visiting the infirmary.

"Yes?" Teine asked, with a little hesitation.

"Is this the hospital?" he asked.

Teine raised an eyebrow and pointed to the sign on the door that read, "Infirmary."

Sheepishly, the blonde shrugged. "I don't read so good. But if this is the hospital, I'm here to get Cut." He offered a folder of papers to Teine, who took a step back, waving his hand.

"No, no! You'll need the Clinician. I'm just a patient." Teine stepped out of the way, gesturing the newcomer in. "I'll go find her. I'm Teine, by the way."

"Marcus," Marcus added from his bed. He was reading the haberdasher's advertisement again. Some of the other boys called out their names and Seymour was headed their way, drawn to the novelty of a new person like a deer to a salt lick.

"I'm Abel of Bartheim." Looking around the room in wonder, the newcomer blinked. I can't believe I'm really *here!*"

Teine paused on the threshold, surprised by the newcomer's enthusiasm. There was a story here. He could sense it.

"There's nothing particularly special about our infirmary," volunteered Seymour as he marched up and offered his hand to the newcomer. "Well, except we have a lady Clinician. Other than that, it's just an infirmary."

"With horrible radio reception," added one of the fabal fans.

"And a really good view of that storm blowing in," commented another.

Abel grinned widely and clapped his hands together with glee, dropping the end of his trunk with a loud bang that startled everybody in the room. He bypassed Seymour's outstretched hand

and instead threw his arms around the surprised boy. "I can't believe it!" Abel crowed. "I'm really here!"

"Let me go," Seymour whispered, his face smushed against the other boy's shoulder. His one visible eye pled silently with Teine for intervention. "You're... breaking... me," he breathed. Everyone at Solmurry knew that Seymour was to be gently handled and this newcomer had just subjected him to more mauling in three seconds than he'd had in his entire ten years there.

"Seymour, why don't you go get the Clinician?" Teine suggested, gesturing to Abel to let his comrade go.

Abel released him with a distracted, "Sorry," and continued drinking in the room, oblivious to Seymour's panicked flight into Nocdoramus' office.

"Now, why are you here?" Teine asked.

Abel held up a finger to silence him. "Wait! I'll show you!" With that, he started popping the catches on his trunk to open it. Most of the other boys began crowding around to see what was going on. With a flourish, Abel reached into the trunk and pulled out a box. Inside that box, packed very carefully, was a miniature sailing ship built inside a big glass bottle.

The boys all seemed to breathe in at once. "Did you *make* that?" "Is it yours?" "Want to trade for it?" The clamor filled the room, until Seymour returned with the Clinician in tow.

"Abel, is it?" Nocdoramus asked. The tone of her voice was all business, insisting on silence from the other boys without having to ask for it. "May I see your paperwork?"

"Y-yes, m'Lady." Abel averted his eyes as if the delicate Aoife woman might break from the weight of his gaze.

It was an odd gesture, Teine thought. Able's mannerisms looked more like fear than respect. But before he could consider it for long, the Clinician spoke again.

"You've been purchased today and are here to get Cut?" she asked, though it sounded more like a statement. "That's odd. We usually never buy or take outside trades during a production sale. It would defeat the point. Especially not for working stock."

"Yes, m'Lady," Abel replied, in a voice that sounded like it belonged to a boy much smaller. He just stood there, gently cradling the ship in a bottle. "My master did it. He did it for me. For the ships."

Teine was beginning to piece together the puzzle, and was amused. His guess was that Abel really loved seacraft, and his master thought highly enough of him to sell him, probably at a loss, if it meant delivering him right to the doorstep of his big dream.

Nocdoramus must have come to the same conclusion, because suddenly she was all smiles. "Well then, Abel, welcome to Solmurry! You'll have to stay overnight here, and have nothing to eat or drink after midnight to prepare you for surgery, but the boys will show you around. Marcus, can you be in charge of sponsoring Abel?"

"Yes, m'Lady!" Marcus nodded pleasantly, with his usual sunny smile. Teine agreed with the Clinician's choice. Marcus and Abel would probably get along well, and having a new person to introduce would help distract Marcus from his loss.

Seymour, none the worse for wear, had also joined them, "I like ships, too," he interjected. "But I like models even more. You'll have to tell me all about that one you have there. Did you make it yourself?"

Well, my job is done here, thought Teine, with no small amount of satisfaction. He grabbed his letters off the bed next to Marcus' and retreated to his own bunk. While no one was paying him any attention, he applied some ointment to his wound and placed the bag of ice where it belonged. The storm clouds were closer, the fabal game was all but inaudible, and Teine was finally ready. He reached over to his pile of belongings and grabbed the journal. Opening it to the page where he'd left off, he could see Leis's handwriting:

"Miriam knew better than to venture into a cave by herself… but she also knew this was no ordinary situation. Davy could live or die, depending on how she played the hand of cards she'd been dealt. She'd have to come up with something especially clever…"

Teine chuckled to himself. He'd been thinking about it, and he'd decided that Miriam's devious plan consisted of overturning a couple stones on the path, and dragging her heel to make it look as though she'd sought refuge in the cave. But instead, she'd hide, hoping the brigands would take the bait and enter the cave so she could scurry away to better cover. Once they dismounted and moved to investigate, she planned to leap out of hiding, grab one horse to ride back for help, and scatter the rest.

During a brief moment with clear reception, one of the fabal teams managed to score again, but Teine was so wrapped up in his part of their creative venture that he didn't even notice.

Chapter 8: Title Transfers

Inside the main office, within the manor house proper, Lord Solmurrian was hunched over one of the prodigious tomes of pedigrees. Although the room was spacious, with high ceilings, a cut crystal chandelier, and richly appointed furnishings, to him it felt very crowded. His brow furrowed with concentration as his pen scratched out a new entry. Then a pile of binna and senta notes changed hands. He longed to loosen the tight collar of his best suit, shed the velvet surcoats, and get comfortable, but he couldn't with so many people around.

A gangly knot of eight Human children, all wearing the Solmurrian livery, huddled together toward the back of the room near the harpsichord. They gawked in silent awe at the lavish appointments while waiting to be called upon to run errands.

The master was flanked by his two business assistants, identically dressed Aoife gentlemen, Vorogu and Volsney. Although not high-born, the twin brothers had made a name for themselves in the time of the present Lord Solmurrian's father, and had been at the books and records as long as anyone could remember. An auction buyer waited for Lord Solmurrian to complete his paperwork, and another Aoife man stood patiently behind him, staring with poorly disguised awe at the portrait of a strikingly lovely woman above the fireplace. The lord eyed this man furtively, while continuing his transaction with the other.

The portrait of Lord Solmurrian's wife had that effect on many people. Part of him was gratified that others could recognize her incredible beauty and presence even in a painting. Another part of him still grieved so terribly he longed to rip the portrait from the wall and hide it away, so he could begin to forget.

While Lord Solmurrian contemplated his status as a widower and waited for the ink to dry on the transfer, Vorogu, his docent, counted the scrip money to be sure everything was in order. When he was finished, he gave a nod to Lord Solmurrian.

"Salma of Solmurry," the Master said, handing the other Aoife man a fat wallet full of papers. "Dona of Solmurry," he added, placing another set of records on top of the first one. "Cynthia of Dinsdale." A thinner packet of records joined the stack. "And Adam of Solmurry," he finished, adding the last batch of papers. "Now, there are your pedigrees, transfer forms, and of course, the pension program and insurance for the ones from our bloodlines."

He smiled, the expression and his comments smooth and well-rehearsed. "Your new Humans and their trunks will be ready for pickup at the carriage house momentarily." He snapped his fingers to one of the Human children standing nearby the door. "Salma, Dona, Cynthia, and Adam. Go." The girl nodded and bolted for the door, ruffling papers on the desk with her brisk passing.

With a touch of his hat, the new owner nodded pleasantly and exited through the door that led to the formal garden. Master Solmurry, both his assistants, and the next person in line all threw themselves over the desk to protect the neat piles of sorted paperwork from an unruly gust of wind when the door opened.

"It's really picking up out there," Lord Solmurrian sighed. As the door slammed, he stood and straightened his jacket. "We're going to wrap things up a little early so people can beat the weather. Though, I bet we'll end up with our share of overnight visitors."

"Agreed," replied the next man in line. "I think we're in for a screamer tonight." The two Aoife men stood in silence for a second, tense and listening to the wind outside. Finally, the guest shook himself out of his reverie. "My wife, our new girl, and I may end up being some of those overnight visitors." With a nervous smile, he held out a ticket stub, offering it to Lord Solmurrian.

"Ah, Lor...*Mister* Aylmer, is it?" the Lord of Solmurry hesitated one instant, then recovered to reach out and shake his hand. "Congratulations on your winning bid! Samia is one of the finest Solmurry has ever offered at a production sale. I'm sure you'll be delighted with her performance and breeding."

Mister Aylmer beamed, as he pumped the Lord's hand with enthusiasm. "My wife... she's going to be so pleased!"

"Indeed," Master Solmurrian replied, extracting his hand. "Are you here to settle your account, then?"

Pale and nearly shaking, Mr. Aylmer nodded, his expression making him seem as though he expected to be drained of blood at any minute.

"Well, then," Master Solmurrian produced a thin, leather-bound pedigree folder embossed with the Solmurry crest, a stylized tall ship on the sea with the sun behind it. With a little flourish, he handed it to Mr. Aylmer, then located the correct paper and slid it across the desk. "You beat the next bidder by less than ten senta," he told him.

"To be truthful, I didn't think we stood a chance," Mr. Aylmer said, holding up the paperwork to inspect it. "But my wife..." He trailed off, blinking in astonishment as all the color drained from his face when he saw the figure on the page in front of him. "But we can't aff...."

Lord Solmurrian didn't hear him. "Your generous 'up-front' deposit, in case of a tie, was what saved you. As you know, your remaining balance is only forty-five hundred senta."

Still looking stunned, Mr. Aylmer muttered, "I… didn't pay a deposit up front." He imagined having to explain to his wife that they hadn't actually won, that it had been a mistake, and that the real figure was so far above their means he had no way to pay it.

"You didn't?" Lord Solmurrian paused from his paperwork, regarding him coolly. Then, he offered Mr. Aylmer him another piece of paper. "Here's the receipt. You *didn't* send your man? I took the deposit myself, and there is no doubt he was putting in a deposit for you on the Special Reserve auction. Have you changed your mind? We can refund this deposit, if you…"

"No, no," Mr. Aylmer blurted, staring dumbly at the paper, then rapidly fumbling for his wallet. "I can pay. We definitely want her. I… just don't know how this happened."

"Solmurry can be a strange place," Lord Solmurrian answered, taking Mr. Aylmer's bank notes and sitting down to write him a final receipt. He paused for an instant, regarding the other man, his expression unreadable. Then he looked back down to his receipt book and began filling out the form. "I don't mean strange in a bad way. Sometimes things just work out when there seems to be no way they could. It can leave you shaking your head and wondering what just happened."

Mr. Aylmer nodded mutely.

"I believe I saw your wife with Samia earlier today." Master Solmurrian added. "Is she heavy with child?"

"Yes, sir."

"Then I'll make arrangements for your family here at the Demesne for tonight. I insist you stay. Racing a storm with her so near her time could be disastrous."

"Yes, sir," Mr. Aylmer replied. "Thank you kindly."

For a minute, there were no sounds in the room except for the wind outside and the dull scratching of pen on paper. Then, the master handed over the completed bill of sale, transfer papers, and the other documents that rounded out the transaction. The embossed wallet for Samia's paperwork looked considerably more robust when they were done.

"I'm certain your wife will enjoy her." Master Solmurrian nodded sagely. "When you're ready to retire for the evening, come to the front door of the Demesne, and my servants will attend you. I'll tell them to make up a room right away." With that, he gestured to another of the liveried children to go with Mr. Aylmer to fetch Samia.

Aylmer left through the door to the garden, the messenger girl on his heels. Master Solmurrian and his clerks again held the papers down on the desk to keep the wind from destroying their neat stacks.

Master Solmurrian rose to his feet, drifting past the harpsichord and the portrait above the unlit fireplace and wandered toward the window. Resting his hands on the windowsill, he surveyed what he could of the festivities beyond the formal garden that lay just outside the door. He supposed he should be grateful, as he no longer needed to excuse himself to hide the tears that welled up whenever he thought of Brigid. He rarely cried now, alone or in public. For some time, he'd been aware that people spoke about him and how he'd continued mourning for far longer than was acceptable. Perhaps soon those comments would be as dead as his wife.

Under the trees on the lawn beyond the garden, the Lord of Solmurry could see the shaded pavilions set up for the wives and children of his business associates. The first time he'd ever seen Brigid, she'd been there. He'd heard her before seeing her, as the office windows had been open and sound of her mischievous laughter carried on the spring breeze. She'd worn a watered silk gown as blue as her eyes, and had been teasing a younger girl with a woven crown of flowers. Although Lord Solmurrian had been barely over a century then, she'd taken his breath away.

As far as he could tell, she'd never given it back.

He sighed, resting his forehead against the glass of the window while continuing to watch the people outside. Aoife women enjoyed the comfortable seating and refreshments while they watched their children run and play on the neatly groomed lawn. But the weather had turned. Low on the horizon, clouds the color of a livid bruise loomed and the breeze carried the wild scent of rain and ozone. It was a certainty that the coming storm brought more than mere *weather*.

The Lord mentally ticked down the guest list while his stomach did a slow, nervous roll. The Courtiers, the Prince himself, and of course Prior Vihah, the High Inquisitor.

Could the enchantment hold, with a storm raging? Perhaps Madric could spirit the boy away before…

"Master?"

"Yes?" he replied, trying to keep the impatient edge out of his voice. "What?"

"Begging your pardon, my lord," Vorogu suggested gently. "But it's a fine, fair day, at least for a while yet. You should venture outside, perhaps mingle with the guests."

Master Solmurrian gave a brief snort of laughter. He was doing mental gymnastics trying to find a way to keep their darkest family secrets, and Vorogu was trying to get him to chase women.

"You've got nothing to lose by becoming acquainted again with fresh country air—not to mention the elegant, *unmarried* daughters of your business associates," Vorogu prodded, a little less gently.

One of the Human children betrayed their continuing presence with a slight giggle, which was quickly cut off by several "shushes" and what sounded like a light slap from one of his peers. It made Lord Solmurrian want to chuckle, himself.

"Vorogu, you know I hold your opinions in high regard," Lord Solmurrian began. "And I trust your advice, as always. But…" the Lord found his eyes raising to Brigid's portrait, scanning her serene expression as if searching for a clue as to how she'd feel about him formally ending his mourning.

Without taking his eyes from hers, he continued, "That incoming storm looks as though it could become bothersome, in a big hurry. I need to make some alterations to the program to give our patrons time to make it home and give staff time to make arrangements to accommodate those staying." He paused for effect, letting the situation sink in for his associate. "You understand, of course," he whispered, "I'll need to send the boy along with Madric, as soon as possible…"

Vorogu looked as though he desperately wanted to say something, but kept silent.

Master Solmurrian gazed out at the menacing sky, turning his back to the room. "Children, you are to spread the word among the staff leaders that we'll be adjourning early, and that we'll be offering hospitality to those who need it. Now, off with you."

The Human children left, pulling the office door shut behind them.

"It's just not the same without her," Master Solmurrian whispered. His eyes were as grey as the leaden sky.

Emboldened a bit, Vorogu pulled a chair over so Lord Solmurrian could sit and look out the window. Nodding, the Master sat while his docent dragged a second chair over to join him.

"Everyone must grieve on their own time schedule," Vorogu offered. "Just because twenty years of mourning is the norm doesn't mean that sixty, or even a hundred is enough in some cases."

Lord Solmurrian continued to gaze out the window. Somehow it was easier to discuss a topic like this when he didn't have to look anyone in the eye.

"It's always the worst when I'm home," he began, with no intention to say more. But the rest came tumbling out. "She still haunts this place. I expect to just turn a corner, and find her. I see her face everywhere."

And in the face of our son, he thought.

For his part, Vorogu did what he did best: sit quietly and listen. Master Solmurrian had sudden surge of warmth for the man, who had probably sat in the same chair and listened to the previous Lord Solmurrian say the same things when he lost his wife, as well. But with that thought came anger, irrational as it was. Somehow the fact that other men, one of them his own father, had become widowers and still survived felt like it was trivializing his own pain.

"Nothing is the same without her, but when I'm away, sometimes I have a hard time remembering exactly what she looks… *looked* like."

"God made people with many wondrous abilities," Vorogu mused. "Everything from powerful magics to altering their physical form at will. But perhaps the most merciful gift we received was the ability to forget, a little, but still love the same." In a rare moment of boldness, he reached out to Lord Solmurrian with his wiry hand, and clasped him on the shoulder.

"I suppose you're right." Lord Solmurrian patted the old man's hand, returning the gesture with cool affection. He appreciated the concern, even though it had been a breach of protocol for his servant to initiate contact. "Do you really think I have enough time to walk the grounds for a bit of socializing before the mad dash for cover?"

Vorogu nodded, then gestured out the window. "There are many lovely new faces. The Earl of Broshenford brought his youngest daughter and her little boy along. Her husband was killed in a pirate attack, and this is her first venture out since she's come out of mourning. Do you see her? She's the one in the red gown."

Like an obedient child, Lord Solmurrian leaned toward the window and peered out. As Vorogu promised, he saw an attractive young woman with hair a shade darker than Brigid's. Her little boy was a bundle of energy. He yelled and giggled while he tossed a bean bag back and forth with his mother. The cheerful domestic scene touched Master Solmurrian, leaving him with a bittersweet sense of nostalgia.

"I would suppose that the two of you might have a lot to speak about," Vorogu added, an innocent expression on his face. "No one understands loneliness like the lonely."

Master Solmurrian nodded thoughtfully. "I wonder how my son would adapt to having a new mother and little brother," he mused. "Another Aoife child about may do him some good. He spends too much time with only the Humans." He sighed, then chuckled ruefully, shaking his head. "Humans, horses and hounds. That's my son."

"That reminds me," Vorogu interjected, with a snap of his fingers. "I have those files you requested. Hand them over, Volsney," he gestured to his twin, who'd remained behind the desk.

He retreated from the window, to return with two leather envelopes that he offered to Lord Solmurrian. "Marcus, and Teine."

Lord Solmurrian opened one folder, then the other, to glance at the first page dossier. "I'm prepared to give him the one he wants, but I still think he's making a mistake. Marcus is such a fine lad. I've had my eye on him for some time to potentially replace his sire. In comparison, this Teine fellow is scrawny..." He trailed off, his expression intent with concentration. "But he looks to be a fine student, though. Hmm. Artist and writer, too. I can see why Marne favors him."

"Give him the one he wants, and keep Marcus for yourself." Volsney suggested, without looking up from the paperwork still littering the desk. "Then, lease Marcus to your son during show season, and have Marne show them both. He'll be there on your coin anyway, so you might has well get the exposure for your man, as well."

Master Solmurrian blinked twice in astonishment. "That's brilliant."

"I do my best, Sir."

Handing Marcus's folder back to Vorogu, Master Solmurrian sighed, tucking Teine's paperwork under his arm. "Well, at least *that's* settled. I think I'll stretch my legs a bit."

"Go on then," Vorogu urged, rising to his feet. "Go meet the lady. I'll get the proverbial rudder turning. This party is not over yet. Perhaps you could extend her family the courtesy of an invitation for hospitality in the face of this wretched weather."

"You are quite the pair of devious old men," Lord Solmurrian said, a faint but genuine smile crossing his features. He straightened his jacket and checked to be certain the ribbon tying back his clubbed ponytail hadn't come untied.

Vorogu made a playful, dismissive gesture. "You look fine. Now go, before you change your mind!"

With a somewhat nervous chuckle, Lord Solmurrian allowed himself to be chased out of his own office into the garden. The wind tore at his garments and carefully arranged hair, and he paused on the steps trying once again to put himself back together. In the formal gardens, he could see several couples, Human and Aoife, sitting closely on benches, some even sharing a passionate embrace, kissing and clinging to each other.

Momentarily grateful that none of *his* house was engaged in such public displays of affection, he passed them all by without censure. The cycle was as it was, and unbridled passions were accepted and even encouraged without judgment or complaint on this Eaoster holiday. Fixing a smile on his face that he hoped looked charming, Lord Solmurrian strode out onto the lawn to greet his guests.

Inside the master's office, Vorogu watched him leave. After a second, Volsney joined him.

"These books are a mess," Volsney complained, pointing to the ledger on the Master's desk. "I swear the man still counts on his fingers. His father would be appalled."

"I know. That's why I urged him out the door. I suspected we'd need a bit of time to put things right."

"It's so much easier when he isn't being 'helpful,'" Volsney grumbled, a sour look on his face. "In truth, I'm not sure whether it's easier being interfered with or ignored." He drifted back to the desk, glanced at a stack of records, and then tucked them in a folder with an eloquent snort of disgust.

"Never mind. Ignored would be much better. So, did you discuss the deficit situation with him?"

Vorogu nodded, turning away from the window. "Yes, I caught him shortly after he arrived. And I think I might have gotten through to him this time. Either that or he didn't hear a word I said. It's hard to tell sometimes."

"If he'd just rein in on the gambling a bit," Volsney suggested, hopefully. "That would make a big difference. Right now, it's like being on a ship that's sinking slowly. We can only bail so fast."

"Well, hopefully he'll take our conversation to heart."

"Hopefully. We'll see."

Chapter 9: Pumped

Soon auction guests and their families were either bundling up their new purchases to leave, or seeking refuge within the Solmurry grounds. Everyone wanted to be under cover, or *covers*, before the storm arrived.

Leis would have liked to be there to help Samia pack her trunk and listen to her nervous banter. Instead, she was behind the Demesne proper in the garden, up to her elbows in soapsuds and dog hair.

"You're a good boy, yes you are," she breathed. "Stinky," Marne's cherished pet, was a grinning, dripping, foul-breathed wolfhound who'd had himself a nice roll in something revolting. The head housekeeper had banished him from the Demesne until after he'd had a bath. Leis hoped to have him clean and dried by the time Marne was released from the infirmary.

The old hound weighed nearly as much as a full grown Aoife, but fortunately for Leis, she didn't have to wrestle him. He stood obediently by the hand pump, not moving a muscle except for his slowly waving tail. "Such a good, stinky boy." Leis pumped water into the bucket, wishing she had an extra set of hands to pump while she sluiced water into the dog's wiry coat.

"Here, move him directly under the spigot," Madric said, "And I'll pump. That will be a lot faster."

Leis squeaked with surprise, starting to mutter something to the master's brother about not getting dirty, until she looked up.

Madric was *at least* as filthy as she was. It looked like he'd gone ahead with the second well digging after all. He was spattered with mud, and looked very pleased with himself.

"Well, then," Madric urged, "Move him under." He gave her a wry, yet tolerant grin, and began working the pump fixture.

It was then that she realized she was just standing there, staring stupidly. "Thank you, sir."

"Oh, please," Madric chuckled. "It's just Madric. I'm going to need to use it too, before I can go inside for a real bath. Just stick around, and pump for me when it's my turn."

Leis nodded dumbly, unable to think of anything to say. Madric filled the silence with pleasant banter. "After all, I can't be shown up by old Stinky here, not with all the courtiers visiting!" He reached out and affectionately rubbed the dog on his grizzled grey head. "Are you cleaner than me, you old fleabag?"

"Thank you, I really do appreciate it… Madric," Leis added, recovering from the shock of having the original heir to Solmurry rolling up his sleeves and laboring right next to her. "I'd been wishing for an extra set of hands, and here you are."

Madric bowed his head, leaning into the pump, a smile on his face.

"Come on, Stinky," Leis urged the dog under the spigot, accomplishing in seconds what would have taken a good ten minutes to finish without Madric's help. Shutting off the pump, Madric tossed Leis the ragged old towel she'd set aside for Stinky. And just in time, too. She threw the cloth over the dog just as he began to shake.

"Here, I'll save you some time. I think I have one more spell in me." As Leis watched, gape-mouthed, Madric cantellated, summoning a small whirlwind. Within a couple minutes, the hound was blown nearly dry.

"Oh thank you, sir... Madric!" Leis exclaimed. "That's *amazing!* I've always wanted to see something like that up close!" Madric nudged the tiny whirlwind in her direction, and she laughed as it tried to unravel her coronet of braids and whipped her skirts around. "Although, I admit, *this* was closer than I had in mind."

Madric backed his elemental down, and it stayed nearby, whirling a few fallen spring blossoms around like a stage magician juggling for a crowed. "Do you mind?" Madric gestured at the spigot. "Can you pump while I...?"

Leis nodded, "Sure."

Giving Stinky a stern look, she pointed to the ground. "Sit." The hound complied, and she showed him the flat of her hand. "Stay."

While Madric stripped his outer robe, Leis tried not to look. Instead, she applied herself vigorously to the pump. Madric washed quickly and tidily, including rinsing his green ceremonial robe free of mud. When he was passably clean, he held the garment by the shoulders. Ever obedient, the air elemental danced around its temporary master, whisking him and his clothes dry. Leis watched, her hand on the hound's broad head, feeling strangely elated, and somehow... special.

"So," Madric asked, dismissing the elemental with a wave. "Are you one of Teine's full siblings?"

Startled, Leis nodded, "Why do you ask?"

With a lazy grin, like a cat too full of cream to toy with a mouse, Madric stretched and pulled the robe over his head. Leaning forward, Leis whispered, "So, is it *certain*, then? He picked Teine?"

"Oh, aye," Madric agreed. "Not his father's first choice for him, but it's the boy's project. From what I've seen of your line, the boy could hardly make a bad pick. Not a hot temper, empty mind, or lay-about among the lot of you."

"Thank you, sir." Color rising to her cheeks, Leis felt unexpectedly complimented.

"And you've taken over Amagi's position completely?" Madric asked. "I'm sorry, what's your name again? Lisa?"

"Leis."

"Well, Leis, Marne's... a very special child." Madric straightened the collar on his robe, smoothing the shoulder seams. "As I'm sure you've gathered during your training period. I am as fond of the boy as if he were my own son, and I regret that I don't have nearly as much time to spend with him as I would like."

When Leis looked up, shyly, to meet Madric's eyes, she was startled at the intensity of emotion she saw there. He visibly struggled with his next words.

"There are... dark times ahead for Marne, and dangers that exist only for him. He'll need people around him who will *always* put his best interests first. Not to look after him, but to look *out* for him, and still somehow maintain a certain level of discretion." Madric's eyes searched her face, testing, looking for any weakness. "Do you think you and your brother will be up to the job?"

Leis paused for a moment, taking a moment to really study Madric and think about his words, and what was going on under the words. Marne was the elephant in the room that no one talked about. She could see it and feel it. It was getting to the point where it was obvious that something was very, very wrong with Marne. It wasn't just his frequent illnesses. It was clear now that his problems went deeper than him simply being a late bloomer. Marne was not maturing at a normal rate. She suspected she was the first one of the boy's caregivers to ever participate in a conversation quite like this one, on Marne's behalf.

She'd also heard about the "disturbances," but she'd never seen anything unusual herself. Anything she *had* heard, she'd passed off as silly superstition, or just serving wenches who liked to frighten themselves with ghost stories.

"I understand what you mean, sir," Leis replied. "Amagi briefed me, and I've been assisting for six months. We'll never let him down."

"And Teine?" Madric asked. "I read his file. He's a boy with a bright future. He's qualified for several different opportunities, more choices than most boys get."

"Yes, sir. He's very bright. He and Marne also have many common interests. I expect they'll have a lot to talk about, once they get down to it."

"I'm sure," Madric chuckled. "Marne has enough interests on his own that he could find something to talk about with nearly anybody."

Leis couldn't help but smile a little, Madric was so correct.

"But the big question is, how will Teine react to having his choice usurped? He could perceive this appointment to Marne's service as work having almost nothing to do with his intelligence, adaptability, or creativity."

Leis couldn't help herself as her eyes widened. "Sir... I... never thought of it that way. I... well..." Truth be told, Leis *hadn't* ever considered it. She'd just assumed if Marne picked Teine, that Teine would be as happy about the arrangement as she was.

Madric nodded. "Well, I suppose we'll have to wait and see. If he's totally unsuitable, we can find other work for him."

Taking in Leis' crestfallen expression, Madric stepped forward and gave her a stilted pat on the shoulder.

"Don't be too hard on yourself, Leis," Madric suggested. "I shouldn't have expected you to consider his perspective. After all, the high-performing boys have much more of a choice in their vocation than you young women do."

"A person has more opportunities if they're never encumbered by babies or pregnancy," Leis agreed. "Men's and women's lives, well, they're like two different *worlds*."

"And, to completely change the subject," Madric began, examining the threatening sky. "Unless this magic storm diverts or blows itself out, I'll be taking Marne with me when I go back to my tower tonight. Is he well enough to travel?"

"He hasn't been released from the infirmary yet," Leis frowned. "He's usually a little weak and shaky after an episode and he'll need a bland diet for a few days. But he could probably go, if it's important. I'll run up and tell Nocdoramus."

"Good." Madric took a second to pick at the collar of his robe. "I thought you might appreciate as much notice as possible. Is this your first time getting him packed by yourself?"

"Yes, sir," Leis replied automatically. "Thank you."

"If you hurry…" Madric gestured, waving her away. "You'll have time to say goodbye to your sibling. I understand her sale price broke a record today."

"Yes, sir," Leis beamed. But even though she was proud of Samia's success, she was already beginning to anticipate the sadness of her sister's leaving.

"I expect we won't be able to get free until after evening meal," Madric continued "It's likely my brother will want to transfer

Teine's title this evening, to show off his extravagant gesture to his courtly guests."

Leis thought she saw a bit of exasperation on Madric's features. That was a sentiment she could understand.

"So, you probably have a little time, but you still might want to hurry. Dismissed."

"Yes, sir," Leis dropped a clumsy curtsy, made clumsier by the fact that her legs were already trying to obey Madric. "Thank you, sir."

Madric chuckled, "Go on, then. You're welcome." He put a restraining hand on the dog's scruff to prevent him bounding after Leis.

"Stay," he told the hound, as he watched Leis pick up the hem of her skirt and go running toward the infirmary. "And so goes the changing of the guard," he intoned. Releasing his grip on the dog's collar, Madric ruffled Stinky's ears. "She seems like the good sort. Let's hope her brother is just as sharp."

Stinky only grinned a panting dog grin and tried to lap up the water dropping from the pump.

Chapter 10: Summoned

Scattered raindrops clung to the infirmary window, and menacing thunder rumbled outside as Teine was putting the finishing touches on Seymour's picture. The dark-haired boy stood over him, his attention divided more or less equally between Teine's drawing and the spectacular storm front on the horizon, growing ever closer.

Clinician Nocdoramus stood with a slender hand on the window, her attention riveted upon the storm. Although she stood several feet away from the Human boys, her fascination with the storm was evident in every line of her stance. Teine longed to flip the page and take a sketch of her to see if he could capture on paper the tension and excitement he saw in the Aoife as they watched the storms. He hated passing up the opportunity to draw something so challenging from life, but he couldn't shake Seymour loose and he knew it. Tenacity was bred into his odd friend, as certainly as Teine's red hair and amber eyes were bred into him.

"I don't know why you're in such a hurry. You're going to be in here for another day, at least," Teine groused. "And it's not like you're never going to see me again."

"You could get your assignment any moment," Seymour urged. "I mean, you could be in Capital City by this time tomorrow."

"Unlikely," Teine mumbled. He was going back over the sketch, deepening the shadows, and picking up the lightest colors in the highlights with a special rubber eraser made of tree sap. It had a vaguely minty smell, and it was making him hungry. He'd been planning to have dinner in the Commons with Leis, and he was already well overdue. Of course there was no telling if Leis would be able to make it, with her new duties. For all he knew, she could be sharing a meal with the young master. *What kind of meal would they have in the Demesne proper?* he wondered. *Leg of lamb with mint dressing?*

Teine's stomach grumbled.

"Damn," muttered Seymour, raising a dark and bushy eyebrow. "You'd better hurry before you die of starvation."

Holding the sketch out at arm's length, Teine examined the work with a critical eye. He was pleased. The horses were better this time, and the dragon was...

"Scary!" Seymour enthused, enjoying a fearful shudder. "That dragon is even better than the live one in the Zoo. Is it done?"

"Yes," Teine concluded. Tearing the perforated page free of the book, he handed it to Seymour.

"No. No! Sign it!" Seymour held his hands up as if he could ward the unsigned work away. "It could be worth something when you get famous."

Teine couldn't help but chuckle. Out of all the other boys in his Cohort, only Seymour and Marcus could say something like that, not only with a straight face but in complete sincerity. He took the picture back, signed with slightly more than his usual flourish, and then dated it for posterity. On the back, he inscribed: *"For my friend Seymour, who likes scary dragons."*

Seymour took the picture with a grin, his eyes caressing the sketch for several seconds. "Thank you. I really do love it."

"I wish I'd done this one in oil," Teine admitted grudgingly.

"Dibs," Seymour laughed.

Before Teine could give him a hard time, the door to the infirmary banged open. Clinician Nocdoramus jumped, and turned to look.

"Ah, Sigolier Zan, you're early," Nocdoramus moved away from the window. "I really didn't expect you till tomorrow."

"My train came early," The petite Aoife woman bounced into the room, eyes bright and cheeks flushed with excitement. *Her features are cute, almost pixieish,* thought Teine. There was a quality to Zan's expressions that made her seem more approachable than Nocdoramus, although the two of them did look like they should be related. Teine found it hard to look away.

"The train was supposed to make another stop, but it went right through to beat the storm." Sigolier Zan and Nocdoramus took each other's hands and embraced briefly. "So, tell me, how have things been?"

Nocdoramus smiled, catching Teine's eye. She began steering the Sigolier toward her office with a hand on the small of her back. "We'll have plenty of time to get caught up, Zan, since you can't do updates on any of the boys' sigils with a storm threatening like this."

"So, we're dismissed?" Teine asked. "We can go?"

"Yes, yes," Nocdoramus called over her shoulder. "All you IMs are dismissed, as long as you're comfortable and not still bleeding. We'll reschedule your sigil update appointments for after the storm is over. Look for your new appointment postcards in your boxes at the SPED." The clinician opened a pocket calendar and studied it for a second. "Probably next Wednesday. They won't take but a couple minutes apiece."

Seymour made a face, "*We're* still stuck here."

"Teine, can you tell the kitchen that the boys are ready for dinner?"

Pausing with the medical gown pulled halfway over his head, Teine's reply was muffled. "He says, 'Certainly,'" Seymour called out.

Marcus was already pulling his trousers on. "Have you noticed how she always asks you for everything?" he muttered to Teine. "You. Always you."

"*I've* noticed," Seymour added. "I think she just likes redheads." His eyebrow wiggle was playfully lewd and suggestive.

Teine stared at him, wide-eyed. Seymour was irreverent at times, but that was one line he shouldn't cross, even in jest.

"Great Mother in Heaven!" Seymour clapped Teine on the shoulder, dismissing the larger boy's horrified expression with a mischievous grin. "Have you no sense of humor?"

"Hmmm." Teine gave him a stern look that he hoped would hit the mark as he pulled on his trousers.

Seymour sat down on the bed, and crossed his arms. "*Fine.*"

"Someday, you're going to say the wrong thing in front of the wrong person…" Marcus added.

"I said 'fine,'" Seymour looked away from the pair and feigned interest in the other IMs packing to leave.

Marcus looked as though he was going to say something else, but Teine shook his head no. Without further comment, he loaded his personal gear back into his book bag, slipped on his shoes, and headed for the door. Marcus threw his last things into his bag, grabbed his boots, and scrambled out the door behind Teine before Seymour could harangue him anymore.

Once out of the infirmary, Teine slowed down for Marcus to catch up. "I hated hurting his feelings like that," Marcus explained.

Teine shrugged, "Sometimes that's the only way to handle him. I'd rather him have some hurt feelings than some stripes on his back or a Disciplinary on his record."

The pair paused for Marcus to pull on his boots. While Teine stared longingly toward the Commons, noting the extremely long supper line, Marcus was hopping on one leg like a funny-looking bird, trying to shove his boot on without unlacing it.

There were people *everywhere*. Guests from the auction and their Human servants were availing themselves of Solmurry's excellent food and lodging before the storm. Teine recognized some of the musicians in the dinner line. Samia was also in line, standing with her new family. Teine noticed she was holding hands with her new Aoife mistress. The girl looked happy, and so Teine would be able to tell Leis not to worry. Even though he was in a hurry, he longed to go over and introduce himself to see what they were like.

"Huh," Marcus breathed, interrupting Teine's thoughts. The bigger boy had forgotten his footwear problem for the moment, and was staring off into the distance. "That's odd."

One of the children, wearing Solmurry livery, was running toward them as fast as she could pick up her feet and lay them down again. "Teine!" she yelled. "Teine! Wait!"

Teine's heart leapt into his throat. The only reason he would be summoned to the house was if something had happened to Leis. He fled Marcus's company without explanation and met the runner halfway across the lawn.

"What's wrong?" he demanded, grabbing the girl by the shoulder. She was gasping for breath, having run as hard as she could. "What's wrong?" Teine repeated. He had to force himself to let go of the child when she winced away from him. "Is it Leis? Has something happened?"

"No!" the girl huffed. "No, nothing like that." She stepped back out of his reach and eyed him warily. "It's just that you've been summoned. His Lordship wants to see you in his office, right away."

Shamefaced, Teine took in the child's demeanor and immediately apologized. "I'm very sorry. You just surprised me, and I thought something had happened to my sister." He was so relieved that what she said hadn't yet registered with him.

She rubbed her shoulder and gave him a dirty look. "That *hurt.* You should be careful grabbing people smaller than you."

"Sorry," Teine sighed. It was really all he could say. It was a bad mistake, and he felt appropriately guilty.

Raising an eyebrow, the child seemed to look him over. "I suppose you're forgiven. But you're going to catch hell if you don't get to the Demesne proper right away."

"To see Lord Solmurrian?" Teine repeated, feeling rather stupid. It seemed improbable.

"Yes, you fool," she glowered, giving him a visual once-over. "Go now. I suppose what you're wearing will have to do, but you should at least tidy your hair. Go in through the front. He has guests."

"Guests?" Teine muttered, hurriedly trying to pat down his fuzzy auburn curls into some semblance of order. "What in the world?"

"Go now," The girl stood with her feet shoulder-width apart, put one hand on her hip, and pointed with the other. The posture was so bold and dramatic that Teine couldn't help but smile. Apparently someone took the "official" part of their "official duties" very seriously. It was cute.

"All right, I'm going." Marcus was approaching, but Teine waved him off. "It's all right," he called.

"I'll tell the kitchen that the infirmary patients are ready for dinner," Marcus replied, holding out his hand for Teine's book bag. "And I'll drop this off on your bunk."

"Thanks!" Teine agreed, handing over the bag. He'd completely forgotten his errand, with the surprise summons to the Demesne. Marcus nodded, then crouched to finish his battle with his boot.

Teine gathered his thoughts and began the jog to the Demesne proper. In all his fifteen years, he'd only set foot inside a handful of times. Like the girl who had come to retrieve him, and almost every other child born on Solmurry, he'd done a turn at message duty, but that was about it. Leis and Amagorra had described the inside of the cavernous and imposing building, and Teine's curiosity had been aroused. Supposedly, the master had an impressive collection of art, in both paintings and sculpture. Several of the statues in the garden were by well-known sculptors, including a set of three fairies cast in bronze by the noted Meshamis of Adamshead, one of the best known Human sculptors ever. Teine admired the artist's work and looked on him as kind of a role model, even though he'd been dead for twenty years when Teine was born.

The front of the Demesne, with its deep columned stone porch and wide sweeping stairway, was partitioned from the rest of the lawn by a low wall of square, manicured hedges. An elaborate metal scrollwork gate opened soundlessly to Teine's touch. Inside this protected area, about an acre in size, several peacocks strutted amongst the ornamental trees, pausing only to display their extravagant plumage to each other. Two Aoife children Teine didn't know were playing a lazy game of bocce nearby.

As Teine began climbing the stairway to approach the front door, he realized that the closer he got to the imposing structure, the smaller and more insignificant he felt. The leaden sky that churned above was so eerily quiet that Teine could hear each scuff of his soft-soled boots against the stone of the walkway.

The whole scene felt absolutely surreal. Teine shuddered as the hair on his arms and the back of his neck stood up. "I'm probably just here for my assignment," he muttered under his breath. "It's time. I've probably just been assigned somewhere, and the master is going to brief me before sending me along." It made perfect, logical sense. But when one of the peacocks shrieked, Teine still startled and jumped.

Finally, he finished climbing the steps and used one of the ornate brass knockers to rap on the door. By the third tap, the door opened inward, and one of the house wenches, a statuesque and very pregnant Human woman, beckoned him inside. "Come on, boy, come on!" she urged. "The master sent for you nigh unto a half hour ago!" She grabbed Teine's wrist and began hauling him inside.

Teine went without struggle, letting the woman pull him deeper into the house. He tried not to gawk at the thick carpet runners, rich hardwood floors, and crystal chandeliers as he passed. The servants in the house wore much better clothing than the children who were still in school, and Teine saw a couple Humans who were wearing outfits as fine as he'd expect to see on any Aoife.

As they walked through what seemed to Teine to be an untrackable maze of rooms, he found himself relieved he'd been spared too much contact with the Demesne. His sense of direction was normally pretty good, but he was sure he couldn't retrace his steps to find the way back out. However, as they walked, he was able to recognize that they were drawing closer to the sound of lively harpsichord music coupled with rowdy, roaring laughter. They stopped outside an ornately carved mahogany door, and the serving wench pulled out a hankie and began to dab at Teine's face, as if he were a grubby toddler.

"Get off," he muttered, hating the meekness in his voice. "I'm no nursling." Reaching out, he tried to snag the kerchief from her hand so he could see to his own grooming.

"Be still!" she hissed, batting his hands aside and gifting him with a stinging slap across his face. "It'll be hell to pay if you go in there looking all a fright in front of the master himself. If you weren't running so late, I'd insist on a bath before presenting you." Pausing, the woman considered him, wrinkle lines appearing in her forehead. "He's in a foul mood tonight."

Teine's was stunned into complete silence. In his fifteen years, no one had ever laid a hand on him before, and this... this *besom* had struck him as if he were a mongrel dog! His throat tightened, despite the cheerful music and general sounds of revelry clamoring from the other side of the door. Suddenly, he realized he'd never felt so unprepared in his life.

The pregnant serving woman took Teine's silence for compliance, and went about her business of cleaning his face and tidying his hair while his stomach began a slow roll of uneasiness. "Now, that's a good boy," she soothed, speaking quietly, although it was clear no one in the other room would hear her over the music and high-spirited banter. "The master is a bit like the storms. Blows in suddenly, and always unpredictable. But you won't have to worr-"

The door next to them slammed open wide, completely without warning. The maid squeaked with surprise. A gaudily overdressed, obviously inebriated Aoife gentleman almost ran into them in his eagerness to leave the room.

"Where's the head, again?" he asked, swaying back and forth.

"Down the hall, Master Dorian." she answered. Teine noticed the worry lines appearing on her forehead again. "Third door on the left, then through the…" Suddenly, she frowned, taking in the Aoife's bleary eyes and besotted grin.

"Right, then," he said, tottering down the hall.

Obviously torn, the woman hesitated. "Oh sweet Vuaren, Father of Mercy," she whined. The helpless tone of her voice contrasted oddly with her strapping size and obvious strength. "If he pisses in that lily again…" She fixed Teine with a stern stare before waddling off in the same direction as the wayward nobleman. "Don't move!" she called over her shoulder to Teine.

Teine didn't move, even though the door had swung all the way open and he was completely exposed to the crowd of people in the Master's office. Teine eyed the door, wondering if he should close it. But closing it would require that he move. Despite his concerns about the entire situation, Teine could not help himself. Without moving his feet at all, he leaned forward to get a better view of what was going on in the room.

Master Solmurrian and his older brother Madric were sitting double on the harpsichord bench, and pounding out a lively duet. They were laughing and elbowing each other, and seemed to be engaged in a bout of musical sibling rivalry. Several Aoife women clapped in time as they danced around the office. A few of the master's business associates lounged in the comfortable furniture, puffed their clove cigarettes, and watched the ladies with appreciative eyes. A handful of the Doyen Prince's more flamboyant courtiers played a game of cards at one of the tables. Teine could hear low conversation just outside his field of vision, but could not see the speakers.

One of the card players looked up, and trilled a sharp whistle. "Hey, look who finally decided to join us."

Both Solmurrian brothers turned from their music to look, and Teine could feel the hot flush of embarrassment color his face.

There was a creak of upholstery shifting, and another Aoife gentleman joined Teine in the doorway. Teine blinked twice with shock when he realized who he was seeing. The Doyen Prince himself, acting ruler of the Empyrean, was sauntering toward him. He looked Teine up and down, a smug expression on his face. "He looks just like a calf at the slaughterhouse door."

Chapter 11: The Gift

Master Solmurrian stood abruptly from the harpsichord, his mouth a firm line of irritation. "You're late. I summoned you nearly an hour ago." Taking in Teine's dumbfounded stare, he sighed, and added. "Oh, come in already. And shut the door behind you."

Teine complied, wishing he didn't have to get any closer to the Doyen. Feeling as huge as a blue ox and about as clumsy as one, Teine closed the door, painfully aware of how he towered over all these powerful, overdressed Aoife. His relative size brought him no comfort. His cheek still stung from the housekeeper's slap, and he'd never felt more awkward or out of his element. With every fiber of his being, he knew he didn't belong here. With the door closed, Teine shuffled a couple tentative steps toward the Lord of Solmurry. It felt as though he was were underwater, with his feet encased in mud.

"You're Teine?" Master Solmurrian asked, joining the Human boy in the middle of the room.

"Yes, my Lord."

Cold and practical, Lord Solmurrian looked him over quickly, as if he were nothing more than a piece of livestock up for evaluation. Teine couldn't have felt more exposed if he'd stood there completely naked. "Your full sibling brought Solmurry a pretty penny at the auction today," the Aoife remarked.

"An honor, sir."

"Isn't he a bit smaller than the one you wanted your boy to choose?" Teine turned to look at the unexpected voice from the corner, and saw Prior Vihah lounging in one of the chairs, his feet up on a settee. The elderly Aoife priest was feeding tidbits of smoked caviar on crackers to the Prince's magnificent white hound. Unlike the courtiers, the Prior seemed interested and amused, his gaunt and wizened face kindly. "But if you don't mind me saying, I'm certain he'll work out well. It seems your son has inherited his grandfather's good eye for Human stock." Turning from the master, the Prior asked Teine, "You're in the choir, too, aren't you, son?"

Teine nodded and smiled back gratefully at the priest, recognizing him from his many visits. Prior Vihah adored Solmurry's volunteer choir, a club Teine had belonged to as long as he could remember. Although Teine was beginning to suspect the unpleasant truth about why he was there, it did seem as though he had at least one ally in a room filled with otherwise unfriendly faces.

Master Solmurrian made a noncommittal grunt, reaching for a file on his desk. He grabbed the embossed leather binder, flipping casually through the papers while periodically glancing at Teine. Trying not to fidget or get caught trying to read the papers, Teine did his best to stand still while looking both patient and wise. His stomach, however, churned slowly from the combination of unsettled nerves and hunger. "It seems everything's in order here," he muttered.

"I still think you should give him a girl," volunteered one of the card players. "It'd be more... educational. And you'd get a better tax break on the gift."

The courtiers and their women erupted with bawdy laughter, and Teine's ears felt like they'd caught fire. Master Solmurrian ignored them, and the Doyen merely gave the other Aoife a mock-stern glare. "There will be no tax breaks on *my* watch!" The raucous sniggering and catcalls momentarily drowned out Madric's solo harpsichord performance, and also the soft rap on the door.

"Come in!" Master Solmurrian, Madric, the Prince, and Prior Vihah called in unison at the second, louder, rap. Their unintended chorus set the ladies to giggling again, as Dorian returned with the same pregnant Human maid Teine had met earlier.

"Begging your pardon, your Excellency, your Lordships," she began, holding the door open for the drunken Aoife courtier. With a firm hand on his unsteady shoulder, she propelled him through the door. "I wanted to return good Master Vondereen to you and tell you dinner will be served shortly."

"Did he spare the poor lily this time?" Madric asked, a sardonic grin twisting his features. To punctuate his remark, he fingered out a quick, comic tune on the keyboard. "His visits are hell on the houseplants." Dorian chuckled right along with the others as the flustered maid nodded her assent.

Master Solmurrian began rounding up the gaggle of Aoife women, herding them toward the door. "Why don't you go on, ladies? Phoebe, here, can take you to get freshened up, and we'll see you at dinner."

Most of the women obediently allowed themselves to be herded, but one ruby-lipped blonde in a dress to match hung back. "But, Alain," she whined. "I want to stay with you."

The Aoife lord didn't quite scowl, but Teine could see the look of irritation on Master Solmurrian's face. Teine had a brief moment where he wasn't sure whether he was relieved that someone was taking the focus away from him, or alarmed that the Aoife woman was managing to annoy the man who held his entire fate in his hands. "It's time for the men to do business, my dear," Master Solmurrian told her. Taking a firm hold on her arm, he steered the dramatically pouting female out the door, putting her in line with the others. Before she could object, he closed the door to the office. "Why do you insist on bringing them?" he snapped at the Doyen.

The Prince smiled, but Teine recoiled from the coldness he saw there. "Ah, but they are so decorative. And not without their charms." He eyed Master Solmurrian, taking in his scowl and clenched fists. "Come now, *Alain*," he added, inflecting the master's given name with the same cloying familiarity the woman had just used. "I'll forgive your little temper tantrum, just this once, if you can make a better effort the rest of the night and apologize to Haneesha."

"Fine." To Teine's eyes, it seemed Master Solmurrian looked just as surly as the woman he'd ejected from his office.

The Doyen Prince raised one impeccably groomed eyebrow. "Fine?" he asked, irritation creeping into his voice. "*Fine?*"

"Yes, your Highness," Master Solmurrian agreed. His eyes were flat and lifeless, Teine noticed, and his heart didn't seem to be fully in the concession. "I will apologize to the woman and behave myself for the remainder of the evening."

Apparently satisfied with the half-hearted acquiescence, the Prince turned away and wandered over to the card game. Teine shifted nervously on his feet, anxiety coiling even tighter in his innards. He was certain Master Solmurrian was less than pleased after being dressed down in front of everyone. Teine worried that he, himself, might now become the target for his master's ill temper.

"So," Master Solmurrian said, turning from the door to his office. "What are we going to do with you?"

Teine opened his mouth, then closed it quickly, realizing it was a rhetorical question and no response was required. The master glared at him as if he was disappointed he couldn't scold him for speaking out of turn. Madric abruptly ended the piece he'd been playing on the harpsichord. The magician tugged on his formal ceremonial robe absently as he turned to watch the exchange between his younger brother and Teine. The room was still as a few big drops of rain splattered on the glass of the master's conservatory windows.

"Oh, do get on with it," muttered the bored Prince. He scowled, leaning forward to get a light for his clove cigarette off Dorian's.

"We're waiting on the notary," Master Solmurrian answered. "He's probably finishing off paperwork for people who are leaving now."

Sighing his annoyance, the Doyen took a drag on his cigarette, then picked up a shot of whiskey sitting on the card table and downed it. "I'll notarize, if I must. Just get it over with, before I expire from hunger. That's an executive order."

Teine's eyes darted to the Prior, who was still placidly munching his way through the tray of dainty consumables. The priest looked completely unconcerned, and still mildly amused. He slurped down a sea dragon larvae garnished with a sprig of parsley, then eagerly crunched on a whole wheat cracker that was left over.

"As you wish, your Excellency," Master Solmurrian turned his attention back to Teine, and stepped forward to close the distance. Suddenly, he smiled. Teine blinked, surprised by the sudden change of demeanor as the master began speaking to him in an almost personable manner. "Teine, my boy, I'm sure you're well aware of the many traditions of excellence we nurture, here at Solmurry."

Nodding wordlessly, Teine listened. The master's joviality was obviously superficial, and seemed to be a part of some internal script he'd prepared for the occasion. Teine pasted an expression of polite, rapt attention on his features. It was a trick all Humans learned nearly as soon as they could walk, feigning interest in anything any Aoife had to say. But never before had Teine needed to squelch back fear and uneasiness at the same time.

"As you probably already know," the lord continued, without skipping a beat. "My son is the sole heir to Solmurry."

Teine willed himself not to look at Madric, the master's elder brother, to see how Solmurry's *rightful* lord was taking his younger brother's proclamation of inheritance. However, Teine's eyes betrayed him. His gaze flickered to the side. The magician's expression was tranquil, but his angular jaw was clenched tightly.

When Teine glanced back at the master, he realized his faux pas had been noticed. Lord Solmurrian's face had turned an alarming shade of furious red, his veneer of goodwill gone as quickly as it had arrived. However, he continued his speech. "He has recently celebrated his centennial birthday. As is customary, he has the privilege of choosing his first manservant from my private stock. To my chagrin..." he raised an eyebrow, a jaded, twisted smile marring his otherwise handsome features. "He chose you."

Teine could only nod solemnly, while fighting the urge to sit down on the floor and bawl his eyes out like a nursling.

"In addition to your duties as manservant, you'll also be trained for Display," the Master added, oblivious to Teine's mental state. "Display training is physically intense, but not time consuming. You won't be eligible for the right Display classes until your eighteenth year, so you should be able to continue your studies and extracurricular activities, if Marne permits it."

"He's in the choir, too," the Prior added, giving Teine a kind smile. "You can probably count on that."

"And, your manservant duties will only be part-time, at best. After some consideration, I've decided to leave your full sibling Leis on as Marne's sole nanny, since your Amagi is retiring."

"Nanny?" muttered one of the card players. "He's of age—why a nanny?"

Teine wondered the same, but didn't dare ask. Lord Solmurrian either didn't hear, or pretended not to. Teine supposed he could ask Leis if the boy was deficient in some way. *Perhaps I'm being a little fatalistic,* he thought, *but given the turn my luck seems to be taking, nothing would surprise me at this point.*

Meanwhile, the master had gone back to flipping through Teine's record. Madric, as if taking a cue from his younger brother, had resumed his harpsichord playing. His nimble hands danced along the keyboard, weaving a complex, but soft and moody tune that Teine recognized as one of his grandmother Amagorra's favorites.

"Here's how your transfer works," the master said abruptly. "Tonight, once His Excellency notarizes the paperwork, you become the sole property of my son, Marnariel Emerys Solmurrian, to do with as he pleases. He may choose to sell you, keep you, change your name, pay for your additional schooling, show you in Display or stud you out. But from that moment on you are *his*. Is that clear?"

Wordlessly, Teine nodded. In the background, he could hear Madric changing the music, skillfully improvising it into something darker, more sinister.

"There is only one exception to his absolute and total rule over you, and it's written in the transfer agreement. Until his age of majority on his one hundred fortieth birthday, I may exercise my right as head of Demesne and have you castrated if you prove to be an unworthy sire for our ongoing Solmurry line. In that case, I might also choose to have you sold into heavy labor or even put down, if you are deemed disobedient or violent."

Teine felt his mouth go dry.

"Do you wish to see the clause in your paperwork?" Master Solmurrian asked, extending the paperwork toward Teine, his eyebrow raised as if daring him to take a look.

"No... no, master."

The tune, now turned dark and dramatic, increased in volume to a crescendo, and Master Solmurrian turned to snap at his brother, "Oh, *do* stop it, Madric! I'll not have you make me out to be some comic villain!"

"No, you definitely don't need *me* for that," Madric agreed, his expression mischievous and flushed with amusement. The magician made a point to catch Teine's eye, and for the briefest second Teine thought he saw some sympathy there.

With an extravagant flourish, Master Solmurrian approved the paperwork, passing it to the Doyen Prince, who looked it over briefly before adding his own mark. He offered the folder back to the lord, but instead the Aoife pointed to Teine. With a shrug, the Prince pushed the folder into the stunned young man's hands. "There you go, boy. Don't lose them."

"You can deliver those to Marne when you see him this evening," Lord Solmurrian added. To his guests, he cried, "We're done here. Let's go celebrate!"

"Great!" Dorian enthused. The inebriated Aoife wobbled to his feet using the card table for support. "Let's eat!" Madric also rose from the keyboard, pecked out a quick "shave and a haircut" tune, and then swept out of the room without saying anything or even waiting to be excused.

"Well, that was rude," Prior Vihah blustered, visibly taken aback by the magician's slight.

Teine blinked, feeling utterly and completely lost.

"Go on then, boy," urged the Prince, giving Teine's back a shove toward the door. "Go bring honor to the Solmurry line, or some such nonsense."

Glancing at Master Solmurrian for direction that never came, Teine swiveled on his heel to follow the mass exodus from the master's office. He was about to file out behind the courtiers when he noticed the Prior struggling to get up from his low, overly padded chair. Without thinking, he offered the Aoife a hand up.

"Thank you, my son," Vihah muttered, groaning to his feet. The Prince's beautiful hound danced around Teine's legs. She shook her soft white coat and grinned at Teine with an almost human expression of approval. Teine could not help himself, and reached down to stroke the hound's silken head and folded ears. "That's a good, strong lad," the Prior added.

"Where should I go?" Teine asked Prior Vihah, feeling like he should capitalize on the cleric's goodwill. It seemed he'd probably need all the friends he could get.

"To pack a bag, I believe." Straightening his robes, Prior Vihah spent a moment putting himself in order at the mirror by the door before stepping out, while he considered Teine's question. "If rumor serves me, I believe young Marne will be making a rapid exit to stay with his uncle this evening."

Puzzled, Teine frowned. "Why? That doesn't make sense. It's dangerous to travel during these storms, especially with a magician!" He paused, thinking about all that he'd heard through the Solmurry rumor mill that day. Then he added, "Besides, isn't the young master ill?"

"It *is* a mystery," the Prior agreed. Something in his voice sounded both ironic and cryptic as Teine weighed it in his mind. "And it's not the *only* mystery. Perhaps you can find out, and let me know." He kindly patted Teine on the shoulder with one spidery, veiny old Aoife hand, then tottered off down the hallway after the Prince and his retinue.

Chapter 12: A Matter of Perspective

Like a sleepwalker, Teine shuffled his way back toward his Cohort's barracks, ignoring the performers, Aoife businessmen, their families, and other Solmurry residents. Everyone was on the move, heading to or from somewhere, breaking down the booths and stages, going about their business. Teine found himself envying them. They had their own ventures to go about, whereas it seemed unlikely that Teine would ever have business of his own, ever again. All the careful planning and preparation, classes he'd taken, all wasted. Because it was his nature to be proactive, he'd tried to be ready for any and all alternatives, but this was the one scenario he'd never foreseen as a possibility. He'd been completely blindsided.

And what a rude awakening it was! Teine had always found his existence comfortable and felt it made sense. He'd always been treated fairly by his teachers and superiors, been popular with his peers and tutors, and was used to receiving lots of encouragement from the authority figures in his life. Never one to cause trouble or be lazy, Teine had always followed directions, did well in his studies, and excelled at every task put in front of him. Everyone from cohort to chore boss had promised him a bright future. He'd felt certain that he could achieve his personal goals because that was the logical conclusion to working hard and following all the rules.

Teine knew on some level he'd been cheated out of something very vital, something very *human*. And part of him expected to be angry, to desire recompense. But all he felt was a kind of numbness.

It seemed that the numbness was concealing, perhaps mercifully, the emptiness in his chest where all his hopes and plans for the future had once resided. He felt the cold air on his damp cheeks, and realized that he was crying.

"Don't be such a baby." he admonished himself under his breath, as harshly as he could.

But the tears kept coming. As if in sympathy, the ominous sky loosed a few drops of rain. Then, the wind kicked up and a steady drizzle began, pausing only to produce gusts of sideways, stinging rain. Alarmed, Teine scrambled to get the folder with all his paperwork under his shirt, feeling grateful that the folder itself was made of leather. Within seconds he was soaked.

A quick glance up at the sky showed dark menacing clouds blotting out the afternoon sun. The main mass of the storm was much closer now, its bruise-colored heart ever nearer their coastline. It would make landfall well before dark. The sky itself seemed to let out a low groan, answered by the trees, and the leaves hissed under the steady fall of precipitation.

Teine knew he should go back to Mastiff Cohort and pack a bag, even though he had no idea what his new master would want of him, if anything. Prudence seemed to dictate that he make good use of the information the Prior had given him and be prepared. Wiping his eyes on the sleeve of his tunic, he attempted to put himself in some sort of order. But envisioning the curiosity, chaotic questioning, and well-meaning sympathy of his cohort did nothing to put him at ease.

What he found he really wanted, he realized with surprise, was to speak with Leis. Although the other boys sometimes teased about his friendship with her, she'd been a constant source of wise counsel and unique perspective. Teine valued her opinions far more than he'd ever let on to his friends. Besides, he knew many of them were jealous and wished their own siblings had any kind of an interest in them. He decided immediately that he should stop at the Commons in hopes of catching her there. She would have good, detailed, first-hand information on his new master, as she'd been assigned to him for several months, if only on a part-time basis.

As Teine approached the Commons building, he could see that the efficient kitchen staff had managed to seat and feed enough people that there were no longer any lines. The only people outside the Commons were a pack of boys from Ram Cohort, who were goofing around in the rain. They looked as though they might have planned to get a pick-up baseball game going, but for now their hardwood bats were abandoned to lean against a tree, while they pitched the ball back and forth. A few adult Humans wearing the livery of other houses and some of the Solmurry residents with whom they were flirting had taken shelter under the broad wrap-around porch of the Commons building.

Skirting the front entrance that led to the main lounge, Teine ducked into the entrance to the dining hall, then paused to pull the folder out of his shirt. He passed a startled cook, a gangly woman about the same age as his amagi, who asked for his meal chit.

"Not eating, Maggie," Teine replied, waving her off and scanning the mixed crowd of working-class Aoife, Human servants from other houses, and the usual Solmurry diners. "I'm looking for Leis." Although Teine had been absolutely ravenous before his meeting, the thought of food now made him feel slightly nauseous. He wasn't ready to eat. But he was ready to talk.

"Not eating?" Maggie repeated, stunned. "Are you kidding? Are you feeling alright? I've never seen a storm put you off your feed." She made a playful show of checking him for fever by clamping her hand over his face. He struggled meekly, his heart not in the game. Sensing his mood, Maggie released him. "Your sis is over there, with Samia and her new people." Maggie gestured toward Teine's siblings and the Aoife couple.

Leis and Samia seemed to be telling some kind of story together, flapping their arms in unison, while the steady rain pattered against the windows. There were smiles all around, and it was contagious enough to have caught Maggie, too. "They seem like good ones. I bet they'd like to meet you," the cook added, giving Teine a nudge in their direction.

Teine made his way across the dining hall, noticing the radio station was playing a cheery dance number with lots of horns, in between bursts of static from the weather. The music seemed to ease some of the tension in the room and distract people from fretting over the incoming storm. A large knot of Solmurry Humans, mostly mature adults, gathered around one of the tables nearby. Noticing the traditional candled cake, decorations, and presents, Teine assumed it was a birthday party. Looking closer, he recognized the guest of honor. Boric of Solmurry was one of the premier characters of the closehold, the lands of Solmurry that were nearest the Demesne. He was a celebrated stud, sire of many of Solmurry's finest, including Teine's friend Vosh. Aside from siring children, Boric had the equally important duty of assigning the crop rotations to the fields and vegetable gardens, as well as overseeing every work crew for the acreage put to crop production. He was important, influential, and enjoyed the privilege of his own cottage, which he shared with a few of his chosen fellows.

Teine had always admired Boric, his easy way of command and effortless talent for making decisions without any obvious deliberation. When he was younger, Teine had dreamed of securing a position for himself like Boric's, something where he'd have challenging, interesting work and his value to Solmurry could be well proven. Teine craved that influence and comfort, desiring nothing more than to reap the rewards of his talents and be surrounded by good friends. As he passed by, he caught Boric's eye and raised a hand in greeting. Boric did the same, his weathered face wrinkling pleasantly at Teine, his grin baring a perfect white smile.

Teine's two rosy-haired siblings were oblivious to the music and the weather as they pantomimed being dragons, banking and breathing fire on each other. Samia's new mistress watched, as transfixed as if she'd been charmed. At first glance, Teine thought she was rather plain for an Aoife, but she had a smile so radiant it transformed her into a real beauty. She was obviously delighted, laughing, clapping, and giggling at the girls' antics.

The tight knot of anxiety in Teine's chest returned as he looked on. It was hard to imagine this happy scene as being a part of the world of cruelty and injustice he'd witnessed earlier that afternoon. Hard to believe that they could all be just *sold*, like cattle or hounds or wheat, their own wishes disregarded and tossed aside. Out of the corner of her eye, Leis noticed Teine and inclined her head to acknowledge him. Looking closer, she raised an eyebrow at his brooding expression, and paused mid-flap.

"Oh, it's Teine!" Samia squealed, noticing her sibling for the first time. "It's Teine, my brother!" Without waiting for an invitation or a by-your-leave, she launched herself at him, wrapping her arms gleefully around his middle.

Consciously aware that he might never see Samia again, after this day, Teine accepted her embrace without a struggle. Then he made the expected pleasantries with Samia's new family. Despite the very obvious fact that they were neither noble born nor had attained any other status than being successful merchants, Teine found himself admitting a grudging liking for them. He was certain that Samia would be safe there. She'd be cherished as a valuable member of their household, and she'd have a variety of interesting duties to keep her active mind busy and challenged.

It would have been fair to say he was jealous.

"Samia tells us that some congratulations are in order for you, as well," Mr. Aylmer said. His hand was small in the grasp of Teine's handshake, but did not feel delicate. Its wiry grip felt strong and capable, unlike how he'd imagined the nobles might shake. His favorable impression of the Aylmers increased. "Is it true that you've been gifted to the master's son and are going on to a career in Display?" the Aoife man asked, before releasing Teine's hand.

"That's the way of it," Teine replied, attempting to arrange his features into something resembling serene acceptance. It wouldn't do to have these strangers to Solmurry left with a negative impression of his willingness to perform his duties. It wouldn't reflect well on his bloodline.

Samia jumped up and down and squealed with delight, hugging Teine again. Leis smiled at him, but with less exuberance. Teine knew Leis was picking up on his discomfiture, and longed for a few words alone with her.

"I've seen a Display meet," Mr. Aylmer added, looking down to his wife. "It's quite the show. The participants all have to be real athletes, at the peak of their physical conditioning. They then perform feats of strength and agility, plus oration and some other skills to showcase their intelligence and versatility."

"You must be so excited!" Mrs. Aylmer exclaimed. "Coming from Solmurry, everyone in the Empyrean will know your name before long! I'm so happy for you!"

Teine's smile was genuine this time, and not at all forced. It was hard not to like these people.

Suddenly, Mrs. Aylmer went pale, her hand fluttering reflexively to rest on her protruding lower belly. A mere instant later, there was a deafening crack of thunder, and a collective cry from everyone as the lights in the Commons first flickered and dimmed, then went out completely. Although the room was far from dark, all the diners began murmuring among themselves.

"Ah, and so it begins," Mrs. Aylmer quipped.

"What?" squeaked her husband. "Now?"

"No, no," the Aoife woman giggled, her voice both musical and warm. "I meant the storm!" Her laughter was cut off shortly by her hissing intake of breath.

"Are you alright, ma'am?" Teine asked, speaking loudly to be heard over the muttering conversations of the other diners. He felt a bit guilty at his relief they were in a crowd—surely in that press of people there would be many folks knowledgeable about childbirth. Delivering a baby was *not* something he felt like adding to his resume right now.

Before she could answer, the power was restored. Dimly at first, but gaining in strength, the overhead lighting hummed softly, then brightened back to its original luminescence. There were scattered cheers, a few claps, then everyone simply resumed their conversations as if nothing had happened.

"Oh, I'm fine," Mrs. Aylmer added. "The little one always gets more active during this kind of weather. I suppose it would probably be prudent to head to the main house before it gets worse."

Samia was instantly at the ready. "Would you like me to go and secure you a ride?"

The Aoife woman waved her off. "No, no… that's not necessary. It's not far at all, and I do have an umbrella." She allowed Samia to help her to her feet, then rummaged through her tapestry valise until she found it.

"Please, ma'am," Samia begged. "Allow me."

Mrs. Aylmer handed over the umbrella and Samia rested it on her shoulder while reaching for her mistress' valise with her other hand. Mr. Aylmer apparently had the same idea, for the two of them rapped knuckles as they both reached for the handle. Samia rubbed her hand, looking horrified. She began to apologize, but Mr. Aylmer simply laughed.

"How about you carry the umbrella, and provide an arm to her support?" he suggested. "Then I'll follow with the bag."

"But you'll get wet!" Samia protested.

"It's a big umbrella. Besides, a little rainwater won't do me any harm," the Aoife quipped. His eyes sparkled with mischief as he shouldered the valise. To Teine, he added, "I'm a field reporter for the *Empyrean Gazette* and I write a regular humor column, as well. I go where the stories are. You'd be surprised how often good stories happen in the rain."

Despite himself, Teine found himself wishing he could speak more with Mr. Aylmer. He'd dreamed of being a reporter himself, until he'd found out that being an Aoife was a qualification. Humans could work for the papers, but rarely had the opportunity to write for them, instead serving in a sales or distribution function. But before he could say anything, Mr. Aylmer was patting him on the arm. "We'll take good care of your little sister. My wife has been waiting a long time for a Solmurry handmaiden." With the valise strap secured on his wiry shoulder, he pulled his wife close and kissed her gently on the cheek.

"Thank you, sir," Teine replied, charmed by Mrs. Aylmer's girlish blush and the genuinely adoring way she looked up at her husband. But, feeling the Aoife deserved a little more personalized response, he added. "It's probably best that you head for the big house. Now that I know you're a reporter, I'd be likely to monopolize your evening with endless questions about your profession. I'm sure it's fascinating work."

"Indeed, it is. If you make it to Empyrea and care to stop by for a visit, you'd definitely be welcome." Mr. Aylmer reached into the inner pocket of his jerkin to produce a folded leather case, which held monogrammed business cards. He offered one each to Teine and Leis. "Here's our address," he said, pointing to the back side of the card. Then he flipped it over, revealing the Gazette's distinctive logo and another address. "And here's the address for my office in the city. Let me know if you hear any good jokes." He also produced a booklet of postage stamps, tore off two sheets of four, and handed those over as well. "Don't forget to write your sister while she's settling in. It would only be natural for her to be a little homesick at first."

Teine accepted the business card and postage stamps, sliding them into the pouch on his belt while he nodded his agreement and made his thanks. He'd grown even more impressed with Samia's new family with each passing minute. Their unabashed affection for each other, and open-handed generosity had been a surprise balm for his earlier fears and hurt feelings. He'd heard it said before that common folk were the salt of the earth, and he was beginning to see that it might be true. Emboldened by the exchange, he shook the Aoife man's hand again and grinned. "You know, it's not too late to see if you can arrange a trade with the young master," he nudged, giving Mr. Aylmer a playful wink. "So I could come and assist with your reporting!"

The Aoife man roared with laughter, and Teine was rewarded with playful swats from not just Samia, but Mrs. Aylmer as well. "Teine, you stinker!" Samia scolded him. "Mine! Go away! You can't have them, they're mine!"

"See, I'm outvoted." Mr. Aylmer countered. His ivory complexion was ruddy with good humor. "But truly, kids, don't be strangers. We'll be happy to hear from you and can put you up if you're ever in town." They all said their goodbyes, Teine and Leis even accepting a kiss on the cheek each from Mrs. Aylmer, before Samia and her new family departed.

"They are really, truly kind people," Leis mused. "So…" she trailed off, at a loss for the correct word."I don't know. So *genuine*, perhaps?"

Teine nodded his agreement, and the two siblings stood in companionable silence for a moment, before Teine's attention wandered back to Boric's party. His guests were all laughing at some joke while Boric himself was carving up the cake and putting it on small plates to share. Enviously, Teine watched. He couldn't begrudge Boric's good fortune, but he could mourn the death of every possible option that had been taken away from him. Then Leis's hand was on his sleeve, and her enthusiastic chirps shook him out of his moodiness.

"Congratulations, by the way. Isn't it exciting?" It sounded more like a statement than a question. "Just think! We'll get to see each other every day now!"

"I suppose that's true," Teine agreed, somewhat reluctantly. He'd been so wrapped up in his own unexpected assignment, it just now dawned on him that Leis had been promoted as Marne's full-time nanny. And a year ahead of schedule, to boot! It was likely that they *would* be seeing a lot of each other. No wonder she felt like celebrating.

Leis eyed him, taking in his uncharacteristic lack of enthusiasm. "Well, you don't have to act so overjoyed," She countered, raising an eyebrow and turning on the sarcasm. "I'd have thought you'd be pleased."

Teine sighed. "Pleased" wasn't exactly how he'd describe what he was feeling. In fact, he was getting downright annoyed by her exuberance. "You thought I'd be *pleased?*" he muttered, turning his back on Boric's party and slumping down in a chair. He beckoned Leis close, so no one else could hear. "You thought I'd be overjoyed? To be threatened with castration and being sold into hard labor?" He paused, taking in the stricken look on her face, and feeling an unlikely mixture of both shame at his outburst, and satisfaction his comments had hit home.

"No, no." he continued, lowering his voice even more, so it was only a hiss slightly louder than the rain. "You thought I'd be utterly *delighted* to go on to a job where a brain is optional, and to have every twist and turn of my own fate from here on out decided at the whim of some spoiled, deficient, selfish little Aoife brat?" He choked off his tirade, realizing he was dangerously close to having more tears fall. Besides, he really did want to hear what Leis had to say to him. He was ready for her heartfelt sympathy, or perhaps a silver lining he'd overlooked.

"Hush, you fool!" she snapped. "If I wanted to hear babies wailing, I'd have asked for a post down at the nursery. Are you too dumb to realize that you've utterly and completely *won?*"

Teine stared at his sister stupidly, surprised by her sharp tongue and the fire in her eyes. He could count on one hand the times he'd seen Leis lose her temper. And, truth be told, he was having a hard time figuring out what she was so angry about.

"Won?" he repeated, feeling like a complete simpleton. "How could I have won?" he sulked. "I'm never going to get to go on to a real job, a real career! I'm never going to have the chance to prove myself, or gain any influence. To maybe have my own cottage someday, or get known for my art or writing…"

"Yes, *won*, you idiot!" she countered, giving him a completely exasperated look. "First of all, if you'd been sent to almost any of the trades on your list—including fabal with that dumb Vosh friend of yours—you wouldn't get to keep up with the things that *really* matter to you. You'd likely have to forget your art and writing completely. You'd be too busy. Now, you're going to not *only* be allowed to keep doing the things you love, you'll be actively encouraged. And you'll get to keep taking classes, too. Any classes you want!"

Teine blinked. He'd never considered what would happen to his hobbies once he'd taken his place among the working ranks at Solmurry. He'd always envisioned having plenty of time for his sketchings and scribblings, during lectures or in his free time. But Leis had a point. There was no place for a sketchbook or journal on the fabal field, at the shipyard, or at the power station.

"Second," Leis added, "I know you crave the comforts of station. But you're about to get something far more valuable! Something nearly everyone—men like Boric included—would trade you for in a heartbeat!"

"What's that?" Teine asked. He couldn't help but be skeptical. If he were in Boric's place, he couldn't see anything worth trading for.

"*Adventure*," Leis threw back at him. "*You* are going to get to go places and see things most of us will only dream of." She gestured wildly, enthusiasm and envy soaking every word. "When Marne goes skiing with his uncle, up north in the mountains, who do you think will go with him? When he and our master take the new ships out on the open sea, with the waves crashing all around and the sails flying, who do you think will be standing there on the bow? While our choir might get to go to Empyrea and sing at the temple once every couple years, you'll be there several times a season, watching fabal from the Solmurry private box. While I do mundane household chores and ruin my figure with baby after baby, you'll be learning how to defend your charge with blades and staves. Perhaps you'll even be given a horse of your own to ride!"

She paused, her eyes wild with more passion than Teine had ever seen from her. It startled him a bit; she had always been so collected. "Honestly, Teine, how can you *not* see the possibilities?"

Teine muttered his assent, hoping to deflect some of her excitement. She had painted a pretty picture with all her talk of adventure and it had given him something to think about. He had to admit that she was probably spot on, at least about some of it. Even their Amagi had spoken of the trips she'd taken with Marne. Amagi had told them of the unearthly beauty of the mountains she'd seen, and a voyage on the steam-powered riverboat. Perhaps there were possibilities he had overlooked.

"And third…" Leis added, her eyes darting back and forth to be sure no one was about to hear what she said next. "Marne isn't *anything* like how you believe him to be."

"Well, how is he, then?"

"You haven't even *met* him yet?" Leis asked, her eyes widening as she suddenly noticed the folder of registration papers tucked under Teine's arm. "Wait, what are you doing *here*?"

Teine shrugged, gesturing in the direction of his cohort's barracks. "I stopped in to tell you the news before I went to pack a bag. They might want me to go with Marne tonight to his uncle's tower."

It hit him, then, that Leis was probably right. His adventure was beginning, and he was late to the starting gate. The note Leis had sent him in the infirmary made all kinds of sense now. "I know something you don't know," he mouthed. Apparently, she had, indeed.

"What?" she asked, not following his train of thought. "Never mind. Forget it! Just go!" She swung her arms at him, as if she were chasing a goose out of the garden. "Get on, and get your bag packed! They could be leaving any minute, and they'll be expecting you! We'll move the rest of your things to the Demesne for you, or you can do it yourself when you return."

A spectacular chain of lightning blazed across the sky, throwing the entire dining hall in sharp relief and adding emphasis to Leis' words. The others in the hall exclaimed in appreciation at the light show, Humans tense and slightly fearful, Aoife fierce-looking and excited.

"To the Demesne? I'm moving to the big house? Are you sure?" Teine asked, hearing his voice crack. "You'd think they could have actually told me," he grumbled. Rising to his feet and running a hand through his unruly damp hair, he quickly added, "I'll go now. But what were you going to say about the young master? He's not what?"

"Yes. I'm sure you're moving to the Demesne," Leis told him. "I've seen the room, it's right off Marne's and it's smallish, but very nice. And," she whispered, leaning in. "He's *not* a selfish brat. And he's definitely not deficient, either. But he's, well, he's kind of hard to describe." She looked thoughtful, as Teine watched her struggle. "Well, our amagi adores him," she finished weakly. "Says he's just the sweetest thing."

Teine was unconvinced. "Amagi has never met a child she didn't love, Human or Aoife. She's hardly choosy that way."

"I don't really know him well, yet, myself." Leis admitted. "But, he's no trouble. Actually, he seems kind of shy and unassuming. He watches everything. Doesn't miss a trick."

His brow furrowed as Teine considered the implications of belonging to someone who "watches everything." Perhaps he was being a bit paranoid, but the possibilities were kind of chilling.

"Quit scowling, you dunce!" Leis reprimanded him, again shooing him toward the door. "And get going! You have no time to waste! You *do* want to make a good impression, don't you?"

Nodding, Teine turned and began to walk away. "Yes, I suppose I'd better, if I want to keep the *rest* of my man-parts."

Leis ignored his fatalistic speculation, following him to the door. "Don't forget our story! It's still your turn, and you can work on it if you have time. And, Teine?" She caught his sleeve, as his hand was on the latch.

"What?" he asked, turning back once more to face her.

"This," she said, pecking him on the cheek. Out of habit, he groaned and pretended to try and escape, but it didn't deter her from hugging him, too. "It's not that I'm unsympathetic," Leis whispered. "But I think you're not seeing the silver lining in this dark frightening cloud." She paused, looking at him as if she could see right in through his eyes and read his mind.

"You know," she added. "Any control we seem to have over our lives is really just an illusion. It's probably easier to learn this lesson sooner rather than later." She smiled, almost maternally, and brushed the wet bangs out of his face. Teine was fervently glad none of his cohort were there to see.

"And, I'm selfish enough to be glad I'm not going to lose you, too." She looked up at him, her long lashes damp, and her eyelids slightly reddened and puffy. Now that he looked closely, it was completely obvious she, too, had spent part of the day in tears.

Surprised, Teine paused. He hadn't considered Leis' point of view at all. Samia, her favorite sister, was soon to be gone forever.

And he, too, could have been assigned elsewhere. From where Leis was standing, Teine staying at Solmurry and getting assigned a post so close to hers must have looked like a minor miracle.

"Uh… I'm sorry I was such an arse," he muttered. She deserved his apology, but it seemed trivial and not nearly enough to begin to make up for his appalling selfishness. "It will be fun to get to see each other every day."

Leis smiled, tears welling up in her eyes. "See. Now there's my Teine. You'd better go. Good luck." She turned him loose, and held the door open for him.

"Stop crying already," he returned, embarrassed. "I'll see you again soon." Leis nodded, then pushed him out the door, closing it behind him.

Chapter 13: Leaving Mastiff Cohort

The barracks for Mastiff Cohort were close, but Teine broke into a jog the instant he left the porch of the Commons. He had a lot to think about. However the sky was so distracting with both the sunset and the oncoming storm.

"Breathtaking," he muttered, pausing for an instant to admire the view. The sky was filled with colors, textural interest, and the feeling of depth and hugeness. Teine so wanted to stop everything and paint the scene right then, using the good oil paints and canvas he'd been hoarding in his locker. The old oaks creaked and danced in the freshening wind, and it was raining in patches. Teine didn't want to get caught in one of the erratic downpours and turn up back at the Demesne looking like a wet dog with soaked paperwork. With a sigh, he dragged his eyes away from the sky and continued onward.

Barely out of breath from the four-story climb, Teine paused before the grey and maroon door of Mastiff Cohort. He admired the stern-looking figure of a mastiff he'd painted in black over the background colors, realizing that four years had passed since he'd painted the door. And after today, he'd likely never see it again.

Teine, Seymour, Marcus, and the others from the infirmary had all been members of their cohort since leaving the nursery building. Like many cohort mates, the boys of Mastiff were close, like brothers. Living together, going to school together, and playing on sports teams together forged relationships between boys of the same cohort that were often more durable than the ties they had with their own flesh and blood siblings. But by this time next week, Mastiff Cohort would be gone, its boys—now young men— scattered like chaff in the wind. The mastiff on the door would be painted over with white, and either the Boar Cohort or the Falcon Cohort would move in, inheriting the duties of their age and becoming the next link in the chain.

Teine hoped they'd do a good job decorating their door.

The instant Teine entered the dormitory building, something seemed out of place. It was simply too quiet! With most of the cohorts empty, the whole floor had a strange, echoing quality, even though there were still a few boys about, and it was far from silent. Mastiff and Holidocrith, Peregrine and Ponar, most of their agemates had either moved on to advanced schooling or apprenticeships, or were still in the infirmary after their surgeries. Only a scattered few remained in each cohort, all IMs who had been released from the hospital but not yet assigned.

As Teine pushed past the sentry mastiff on the door, his uneasy feelings lifted. So did the peace and quiet. Marcus was playing a game of cards with a couple of the boys from Ponar, one from Peregrine, and a younger lad he didn't recognize, until he realized it wasn't a lad at all! The girl had curly dark hair and startling blue eyes, and was dressed in trousers with a cap on her head, like a newspaper boy from the big city. "Uh, hey!" he said, somewhat alarmed. "What's that girl doing here?"

"She's my cousin," muttered Billy, from Peregrine. "She's from Mahoney. We penpal it, and she got to come up and see me."

Teine grinned, the numerous conversations he'd had with Billy about his cousin all coming back to him. Billy had originally come from Mahoney himself, and like Seymour, had been purchased as a stud prospect a few years ago. Over the years, Billy had gone Solmurry all the way but, like Teine, still cherished his blood relations. He'd stayed in touch faithfully, and had always found Teine a willing ear for his commentary on the girl's entertaining antics.

"Hi, Alice," Teine offered, to make up for his blunder. The girl seemed to be examining him, as he'd looked her over. Although she dressed in the clothing of a boy, she had the subtle start of womanly curves under her baggy tunic and trousers. "N-nice to meet you, finally," he added, hoping he didn't sound like a complete twit.

"Ah, Teine. Be nice to her—but not *too* nice. Little wench deals from the bottom of the deck," Marcus chuckled, and Teine joined in.

Laughter echoed around the barren room, and Alice herself chimed in, laughing long and loud with her open mouth full of chewed peanuts. Teine winced and looked away, moving toward his bunk and wall locker to retrieve some of his things and be on his way. Although Teine would have liked to speak with Marcus some, he didn't want to interrupt their game. But before he got far enough down the row to see his own bed, he heard the turn the conversation had taken at the card table.

"Has he seen it yet?" Alice asked. Her higher voice carried across the mostly empty room.

The rest of the boys all shushed her in unison, and Teine turned to look. "Seen what?"

The girl cackled and the boys all shushed her again, "Don't say anything," Billy admonished her under his breath. Even though he spoke very softly, Teine could still hear him. "It's his surprise. Don't spoil it."

Teine sighed and turned back toward his little area of the room, a feeling of pleasant anticipation distracting him from the unpleasant girl. Alice was a little off-putting, and Teine was not impressed by her. She was very un-ladylike, a far cry from the polite, cultured girls of Solmurry. Teine was certain that Solmurry girls would never chew with their mouths open and would rather be caught dead than playing cards in the barracks with a bunch of strange boys!

Teine strode to his bunk, wondering what he should take, when something unusual caught his eye. Sitting on the small rug by his bed was a large, rectangular shape, covered from top to floor by one of the blankets off Teine's bed. His eyes widened reflexively and he looked over his shoulder to see all the card players either standing up or craning their necks to see what would happen next.

"Have you seen this?" Teine asked them.

"Oh, yes!" called Marcus. "But I think we'd really like to see *you* see it!"

Teine shrugged, "Well, come on over then." He tossed the folder that contained his transfer paperwork on the bed and sat down.

Moving his book satchel out of the way, Teine feigned indifference to the large parcel while he waited for the others to join him. After all, he did know exactly what it was. It was a trunk. A monogrammed trunk was the traditional gift from any holding to a young adult about to take their place in the world. Solmurry made them on site, enough to cover their own crop of youngsters each year, but also for resale to the other holdings that produced Humans.

Teine had seen many kinds of trunks over the years, as every adult at Solmurry had one of their own, and many had inherited others from their kin and friends as they passed on. He'd decorated his old footlocker in the childish artwork he'd painted years ago. He'd been eagerly awaiting the day he could dump it in the refuse bin to be picked apart for recycling. Now, it seemed that moment had arrived.

The card players dropped everything. Cards flew this way and that, and at least one beverage was spilled and ignored in their mad dash to see Teine's reaction to his trunk.

"Open it!" urged Alice, launching herself onto the bed next to Teine. "It's the biggest one I've ever seen!"

At least Seymour's not here, Teine thought with relief. There was no way his friend could have let that comment lie without turning it into a crass joke. But he said nothing, only waited for his audience to get in place. Then, Teine pulled the blanket off the trunk with only the slightest amount of flourish.

Stripped bare of its covering, the trunk looked even larger and more imposing. It was made of rich, honey-colored wood, with a subtle engraved pattern along the border where the lid opened. Teine had never seen a trunk designed like this before. It had a handle on one end, a sliding wooden rack that pulled out from the other end, and rolling wheels on the bottom.

"What's with those wheels?" asked Alice. "Is it trying to be a carriage or a sled-cart?"

"It needs those wheels, it's so big," muttered Marcus.

Teine could not take his eyes off his new trunk. It was easily one of the grandest things he'd ever seen in his life. Even the corners and edges had been painstakingly rounded off, so as to not snag or catch on anything or hurt anyone when the trunk was moved. It was definitely a show trunk, designed for use by a person who traveled a lot and needed a chest that would stand the test of time and many, many miles. It would last him a lifetime. And, best of all, his full name, *"Teine of Solmurry,"* and the Solmurry crest were engraved on a recessed brass plate on the front of the trunk by the keyhole. Few Aoife would have anything finer.

"Wow!" breathed Alice, leaning in for a closer look. Her earlier skepticism was melting away as she viewed the trunk up close. She stole a quick glance at Teine before looking back at the trunk and demanding, "Who bought you?"

"No one bought him," Marcus told her. "The young master's centennial was last week, and since he's going to show in the Displays, he chose Teine." Turning to Teine, he added, "When the guys brought it over from the workshop, they mentioned that the young master had designed the whole thing from scratch himself!"

"Bullpuckey," Billy sniffed. "I heard it too, but I don't believe it."

Teine pried his eyes away from the trunk to look at Marcus. "I'm sorry about steering you wrong. I really thought you were going to Display instead of me," he confessed. "It was just what I'd heard. I hope you didn't get your hopes up."

Marcus allowed himself a small, self-satisfied smile. "I can't believe you fell for it so completely. I was doing everything in my power to keep it a surprise."

"You *knew?*" Teine was amazed. He'd known Marcus since they were infants, and until that moment he'd have sworn that Marcus could sooner fly away than lie convincingly or deceive anyone about anything. He grinned lopsidedly at his cohort-mate, then flung himself at Marcus to wrestle. As usual, the bigger boy fended him off easily.

Teine chortled, "You sneaky *dog!* Really, I'm impressed."

Looking uncharacteristically smug and pleased by Teine's praise, Marcus gestured to the trunk. "Now, quit flattering me and open that thing up. The key's on your desk. We're all dying to see how it's put together inside."

Eagerly Teine fumbled for the two keys that were tied together with a red ribbon. They jingled musically in his grasp as he fitted one to the lock and turned it. There was a subtle pop when a catch inside the trunk was released, and the lid opened just a crack. All the others crowded close to see what was inside.

"You got clothes, too?" Marcus exclaimed, looking in at the small assortment of neatly folded garments, sturdy canvas and gum-soled walking shoes for everyday wear, plus a pair of leather ankle boots. "All right, now I am *officially* jealous."

Not an inch of space inside the miraculous trunk was wasted. Even the interior was lined in more of the same blonde wood and rich golden velvet. *The clothes were a very nice surprise,* Teine thought, but he just couldn't get past the sheer craftsmanship of the trunk itself.

The way it was laid out inside was nothing short of brilliant. No details were spared. There were compartments laid into the lid that closed tight, but had glass partitions so the contents could be easily seen. There was also a section of the trunk that was divided off, as if to carry books. The ankle boots weren't just thrown in haphazardly, instead they were resting on cylinders that looked like they were made for storing riding boots. And as if that weren't enough, all the organization accessories had been designed so they could be removed and left behind, if Teine needed the space to carry something big.

"Are you going to try those clothes on?" asked Alice.

The girl's teasing voice cut through Teine's reverie and startled him back to the present. "Oh, damn!" he exclaimed as he suddenly remembered he was in a hurry. "I was so surprised, I almost forgot!" He began frantically emptying his satchel onto the bed and repacking only the items he needed. "I have to get back to the Demesne, now!"

"Why?" Marcus asked, picking up on his friend's sudden distress. "Are you leaving?"

"No," Teine answered, sniffing an old tunic before stuffing it into his satchel. Then he immediately contradicted himself, "Well, yes, but not for long. I think they want me to go with the boy and his uncle back to the tower, but I can't swear to it. No one's given me a definitive on what's going on. I've just been guessing." With a shrug, he snatched the folder that contained his transfer paperwork and slid it between his sketchbook and notebook for safekeeping. "But I know I'm supposed to move all my things to the Demesne. They have a room for me there now."

Quickly, Teine pawed through the new clothes in the bottom of the trunk. All of them looked magnificent enough to wear to any function at the Demesne proper, so he grabbed a few of the new items and added them to his bag as well.

"Lucky," Alice muttered again. "I really mean it, too. I've never even *been* in our Demesne, much less ever dreamed of living there."

"Don't panic, Teine," Marcus advised. "Just get what you need for tonight, and I'll get you packed and see your things make it to the big house safely."

Marcus's calm, generous offer stopped Teine in his tracks and he felt a great weight slide off his shoulders. "You really mean it?" he asked, trying not to squeak as his voice cracked.

"Sure," Marcus shrugged. "I have the time. You'd do the same for me. Let me help."

If there hadn't been so many other people there, Teine might have hugged him. Instead, he busied himself by stuffing a complete change of clothes, a night shirt to sleep in, and some other essentials into his bag. "Thanks, Marcus. I owe you big."

Marcus simply grinned, "Sure." He turned back to the card players and waved them off. "Well, now I have things to do. You can just-"

"Start over!" Alice interjected gleefully. "We'll just start a new game."

"Hey! But I was winning!"

"Too bad!" The throng retreated, heading back toward the card table to resume their entertainment.

Once they were gone, Teine grabbed Marcus's shoulder in solidarity and gratitude. "I really mean it. Thanks."

"Hey, do you want all your things from your footlocker packed into the new trunk?" Marcus asked. "Oh, you'd better leave me one of those keys."

"Good idea," Teine reached under his bunk and grabbed his old pair of workout shoes. They were worn and filthy, but at least the laces were salvageable. He tossed one to Marcus to unlace, and he worked on the other one until both shoes were picked clean, and each key was threaded on a shoelace.

"What do you want to do with your old footlocker?" Marcus gestured to the offending piece of furniture. "Is that going, too?"

"Oh yeah, it's going—straight to the *dump*!" Teine ordered, making the hand gesture the Doyen Prince would make to send a fallen gladiator to his grave. "My god, but that thing is ugly."

"I'll take care of it," Marcus promised. "Anything else?"

Teine hesitated. There was nothing of his that he was shy of Marcus seeing. "Just fit it all in the trunk, and I'll sort it out later," he suggested.

"All right." Marcus nodded agreeably. "Are you ready?" he asked, as Teine threw his bag over his shoulder.

"Ready as I'll ever be." Teine found himself glancing around the room, trying to embed it permanently in his memory, knowing that this was his last look at his own childhood. From Seymour's perpetually unmade bed, to the goldfish bowl on the nightstand next to his, Teine didn't want to forget a thing.

"Good luck! You'd better get going," Marcus urged. "I'll leave your spare key with Leis."

Not trusting himself to say anything else past the huge lump in his throat, Teine simply nodded, then headed for the door. As the card players all called their well-wishes, Teine paused in the open doorway and waved. Then, impulsively, he kissed his own palm, and slapped the painted mastiff on the door. "So long, friend," he muttered. As he pounded his way down the stairs, Teine heard the door swing shut and latch behind him.

Chapter 14: Hat Trick

Dodging the puddles and other people as best as he could, Teine took advantage of a break in the scattered showers to head toward the Demesne at a flat-out run. He was already wet enough, as it was. As he pounded his way down the footpath, his satchel hammered his kidneys with each step. Fortunately, the bag was sturdy waterproofed canvas, and although it was heavy, Teine did not worry about the safety of his precious paperwork.

"Where's the fire?" called a couple of oldsters, as he barreled past like a racehorse down the homestretch. Teine didn't bother to answer.

As he neared the main house he nearly wept with relief. The grooms were just driving up Madric's distinctive candy-apple red carriage. It seemed as though he was not too late, after all. The horses, a matched pair of sleek bobtail grey thoroughbreds, danced and tossed their heads. Behind them, the sky loomed large and angry. Although the rain had momentarily paused, it seemed as though the whole world stood still, waiting for nature and magic to both unleash their wrath.

Once he passed the low hedge perimeter that outlined the lawn, Teine slowed from his breakneck pace to a light jog. He headed for the back entrance this time, as was only appropriate. His sense of decorum told him that no matter who he belonged to, there was only one place for a sopping wet Human to go: through the back, where nobody important would see him. As it turned out, someone was waiting for him. He nearly groaned out loud when he saw who it was.

"Where *were* you, boy?" snapped Phoebe, the pregnant maid who had taken him to the master's study earlier. "I sent a runner for you a good half an hour ago."

"Then they're probably still looking for me," Teine shrugged. He could understand the crabby woman's wrath, but he was unwilling to accept any real blame. "I wasn't given any orders to report here. Leis just told me it was a good idea, in case I was needed." Hoping to distract her further, Teine reached into his satchel and produced his leather bound folder of transfer papers. "Here's my paperwork."

Phoebe squinted at him with a skeptic's eye, then took the folder, but immediately handed it back when she saw what it was. Teine figured she must have decided he was telling the truth, as her demeanor softened. She stood aside to let him pass into the mud room. There, on practical cubby shelves, were items ranging from garden shears to berry baskets, with lower divisions for different pairs of wooden clogs arranged by size. An assortment of hooks and bars for hanging coats and rugs adorned one wall, as well as a big, durable hamper woven from small saplings.

Phoebe draped Teine's shoulders with the biggest, thickest towel he had ever seen. "I suppose it can't be helped, then. Lord Solmurrian has had a busy day. Perhaps he thought he mentioned it to you during your meeting." She rubbed the towel on his shoulders, and Teine froze out of sheer surprise as she began toweling him off, paying special attention to his mop of dark red hair. "My, but you look a fright," she grumbled, "But I suppose that's not of concern to anyone tonight. You'll be riding in an open carriage in a bit, anyway."

"Open?" Teine squeaked, unable to help himself. "But... the storm?"

"Open," Phoebe confirmed, cracking the first grin Teine had seen from her. "Madric says it's actually less dangerous, with these gusty winds. Apparently he was riding in a carriage with the bonnet up once, and the wind ripped the whole rig right off the road. Horses, too."

Unwilling to admit he was a little frightened of horses in the first place, Teine decided to change the subject. Noticing the change in Phoebe's demeanor, he took the opportunity to try and gain a little more knowledge so he could insulate himself from any social gaffes. "He lets you call him Madric?"

Phoebe nodded. "It's confusing to have two 'lords' running around, and he's technically not our master," she told him, keeping her voice low. "There, you've stopped the worst of the dripping. Now it's just what us ladies of the house like to call 'hurry up and wait' time." She took the damp towel from his shoulders, draping it tidily over a bar on the wall. "Would you care for a cup of something warm? I've heated up some milk for the boy. There's enough for two cups of chocolate, if you'd like."

It took all the discipline Teine had to keep his jaw from dropping to his chest. Chocolate was very expensive, and therefore was reserved as a treat for only the most special of special occasions. He could count on one hand the number of times he'd tasted it in his entire life. Like most Humans, he had a sweet tooth that was easily sated by other confections, and he indulged on a regular basis. But chocolate? That was a real surprise.

"Yes, please," he answered, as quickly as he could.

"It will be ready shortly, and then we'll bring it to him," she promised. "We've been readying your room, but the linens haven't been brought up yet. I don't expect you'll be staying here tonight, anyway. Why don't you wait in the playroom until Madric is ready to leave? C'mon…," she said. "Don't worry. I'll take you there."

Now that Teine was safely accounted for, dried, and reasonably presentable, Phoebe seemed to slowly unwind. Teine found he could almost forgive her for the slap, earlier. She continued with the pleasantries as she led him through the thickly carpeted, maze-like halls and up a flight of stairs. "I know it's probably a bit overwhelming finding your way around here, but trust me, it will be second nature after a few days. Here we are!" Phoebe paused at a double-sized door covered by a heavy emerald-colored velvet curtain. It sounded as though someone was playing a radio on the other side. The reception was good enough to tell that it was a fabal game. Teine hoped it was a replay of the game he'd missed earlier.

Phoebe pushed the curtain open and stepped into the room. Teine followed closely on her heels, noticing the room was decorated much less formally than the master's study. The furnishings were all well-padded and comfortable, with sizes to accommodate adult Humans and the smaller-framed Aoife as well. On an intricately woven rug, a grizzled old wolfhound grinned and thumped his tail in welcome. Teine liked dogs, but he hardly noticed the hound's friendly overture, his attention was so completely taken up by the box across the room. It sat on a pedestal against the far wall, and although there was glass set into the front of it, it was nothing like a mirror or a window because it was neither transparent nor reflective. Teine squinted, trying to make sense of what his eyes told him could not be. He then moved forward to get a better look.

Chuckling at his reaction, Phoebe left him to his investigation. "Cocoa will be ready in a minute," she called out, then turned and left. The curtain swished shut behind her.

Ruffling the dog's ears as he went past, Teine walked right up to the strange box. First, a conservatively dressed elder Aoife man sitting inside the box looked Teine right into the eyes and told him about a report on something called the "stock market." Nothing the Aoife said made much sense; he spoke about "trading futures." *How could you trade a future?* Teine was just about to peer behind the box, to examine the workings to see if the device was perhaps some kind of mirror that reflected from another location, when the scene changed suddenly to a green field covered with fabal players in their brightly-colored armor. Teine stopped and stared in wonder as the amazing box showed the fabal game that had been played earlier that afternoon. An announcer commented on the action, which was limited only to the most exciting parts of the game, the parts the Teine would most have liked to see.

"Excuse me," came a soft child's voice from the far corner of the room. Teine started, caught completely off guard. He looked wildly around the room as if caught red-handed at some nefarious activity. Then he saw a small form huddled between the overstuffed leather couch and a comfortable-looking armchair, tucked neatly behind one of the footstools. Teine saw the child seemed to be wearing some kind of metal helmet. But before he could say anything, the boy spoke again. "You make a much better door than a window."

Teine blinked, feeling stupid, then realized he was blocking the view to the box. "Oh, sorry," he said. He stepped to the side, checking to see if he was out of the way.

"That's better. I want to see how the game ended. Then we can talk."

Shifting his weight from one foot to the other, Teine nodded. Apparently, he'd just met his new owner.

The curtain swished open and Phoebe padded in. She carried a silver tray with two earthenware mugs filled with steaming liquid and overflowing with a white, sweet-smelling froth. Teine's stomach rumbled loudly at the scent. He'd been hungry hours ago, and now his body reminded him of his neglect. Phoebe handed the tray to him, and to his delight it also held a plate of sandwiches and a bowl of crisps. Teine glanced hopefully at the food while Phoebe stepped over the dog and set up a small, low table next to Marne's entrenchment. She served the child first, bringing him his cocoa and a few sweet cookies on a plate. Teine watched, hoping to get a better glimpse of him, but all he saw was a slender arm wearing a heavy, clunky golden bracelet.

"Can I have my colander back?" Phoebe asked. "I'd like to get those good noodles cooked for tomorrow, and I'll need it to strain—"

"After the news," Marne replied, not taking his eyes off the box. "Then I won't need it anymore."

Teine blinked. His new master was wearing a kitchen utensil on his head? That did not bode well.

Phoebe seemed to take the news in stride. "So, it's safe to start the water?"

The colander bobbed up and down as Marne nodded. "Boil away!" The playbacks of the fabal game continued, and then the scene switched to some baseball players practicing at their spring training camp.

As Teine turned many unlikely explanations for the odd scene around in his head, Phoebe took the tray from him and set it on his own table. Snagging one of the crisps from Teine's bowls, she held it up in her fingers, showing it to the dog. "Stinky—catch!" Turning to the sound of his name, the slobbering hound snatched the cookie expertly out of the air, looking proud of his trick. "Yay! Good boy!" Without further comment, she tucked the silver tray under her arm and ducked out through the curtains.

Experimentally, Teine took a nibble of one of the sandwiches. Filled with some kind of rich meat paste, cucumbers, and cream cheese, it tasted heavenly. Too hungry to be coy, Teine sat down in one of the chairs and began tucking in while the chocolate cooled to drinking temperature. Between the excellent food and the amazing box, it took only a few minutes before he was warmed and feeling comfortable enough to ask a question.

"So... why are you hiding back there?" he asked Marne. Between Leis' stories and his own memory, Teine recalled that the boy loved to read and that his tastes ran toward the adventurous. "Are you playing soldier or something?"

Without warning, the picture on the box went all fuzzy. Stinky the wolfhound raised his head and pricked his ears, tail beating the floor with glee. As Teine turned his head to see if Marne knew what had happened, he realized that the boy had risen to his feet and was looking at him from his sanctuary in the corner behind the footstool. The Aoife child was taller than Teine expected, about the size of a five- or six-year-old human, or an Aoife boy of about seventy. Although it was hard to get a clear picture of his face, obscured as it was by the colander, Marne wore an imitation of the garments any adult Aoife would wear. He was a frail-looking lad, pale and clammy, and Teine suspected the boy would be more comfortable in pajamas. *Did Aoife even wear pajamas?*

Even as Teine cataloged these details away, Marne swiped the colander from his head and bowed deeply, as if he were doffing his hat to a person of standing. The instant the colander cleared the boy's head, the fuzzy picture on the box dissolved completely into a blast of static and the sound twisted into a high-pitched squeal.

"Oh," was all Teine could think of to say.

As soon as the colander was back on Marne's head and he was tucked back safely behind the footstool, both the picture and the sound from the box returned to normal. But an instant later, there were sounds of running footsteps out in the hallway, and the curtain blew in to reveal Madric. Teine recognized him from his regular trips to Solmurry, but had never spoken to him before.

The Aoife magician seemed to be on high alert, looking around with alarm. Ignoring Teine as completely as if he did not exist, Madric went right to his nephew, standing over him protectively. "Are you all right?"

Outside, the wind began to pick up, sounding a low moan through the shutters.

"I just took off my hat," Marne replied peevishly. "Just for a second, I swear."

Madric relaxed, dropping into a fluid crouch so he was down on Marne's level. "You gave me a fright when the music cut off like that. But you also gave me an excuse to leave the dining hall, so perhaps I won't die of boredom tonight, after all." His grin was genuinely playful, and Teine looked on with amusement. "Are you nearly ready to leave?"

"That depends," replied Marne, a mock-angelic expression on his face. "If you *do* die of boredom tonight, do I get your greys?"

Madric chuckled, "You and your horses, boy, I swear. Have you ever met a horse you didn't want? No, wait, don't answer that. I don't want to think about how many your father would be feeding if he hadn't set your limit at five. And that means you have six, still?"

"Ponies only count as a half," Marne reminded him. "So, technically, I could have another pony before he'd complain. Besides," he said, changing the subject. "If we wait a bit longer, we'd be traveling in the thick of it."

The boy's voice was soft, but Teine could hear the anticipation, the excitement. He glanced at Madric to try and figure out what

Marne was talking about, and saw the magician pale visibly. It was then that Teine realized Marne had been encouraging a delay of their departure so they could travel while the storm was at its strongest. Unconsciously, Teine wrapped his arms around himself, picturing the horror of such a scene. Once, the year before, he'd delayed going back to the Commons after a storm had come on suddenly. He'd seen the gales take the form of a giant man made of wind who ripped a hundred-year-old oak out of the ground, crumpling it into toothpicks.

During that same storm, lightning had struck the Demesne, and a suit of armor that everyone thought had been strictly ornamental had come to life and run amok through the dining room. Four of the serving staff had run screaming back to the Commons while Teine's own Amagi, a couple of enterprising junior butlers, and Vorogu, the Aoife docent, had managed to trap the suit in the pantry until the enchantment had worn itself out. Prior Vihah had been notified, and the suit had been taken the very next day, "for study."

Madric blinked, then laughed a nervous laugh. "Well, then. I think I've made enough pleasantries for one evening. I believe we can safely take our leave without ruffling any feathers." He raised his voice and called for Phoebe. When she arrived, slightly out of breath and wiping her hands on her apron, he caught her by the arm. "You know the drill, my dear," he said, looking up at the Human woman with a sparkle in his eye.

"Indeed," she confirmed. Turning to Teine, she pointed at the box. "Would you be a dear and turn that off?" Teine stared blankly at her. "Oh, never mind. Look—here's how it works." She strode over and turned a knob on the side. There was a satisfying click as the picture folded up and disappeared like a book closing. Then she returned to Madric, "I'll wait a few minutes, then make the usual apologies for both of you." Madric nodded his approval.

Marne rose to his feet, rolled the colander down his arm like a gentleman doing a hat trick, and handed it to Phoebe. "Thanks."

"I'll keep it on the low shelf, in case you need it when you get back," she promised.

Once Marne was standing, the wolfhound also stood and began dancing around, his paws making muted thuds on the dense carpet. "No, Stinky," the boy chided. "You can't go this time. There's not enough room in the carriage with Teine along." The dog's excitement evaporated and he sat on his haunches, watching the boy with mournful eyes. With a sympathetic expression on his face, Marne padded across the room, his footfalls almost silent compared to those of his lumbering hound. "I'm sorry," he said. The dog was so tall and the boy so small that they were very nearly eye to eye as Marne gently stroked the hound's grizzled grey face and rubbed his ears. When he hugged the dog around the neck, it was almost as if the dog hugged him back, leaning his entire body into Marne's embrace.

Madric smiled, and Teine noticed his expression was kind and almost paternal. "Come on, now. Stinky will live without you for a day or two."

Marne pulled the dog close again, and Stinky responding by leaning hard enough to nearly knock him over. "He's had a bath today," he explained, scratching the dog on the sensitive skin under his collar. Stinky looked as though he'd been transported directly to heaven, stretching his neck and raising his head to facilitate Marne's attention. "Being too clean makes him itchy."

Nodding, Madric replied, "Well, you take advantage of that. I'll go get your hood."

Within moments, Phoebe had herded Teine out the doors near the carriage house, where Madric's carriage was sitting under the awning. The greys waited more or less patiently, with only an occasional snort or stomped foot, under the care of the Solmurry grooms. Teine went around back and placed his bag in the compartment under the seat. Marne stood quietly on the threshold, his arm companionably around his dog's withers. As Teine slowly approached the seating of the carriage, delaying the inevitable as long as possible, he could see the whites of the horses' eyes. The greys were hyper-alert, their heads held unnaturally high. He was about to ask one of the grooms for some assurance that the horses were safe to use when he noticed Madric had arrived at his nephew's side.

Madric nudged the dog away in order to pick Marne up. Marne cooperated as Madric maneuvered his feet into some sort of sack, which Marne pulled up to his armpits and held in place. Then, Madric produced another cloth sack, identical to the first one, except that this one had some type of writing, some unreadable symbols around its edge. While Teine looked on, staring blankly, Madric put the other sack around and over Marne's head and arms, pulling it down to overlap the other sack by about a foot and a half. "Are your arms tucked in?" Madric asked. Teine couldn't hear Marne's reply, muffled as it was by all that fabric, but Madric seemed satisfied with his nephew completely covered like a giant laundry duffel. Suddenly, one of the greys nickered, and Teine jumped, badly startled.

"Look at that," one of the grooms muttered, after they were done chuckling at Teine's reaction. They pointed westward toward the storm. Teine was almost afraid to look. Although the quiet part of this storm had yet to pass and was still overhead, Teine could barely see the remnants of the setting sun behind the low, dense, swirling front that was thick with flickers of lightning. An oncoming mass of clouds had the fuzzy straight lines that heralded heavy rain, and it looked as though it was traveling nearly as fast as a horse could gallop. It was so still and oppressive, Teine thought he could hear the sky itself groan. His mouth went dry, but he wasn't certain if it was from excitement or fear.

A loud peal of thunder, close enough to make the horses dance, brought Teine back to the moment. Glancing over to see what was taking Madric so long, he blinked twice at what he saw. The Aoife magician had produced a metallic cord, and was binding Marne's sack while murmuring something that sounded like a cross between a rhythmic poem and a church hymn. As Madric chanted and gestured with his hands, it occurred to Teine he was probably casting a spell on the bag. His suspicions were confirmed when the strange runes around the edge of the outer sack began glowing with a bright green light.

Huge, wet drops of rain began to fall. First one, then several, expanding within seconds into a downpour that obscured buildings just a few feet away.

It didn't take long for the runes to fade, and when they did, Madric stooped to pick Marne up and sling him gently over his shoulder. Phoebe stood at the ready with Madric's traveling hat, which he donned, his cape, which he threw over his other shoulder, and a magnificent wooden staff carved all over with vines. Speaking a few words of reassurance to the maid, Madric then stepped out over the threshold and strode toward the carriage.

The horses, seeing their master, fidgeted in anticipation. "Good evening, Madric," the chief groom greeted the wizard pleasantly, as if this was no unusual occurrence. "Your horses are fit and ready. Is there anything else you wish before you depart?"

Madric looked up, admiring the bricked arch that protected all of them from the rain. A mere ten feet away was a sheeting downpour. "Do you have a really big umbrella?" he asked. As the grooms laughed at his humor, the Aoife magician turned to Teine. "Hop in... Teine, is it?" Wordlessly, Teine nodded, then clambered into the carriage. "You'll be sitting in front with me, but get into the back and I'll hand Marne to you." Teine did as he was asked. Even swaddled in heavy layers of cloth, Marne weighed hardly anything.

"I won't drop you," Teine told the boy as he eased him onto the nest of blankets and canvas cushions behind the bench seat.

"I know," Marne replied. If it was possible, his voice sounded even smaller, more vulnerable than it had in the room. "Don't be afraid."

"I'm not." It was a lie, and Teine suspected that Marne probably knew the truth, but he had to try and save face if he could. Meanwhile, the air had grown so thick, so pregnant with curbed power, that Teine had the impression of sitting in a boat that was paused in mid-air, the instant before it fell down a massive waterfall. As Madric climbed onto the front bench and settled himself on the red leather seat, Teine couldn't help but ask the one question that had been nagging at him for the last few minutes.

"Hey, Marne," he whispered, getting down low next to the bag. "Why are you all wrapped up like that? Are you hiding from someone?"

"Sort of," Marne answered. "It's so the storm won't see me."

All the hair on Teine's arms and the back of his neck stood up at once. It was such an eerie feeling that he startled when Madric turned around to lay his staff behind the seat with Marne. "Come on up here, Teine," Madric said. "It's going to be a bit bumpy. You'll be more comfortable on the seat." Teine scrambled to comply, trying hard not to think about what the Aoife boy could have meant.

Suddenly, Madric stood, tossed his hat casually in the back, and unchecked the cart brake. "Let's roll," he whispered. The horses surged forward as if they were one, their momentum shoving Teine back into his seat as he clutched blindly for the railing. Lightning flashed and the wind shrieked while Madric stood laughing, his expert hand on the reins. They careened down the Solmurry driveway, heading hell-bent for the little dirt road that led to his tower, with the maelstrom raging like a hungry animal hot on their heels.

Chapter 15: The Shepherd

It wasn't that Teine had never been in a carriage before. Many times the grooms had hitched up a few of the hay wagons and taken the students on a field trip, or to Emmett, the closest small borough. But the matched sets of placid draft horses that pulled those wagons were a far cry from the wound-up, hot-blooded racers that drew Madric's carriage.

The horses' hoof beats came faster than Teine thought possible, their rapid thuds dampened by the soft footing and occasional puddles of standing water. The relentless staccato pounding of hooves was mesmerizing, an auditory anchor holding Teine in the present while thunder roared and the maelstrom howled all around him. He was soaked to the bone in an instant, but all he could do was brace himself in the seat next to Madric, knuckles white on the bar and toes locked under the footrest. Teine had never in his life been as certain that he was going to die.

As they turned onto the small wagon trail that marked about ten miles to Madric's Tower, the downpour slacked off a bit. Three terrified deer skittered out from behind hedgerows to startle in the center of the road, then bounded alongside for about a furlong. Madric only laughed more as the horses leaped to the side and the carriage careened dangerously on one wheel. However, he managed to keep the team on the road and the cart behind the team. Teine snuck a cautious look up at the magician. Madric was still standing, plying both the lines and the whip with delicate skill as he weathered all the bumps and rattles from both the terrain and the buffeting wind. His hair was soaking wet, streaming out behind him as the lightning crackled all around.

"Woo-hoo!" he yelled, urging the horses to race the deer. "Isn't it great to be alive?"

Teine agreed, and fervently hoped he'd stay that way. He wondered what Marne's reaction to all of this would be if he weren't wrapped up in a bag and he could see everything. Would the boy show the same wild exhilaration that the rest of the Aoife did? What was it that drew them to the storms? What wildness lurked under the surface of even the most staid and stodgy Aoife that could turn even polished, genteel Madric into a raving, whooping daredevil? Teine wanted to know. Preferably, that knowledge would come when he was wrapped in a warm blanket before a roaring fireplace.

"Oh, don't look so tense, boy," Madric teased. Lightning flashed, and Teine was sure it hit a tree not far behind them. "We're well ahead of the worst of it. So far, this is just a normal storm."

"Do you think we'll outrun it?" Teine yelled.

"Mostly, yes!" the magician returned. "Believe me, you'll be able to tell if we don't!"

Teine gave him a skeptical look, which set Madric off laughing again.

Teine was already exhausted. Another ten miles or so would be a mind-numbing exercise in endurance and self-control. His dinner of sandwiches and hot chocolate, hastily consumed, was far richer than the fare he was used to. It sat temperamentally in his stomach, waiting to be either jostled loose or settle down. Teine would rather be dragged behind the carriage for ten miles than throw up on Madric, so he tried hard to will his stomach to be steady and the carriage to stay in one piece.

The road to Madric's Tower was a little-used wagon track, more for horse riders than for hauling supplies. It was drug with a blade twice a year to smooth out the ruts, but in Teine's opinion, even twice-a-week maintenance wouldn't make it safe for the kind of breakneck gallop they were doing to outrun this storm.

Despite his terror, Teine felt a nagging disappointment. They were rapidly losing light, and he'd hoped to see the tower as they approached. Would it look like the pictures in the old history books? It seemed the only glimpse he'd be catching would be illuminated by lightning.

A site of historical significance, Madric's Tower had been converted from one of the oldest lighthouses on the coast. Teine remembered reading about how it had been constructed in a time ages past when its dual purpose had been to warn friendly ships off the rocks and to warn the inlanders of impending invasion.

The Empyrean still had its share of jealous neighbors, eager to pluck the riches from this beautiful and gracious land. There were nearly always rumblings of war, though the main threats changed over time with the signing of treaties and alliances built on the whims of short-lived kings and warlords.

In times with strong magics, spells served to spread the necessary alarms. More recently, the coastline drew its protection from the Empyrean's formidable navy and bands of wandering Aoife rangers and knights stationed in the far-flung reaches of the coastline. Over time, all the Empyrean's inland beacon towers had been disassembled and their materials put to use elsewhere.

As they traveled, the overall terrain grew steeper with the road winding up, over, and around small bluffs and stands of trees. Teine guessed that they were probably about halfway there when Madric pulled the team to a halt on the leeward side of one of the hills.

"The horses need a breather," he explained, seating himself next to Teine. Soaked with rain and foamy sweat, the normally light-colored horses looked much darker, especially in the fading light. They humped up their backs, trying to turn their tails to the wind. Teine didn't know horses well, but to his untrained eye they still seemed edgy. Their heads tossed, their nostrils flared, and their ears were pinned flat to their wet heads. Even though they'd been run hard, the pair still twitched excitably at every crash of thunder.

Teine used the break to force himself to relax his death grip on the bar. He rubbed his hands together, trying to chafe some feeling back into them as he looked around. He couldn't see too much of the terrain with the storm obscuring what was left of the fading daylight, but he could make out movement nearby. His heart pounded for a few measured beats until he could discern the shapes. Further down the hill, sharing the shelter of their bluff, huddled a small herd of beef cattle. They had all lain down to avoid the worst of the wind and rain and were clustered close together near some low growing bushes. Teine blew a sigh of relief.

Madric seemed unconcerned. Turning up his collar against the wind, he pulled a flask from his boot, uncapped it, and offered Teine a drink. Teine caught a whiff of the contents and politely waved it off. He suspected liquor wouldn't help him any.

"How are you doing back there, Marne?" Madric asked.

"Fine!" the boy called, then said something else that was lost in the muffling effect of the bag, or possibly the gale.

His uncle heard what Teine missed. "Better than being too cold, I'd imagine," Madric answered. "We're about halfway."

"That's great," Marne replied.

"Where are we?" Teine asked. Now that the carriage wasn't rocking and weaving, and they were sheltered somewhat from the wind, Teine's sense of adventure was returning. "Still on Solmurry lands?"

He had to ask twice to be heard over the din of wind and rain. Madric nodded, leaning closer to hear Teine better. "Yes. It's all ours, all the way to Dunham. Do they still cover the Solmurry Capite in history class?"

Teine nodded, glad to have something to talk about. It would take his mind off his fear for the moment. "History's always been one of my favorite subjects. Especially when it's taught by..."

"Professor Norzic!" yelled Madric, laughing. "I had him, too. What is he, now? About eight hundred?"

"Oh, at least! And he still tells a story like you were there, watching!" Teine chuckled. He'd completely loved history under that tutor. Norzic was one of the best Aoife professors, and had a lively instruction style. The ancient gentleman always presented the material in an interesting, narrative manner, complete with mysteries and cliffhangers that left many a student wondering all winter break what happened next. "And local history is the best of all!"

It was Madric's turn to nod in agreement. "It's very... colorful. You know, in present day, Solmurry remains one of the top twenty largest land holdings in the Empyrean, based on acreage." He took another swig of the brandy and hunkered down in the seat. "So," he said, a sly grin on his face. "Why don't you refresh my memory on the Capite?"

Marne said something that was muffled by the bag, but it sounded like a strong second to Madric's request.

Teine knew he was being tested. "One of your distant ancestors had been a 'Capite'—a holder of land granted directly from the Emperor himself," he began, hopefully speaking loud enough that Marne could hear. Teine remembered listening with rapt attention in class as the master storyteller had spun the tale. He hoped he could do it justice. "The noble Aleric Solmurrian, second son of the Solmurry line in the last Age of Magics, was famous for his undying loyalty to his boyhood friend, the Emperor..."

"'Undying' being the operative word," Madric chuckled.

"Fallen in a vicious battle against a rival to the Emperor's throne, the Solmurrian wizard had cast enough magics on himself to keep his body and soul together, even after he died. He rose from the dead, his corpse mobile and possessed of all his memories and abilities. They say he arrived at the last minute to save the Emperor's life and lay waste to his foes," Teine intoned, hoping he made it sound as interesting as it was. "After that battle, the heroic magician saw the undead thing he'd become and voluntarily severed the spells that had made him live beyond death. After he quietly passed on, his friend the Emperor grieved his loss terribly and granted the Capite to the Solmurrian clan in appreciation for his friend's sacrifice."

"This is why the inheritance of Solmurry is kind of an 'all or nothing' prospect," Madric interjected, leaning an elbow over the back of the seat and turning to be sure Marne heard him. "A Capite can't be divided. It has to remain intact."

Teine found himself nodding. "Oh yes. That's why Solmurry's still in one piece after all this time." He slipped back into teacher mode to finish the story. "Since then, centuries have passed and many of the other noble family holders have had their lands divided and subdivided for their descendants, taxed, and divided more. During the reign of these last four Emperors, Solmurry herself has remained intact."

Marne practically had to yell to be heard over the storm and through the bag. "That's why even ten miles out from the Demesne proper, we're still on our land."

"Good!" Madric encouraged.

"I loved that class, too," Marne insisted. He must have been shouting at the top of his lungs to be heard through the canvas.

"Well, here's a bit you might not have thought about," Madric countered. "It's the Capite that we have to thank for most of our Human population. Without all this vast acreage, we wouldn't be self-supporting on the scale that we are. These pastures and rotated fields of crops are cultivated and maintained by Solmurry's Humans, ensuring a built-in supply of not only foodstuffs, but jobs, too."

Teine was contemplating what Madric said, when suddenly both of the greys snorted. One nickered nervously and began to fidget and they both craned their necks to look out into the darkness near where the cattle were resting.

"What's that?" Teine whispered hoarsely, trying not to think about all of the predators in the area. Aoife had nothing but contempt for things that were "too tame" and so kept a large acreage of their lands unneeded for agriculture in its natural wild state. Thus, each holding had its place where neither Human nor Aoife would dare go unarmed.

Madric didn't answer, just glanced purposefully at Teine then pointed toward his staff. With his longer arms, Teine was able to snatch the weapon from the back and hand it to Madric quickly. With one hand on the reins, Madric raised the staff and brandished it, as though to ward off an attacker. The horses danced, tossing their heads and whickering. The magician glanced back and forth between the staff and the storm front, his jaw clenched, and his eyes wide. Teine's stomach sank as he realized that Madric was not as confident as he had appeared earlier. "Take my sword," Madric hissed. "On my belt, now!"

Teine fumbled with the short blade, trying to get it out of its scabbard without slicing Madric in the process. But his worst fears were confirmed when he saw movement out of the corner of his eye, out among the cattle. A shadowy, sinuous form rose from the ground and began approaching the carriage. Within a few paces, though, it was evident that the incoming animal was not a cow. Long, lanky, and very large, with a row of spines on its back, the creature approached with reptilian grace. Teine fancied he could see the shine of its malevolent eyes and the reflection of lightning dancing along its scaly hide. He held his breath and wondered if having a friend eaten by a dragon would dampen Seymour's enthusiasm for them.

Just as suddenly as the horses began acting up, they quieted. Madric and Teine exchanged a quick, confused look, and Madric shook the staff menacingly at the darkness.

"It's just Willis!" Marne shrieked from inside the bag. "Just Willis! Don't hurt her!"

Almost apologetically, the Holidocrith slunk up to the carriage, ears flat against her neck. Raising her head to Madric's eye level, she blinked her alien, yellowish eyes as if she were dying to speak to him.

Teine noticed with wonder that Willis had the most beautiful, impossibly long eyelashes. He'd seen Holidocrith before, of course, but never this close. They were magnificent creatures, and as a younger artist he'd filled notebook after notebook with sketches of them. Being warm-blooded and giving birth to live young, Holidocrith fell into some strange category between mammals and reptiles. Willis was an average specimen, nearly as tall at the shoulder as a carriage horse, but built to be narrow and swift, like a coursing hound. From a distance, Holidocrith had an almost horse-like profile with long, elegant necks and proud heads. But they had their share of dragon-like features, as well. Holidocrith used their thick, meaty tails, scaly hides, and spines down their back to protect themselves when fighting other predators. They were fierce, intelligent, and noble, respected as sentients and cherished for their loyalty and work ethic. Many drew wages all across the Empyrean and others served kingdoms as cabbies, teamsters, mercenaries, and sentries. Teine supposed Willis was on the Solmurry books as a shepherd.

"She's sorry she frightened you!" Marne shouted, struggling to be heard. "Very sorry. She wants to know if you want an escort."

"Well, I feel like a complete fool!" Madric bellowed. "But it's nice to see you. It's been a while!" Shouting over the wind was starting to make him hoarse. He remedied this by taking a long swig from his flask. Teine grimaced in sympathy. "Do you think we *need* an escort?" he croaked.

There was a pause where Teine thought he heard a little sigh of frustration before Marne spoke again. "She says no, but you should get back underway. It's not good for the horses to stand still too long, and she also thinks it's going to get worse pretty quickly from here on out."

"Thanks, Willis." Madric said. "You should really come to my tower for a visit sometime when the weather clears up and Marne's visiting. It'd be nice to catch up."

"She says that would be delightful."

Madric showed the flask to the Holidocrith, shaking it to show there was some left. "Want the last?"

Willis tossed her head in what presumably was a nod and opened her mouth to invite Madric to pour. Teine stared in amazement at all those sharp teeth in such a horse-like mouth. When Madric had emptied his flask down her gullet, Willis folded her ears back and waggled her tongue playfully at them before heading back to go lay back down with the cattle. Light on her feet,

Willis moved quickly. *Creatures that big certainly don't scamper,* Teine mused as he watched her return to her herd.

"I've never met a 'Liddy' that would turn down a drop of good brandy," Madric nodded, sitting down. "I think we've had enough of a rest. Might be wise to get moving again."

"I thought most people could hear Holidocrith," Teine commented, trying not to sound glum. "I was looking forward to finally getting to talk to one." He handed the sword back to Madric, and the magician handed him the staff.

Madric secured the weapon back on his belt. "Hey, grab my hat, will you?" Teine leaned back to reach behind the seats and exchanged the staff for the hat while Madric answered his question. "Willis is harder to hear than most," the magician told Teine. "But she's not a dumb beast. In the last war, when she was serving as the previous Lord Solmurrian's mount, she had a head injury. Since then, she just can't seem to get through to very many people. I think that's why she ended up here, out in the wilds."

"She's lonely," Marne added. "The cows are too stupid to talk to."

Settling his hat on his head, Madric looked back over his shoulder at the raging storm and winced. "I'm not looking forward to coming out from behind this hill!" he warned.

"I'm ready," Teine said. He really meant it, too. Somehow, the false alarm had done more to bolster his confidence than anything else that had happened to him so far that day.

"Good. Let's go," Marne urged. "I had too much cocoa. So... sooner would be better than later."

Madric chuckled under his breath, pushed the brim of his hat down tighter, and snapped the reins. "Walk on!" he commanded. Obediently, the team leaped forward, eager to run again. As soon as the carriage came out from behind the sheltered area, Madric's hat was sucked straight off his head. "Blast it!" Madric cursed. But he looked far from angry. Just like earlier, he still seemed positively elated, even though the winds were their fiercest yet.

The second half of the journey, while cursed with worsening weather, was actually far more comfortable for Teine. He was beginning to have confidence in Madric's driving skill and general leadership. Battered constantly by the relentless gale, hammering rain, and occasional bits of small hail, carriage, driver, and team performed admirably. Before Teine realized it, they were passing under a stone arch and the horses' hooves began to ring on cobblestones.

"Easy there, my beauties," Madric crooned—if you could call screaming at the top of his lungs "crooning." "It's a slippery one!"

The horses fought for their footing up the hill, hooves scrabbling on slick bricks and stones. Up ahead, a light suddenly sprung up and Teine thought someone must be holding a lantern for them. He started to say something, pointing, when another beacon lit further up the road. The horses slowed to a trot, then a walk. Soon, their heads bowed against the load on the steep, treacherous climb.

"Do you like the lights?" Madric asked, looking cheerfully smug. "I enchanted them myself. They're motion sensitive."

Teine was suitably impressed at how Madric was able to take such a wondrous power and turn it to such practical use and then explain it away as though it were commonplace.

As the horses continued to climb, Teine found himself looking forward to seeing Madric's Tower in the daylight. He'd heard its rambling courtyard and attached housing made of natural stones had a lot of charm and character. The tower and surrounding buildings had been made by Krunal miners, ages ago when the trade relations between the Krunal and the Empyrean had been friendly. Madric's Tower had even been featured on the cover of one of the *Country Style* magazines, a popular title for the well-to-do merchants of Empyrea and the other urban areas in the Empyrean.

Their path had been lit all the way up the cobbled drive, and Madric drove the horses under a lantern-lit covered arch next to the stable. A beautiful escutcheon, made of colored stones, was built into the wall of the stone coach cover. It depicted the ship and sun of the Solmurry heraldry. "Beautiful," Teine mused. He'd have to have a closer look in the daytime.

A burly Human, bearded and dressed in the plain, serviceable clothes of a commoner, was waiting with a stack of blankets. He moved forward to greet the incoming carriage. Although the howling wind had not yet abated, Teine felt a strange sensation of lightness as the rain ceased to beat directly on him.

"Ah, Madric, ever daring the devil, I see," the groom teased the magician, throwing a blanket in his face.

Madric grinned like a kid caught red-handed, then blotted his face and hair while turning to check on Marne. "Teine, help me with him. Your arms are longer."

Teine scrambled to obey, painfully conscious of his own full bladder ever since Marne had so helpfully mentioned his. Between the two of them, the carriage upholstery was in serious jeopardy. He lifted the boy out carefully, starting to reach for the bindings that held the bag shut, but Madric stopped him with a sharp "No!" Startled by the uncharacteristically stern tone in Madric's voice, Teine jumped, half expecting to be slapped.

"No, not here," Madric added, taking a couple of steps to look out over the valley, as if trying to confirm something. "The leading edge is nearly upon us. Magic draws these storms, and Marne's got enough latent talent to be a big lightning rod without the protection of that bag," he explained.

Teine nodded, finally understanding why Madric had looked so nervous earlier when he feared he might have to use his magic staff against an attacker. "So, how do we protect Marne, then?" he asked.

"We'll have to take him to the basement."

Chapter 16: A Short Reign with a Violent End

Teine followed the magician and his groom through the stables and into the base of the tower, carrying Marne in his arms. Unlike the Demesne at Solmurry, the tower was designed not to be pretty, but to be functional.

In keeping with the more egalitarian leanings of the time, there was no such thing as a "guest entrance." All comers and goers to the main floor of the tower would enter or exit through any number of practically designed portals, each equipped with some type of storage or coat alcove. The Krunal talent for design gave the rooms a warm, homey feel, even though most of the walls were bare stone with iron lighting fixtures.

As they made their way to an open workroom outfitted as a kitchen, Madric held his arms out, beckoning Teine to come closer. "I'll take him now. You follow Kenneth." The ginger-bearded groom with the blankets and towels transferred his burden to one arm and respectfully tipped his cap at Teine. Feeling pleased and slightly embarrassed, Teine found himself grinning as he handed Marne over to his uncle.

"There, now," Madric muttered. "And on down to your room. We'll get you all settled in and comfortable in just a moment." Inside the bag, Marne made a noise that could have been interpreted as an affirmative. Then Madric turned his attention back to the Humans. "I think we should all take a spot of tea before bed," he told the groom. "Have Hamoni put on the kettle for us. Teine and I have many things to discuss after I get my favorite nephew settled in."

"I'm your *only* nephew," Marne pointed out as Madric carried him into the open pantry. As they passed, Teine noted the shelves stacked high with glass jars of canned vegetables and other tinned goods, crates of wine, and a stairway that led down.

"Then you're well ahead of the competition," Madric chuckled.

"There *is* no competition." Teine heard Marne's retort before they were out of earshot.

The next thing he knew, Kenneth draped a blanket over his shoulders. "Here you go," Kenneth said, clapping Teine on the back, an amused expression on his craggy face. "You look like you've had an exciting day."

"You have no idea," Teine breathed, once they were alone. He was surprised at the depth of the relief he felt with the Aoife out of the room. With other Humans he could more or less speak his mind without any fear of reprisal. Grinning ruefully, he shifted his weight from one foot to the other, trying to maintain some sense of dignity. "Now, where is your chamber?"

"Oh, right this way, young man." Kenneth gestured toward a room where Teine spotted a very welcome sight: a water closet, complete with the overhead water tank and the chain to pull for the flush. Apparently the plumbing at the tower was as good as that at Solmurry proper.

As Teine was taking care of business, he heard the light patter of a second set of feet followed by the unmistakable clank of the kettle being set on the stove. *Hamoni, perhaps?* Teine speculated, unable to stop himself from wondering what sort of person she'd be, and horrified at the possibility that she could hear him.

"So, did he drain it completely this time?" The woman's voice was surprisingly sultry, and Teine found himself listening more intently. "Or could you tell?"

Teine paused midstream, then realized she wasn't talking about him. "Give me a minute," he muttered under his breath, resuming the task at hand.

"No, I couldn't tell," Kenneth confirmed. "But they were using the bag. Either it worked well enough to keep them from being harassed by free elementals or the worst of the storm hasn't started yet. The carriage was in one piece this time."

There was the rush of running water, and then the clatter of ceramic plates stacking. "Well, at least that's something. It's a shame the child can't just live in the bag."

"Hmm," agreed Kenneth. "That would be... less complicated. And speaking of complicated, Marne brought his new birthday present along."

Teine reached up and pulled the chain to flush, shaking his head ruefully. He hadn't wanted his entrance to be an exercise in comic relief, but apparently it wasn't his scene to write. To take the sting of embarrassment away, he quickly dampened his hands in the sink, lathering them with fragrant soap and rinsed.

"Oh!" chirped the woman, obviously surprised. To Teine's ears, she sounded young and probably pretty. "Did he get the one he wanted?"

Teine quickly blotted his hands on a hanging towel, and stepped back out into the kitchen just in time to see Kenneth's shrug. "I don't know, are you the one Marne wanted?" The groom had settled himself onto a practical wooden bench and was leaning back on the wall with a genial smile. "We didn't get to that part of the introduction."

"I'm Teine of Solmurry." Teine replied, leaning forward to shake Kenneth's strong, calloused hand. "And I assume I'm the one he wanted. It seems unlikely to me that Marne's will is often thwarted."

"A clever answer, Teine of Solmurry," the woman replied, her musical voice coming from the kitchen area. When he turned to introduce himself, Teine jumped visibly, startled by her appearance.

She was an Aoife, yet she was dressed simply and humbly in the stained, practical clothes of a house servant. In all his years at Solmurry, Teine had never seen an Aoife in a servile role. It was jarring to see one as lovely and ageless as any noble drying and stacking freshly-washed dishes. Uncertain of the etiquette for the situation, Teine stammered, then lapsed into silence. He could feel his face redden.

Thankfully she'd continued speaking, and didn't seem to notice. "Betraying nothing, yet still complimentary to your young master. You have good instincts, I think."

Bemused, he realized she'd taken his hand in both of her slender ones, and was pumping it up and down, soundly, as if she were another man. "You'll do well. And, I have to say," she continued eyeing him up and down playfully. "You're a lot easier on the eyes and *nose*, than his usual companion!"

Kenneth roared, "Ah, poor Stinky. But his heart is pure."

"And his breath is pure hell," she giggled, "I'm Hamoni, but please, just call me Moni if you feel like it. Now, pull up a bench." Bustling around the kitchen, she set a tray with cheese and crackers, a bowl of fresh fruit, and a pitcher of water on the table. "You're among friends and the rest of your day is certain to be comfortable and relaxing."

"Promise?" Madric asked, climbing up the stairs from the basement. As Teine was just about to sit, he straightened himself and waited for Madric. The Aoife magician looked exhausted, but seemed to be of good cheer.

"I think the poor lad nearly fell asleep in the water closet." Without any formalities, Madric casually tossed a heavy golden bracelet out onto the table, then slumped down on the bench next to Kenneth and began prying off his boots. Hamoni reached hungrily for the bracelet, but a stern look from Madric sent her scrambling toward the cupboard to get earthenware mugs and the teapot. Teine hesitated to sit, standing awkwardly in place. *What had just happened?*

"What, are you waiting for a personal invitation?" Madric asked.

"Should I be?" Teine asked, swallowing hard and feeling like a complete dolt.

The others laughed heartily, and Teine felt somewhat relieved when Madric gestured for him to take a seat. "You'll discover a few things once you've been here a while," the magician offered. He dropped his first boot to the floor with a sloppy wet splash. "I'm much less concerned with formality and appearances than my brother. I'm not quick to take offense and I don't make idle threats. If you've offended me, I'll say so. And I'll give you plain suggestions on how to amend your behavior so it doesn't happen again. Thanks, love," he told Hamoni, when she offered to help him off with the other boot. As she tugged, Madric continued, "I keep company with whom I please and how I please. And what I please right now is to have a nice bit of tea and talk about your future."

The boot released, and Hamoni nearly sat down from the force. Teine caught her arm to keep her from falling over. "My future?" he asked, as it suddenly dawned on him what Madric had just said.

Hamoni picked up both Madric's dripping boots, and, holding them at arm's length, walked them out to the mudroom.

"Yes." Madric replied. "Hand me one of those blankets, eh, Kenneth? Thanks." The magician pulled off his outer cloak and green festival garb, draping them both over the edge of the bench. Then he wrapped himself in one of the warm blankets and uttered a contented sigh. "Much better. The first thing we'll need to do is test you for any latent magic ability. Then we can see where to go from there."

Teine blinked, "Magic? Could I really be magic?"

Hamoni walked past, heading for the whistling kettle. "It's a possibility. It can happen to anyone."

Madric nodded, "It's becoming more and more common, to be sure. I think we're on the brink of the next Age, and some of the events in the last few years have proven it. Awakening artifacts and animals, strengthening storms," he listed, gesturing to the rattling glass in the window frame. "Not to mention the incredible growth and diversity in the available magics."

"Not just conjuration and summoning anymore," Hamoni added. "Illusion, charm, and enchantment spells are becoming much more common." She dropped the tea ball into the pot and began to pour steaming water over it. "Not to mention more reliable and harder to detect. I heard that there's a cadre of rogue wizards beginning to study the possibility of creating spells that can teleport people and items from one place to..."

Teine stared frankly at the Aoife girl's dissertation, until Madric cleared his throat, "Hamoni, mind your place."

"Yes, m'Lord," she replied, bowing her head and looking genuinely contrite. "Tea's up. Are any of you hungry? Or hungrier than cheese, crackers, and fruit can satisfy?"

"I can always eat," Kenneth volunteered. "But I'm not expiring from hunger. What about you?" he asked Madric.

"I had my fill and then some at my brother's table," he grinned roguishly, then reached for the bowl of fruit to push it toward Teine. "It's true he's a sycophantic little weasel, but he sure sets a good spread."

Teine nearly choked on his bite of pear. Once he was done sputtering, he suppressed a grin. "Thank you, by the way. Thank you, m'Lord," he said, looking directly at Madric. "I really appreciate what you did for me in there."

Madric raised his eyebrows. "What I did?" he asked, tilting his head as though he were trying to remember. "Oh, yes. Well, teasing him is rather second nature."

"I've..." Teine began, trying to decide if this conversation was in any way appropriate. "... I've never been on the receiving end of a dressing down like that."

"Was Lord Solmurrian mean to you?" Hamoni asked, pausing with the teapot in her hand.

"And *then* some," Madric confirmed. To Teine, he said, "I'm about to give you a piece of advice that I hope will serve you well in your life. I learned it myself the hard way, and I would spare you that pain if I could."

"I'm all ears," Teine replied sincerely. Whenever one of the elders, like his Amagorra, had offered advice, he'd always been quick to listen. Now that he was about to get advice from someone with several lifetimes of experience, he couldn't ignore it if he tried.

Outside, the wind screamed and howled, lashing the leaded glass window over the sink. For all its bluster though, Teine felt very safe, safer even than he'd ever felt in his own barracks. There was something comforting about ancient stonework that was perhaps thousands of years old. It felt like he was sheltered by the very bones of Ersa, herself.

"The world is filled with small people," Madric said, reaching eagerly for the tea that Hamoni handed over the table. "People who, in their smallness, will try to play you small."

"He's not speaking of their stature," Hamoni added.

"He gets it," Madric snapped. "He's not a halfwit. You don't need to spell it out for him." To Teine, he continued, "My brother is one of those people. Through a cosmic joke and a bit of betrayal, he managed to secure a station for himself far greater than his talents or strength of character warranted. And the saddest part of this whole tale is that he knows it's true."

Teine wanted to nod, but didn't dare. It wasn't his place to agree or disagree with the Lord Solmurrian's deposed brother. And besides, it could be that the test for magic wasn't the only test Madric had planned for him. This could well be a test of his loyalties. Teine was absolutely certain Madric was clever enough to play that game well, if he chose. His only prudent course of action was simply to give away nothing and just listen.

But it seemed that either Hamoni's interjection had knocked the magician off course, or Madric had already spoken his peace and was finished. Teine sat there, watching Madric watch him, wondering if he should speak next. Finally, the silence got to him. "Thank you for your insights, Lord Solmurrian. I'll be sure to consider them in my next encounter with your brother."

The magician regarded him for a second longer, making Teine feel quite exposed. "You can call me Madric, when it's appropriate. We don't stand on ceremony here, unless we have state guests." Teine nodded again, then decided it was probably all right to have another bite of the pear. Out of season, the fruit was still firm, sweet, and tasted just like it had come off the tree.

"Good, isn't it?" Madric asked. "Well, magic's useful for more than just war and digging wells."

"I'd drink to that!" Hamoni added, reaching over Teine to grab an orange, which she cheerfully tossed in the air and caught before beginning to peel it. "If I were the drinking sort."

The four of them ate in silence for a moment, and it took Teine another moment to realize that he was comfortable. He didn't know what he'd expected, but this sure wasn't it. Perhaps Leis had been right and this was nothing short of a huge opportunity in disguise.

"Well, we'll have a busy day ahead of us tomorrow." Madric poured himself another cup of tea from the pot Hamoni had set down. "First, right after breakfast, we'll do your evaluation. Although the storm is supposed to continue through tomorrow night, the minor magics we'll be using in the tests shouldn't be enough to stir it up. Then, while I attend to other business, I have a couple of projects for you to work on."

"Yes, sir," Teine replied, habitually.

"Don't 'Yes, sir' me," Madric scolded, pointing a finger at him. "The end result is for your benefit, and I expect you'll like it very much. There's a very nice suite up on the third floor that's currently just storing furniture. You'll be cleaning it out to be permanent quarters for when you and the boy visit. Each of you will have your own room, and a spare in the middle for a playroom."

Teine blinked. A suite. His own room. His *second* own room, as he seemed to remember one of the maids mentioning that he had his own room in the Demesne proper as well. No more life in the barracks, at the mercy of everyone else and their sleeping quirks. No more endless nights where Seymour had insomnia and woke up everyone to debate the validity of one fabal team strategy over another, or the nature of good and evil, or whatever else was rattling around in his brain. No more explaining to any and every one passing by what he was writing, drawing, or working on until he decided *he* was ready. "It sounds like heaven," he told Madric, trying to hold his exuberance down to a dignified level.

"It won't when you see how much furniture there is to clear out," Madric retorted. "It's practically floor to rafters in there, and it will *all* need to come down to the main floor if it's to be carted away, or the basement if it's to continue in storage. Hard work. And lots of it."

Teine reached for another piece of fruit, this time selecting a firm, brightly colored orange. "I don't mind the work. It sounds like a pleasant way to spend a rainy day." Madric nodded his approval and Teine was relieved to see the magician had the same reaction that nearly all his teachers or bosses had exhibited when he professed his willingness to work. It seemed that Madric was, as he had insisted, straightforward and probably not difficult to please. Perhaps it was time to see how his *real* personality, not just his polite facade, would be received.

Reaching for the heavy golden bracelet still laying on the table, Teine placed the orange on it, as if it were a crystal ball on a stand.

"Behold, the mighty orange, resplendent upon its throne!" he intoned, wiggling his eyebrows playfully at his audience. "Oh, king of all other fruits, mere apples and berries bow to thee."

"Not the grapes, though," Madric added mildly. "Grapes bow to no one." Kenneth rolled his eyes and chuckled. Teine chalked it up as a win.

Hamoni ruffled Teine's hair. "You're silly," she giggled, "You should fit in just fine here." To Madric, she said, "I'm certain you don't want him to bed down in the basement with Marne tonight. There's only the one bed."

"He can stay in one of the guest quarters tonight," Madric replied, waving her off before standing. The magician was still as barefoot as a newborn Human, and Teine had to forcibly restrain himself from looking. He didn't know if he'd ever seen an Aoife's bare feet before. Completely unaware of Teine's curiosity, Madric continued speaking, "The servant rooms are all full except Kenneth's, and I hear he snores."

"Do not," the groom huffed, sipping his tea. "Well, not unless I have a cold."

"Nonetheless, one of the guest rooms will be appropriate, just this once," Madric confirmed, patting Teine on the shoulder. With Teine still seated on the bench, Madric was still only taller by a few inches. "Consider it my welcome. I think Marne chose well, and we're pleased to have you. Good night." Without another word, Madric padded out of the kitchen.

Teine was still practically glowing from the unexpected praise. "He must be exhausted," Hamoni sighed, watching Madric leave. "I bet he goes straight to bed, and it's barely after nine."

"Forget the magic. Just being at Solmurry takes enough out of him," Kenneth added.

Hamoni began cleaning up, clearing Madric's cup and topping off the tea for the others. "Teine, are you planning to eat the King, or is he going back in the bowl with his subjects?"

"Oh, I think his days on the throne are over," Teine replied, pleased she was taking up his joke. He snatched the orange and began peeling it, noticing with satisfaction the fine mist of juice that sprayed as he dug into the skin. "It was a short, but magnificent reign."

Bending over to wipe the table clean, Hamoni grabbed the bracelet and tucked it away in one of the front pockets of the apron.

"Are you tired as well?" she asked Teine. "Or would you like to have a quick tour before retiring to your chamber for the evening?"

"That's my cue, eh?" Kenneth groaned, pulling himself to his feet. "I'll go see if the louts brought in your bag." He waddled, bowlegged and stiff, out the door to the carriage house, then immediately turned around and came back in. "It's right here. Apparently the boys are at the top of their game tonight." The groom returned to the kitchen, handing Teine his overstuffed satchel.

"Thank you, Kenneth," Teine replied, slinging the bag over his shoulder. Then he turned to Hamoni. "I'm tired, but not overly so," he told her. "And I'm very curious to see more of the building. It's got some historical significance, you know."

Hamoni laughed, mischief in her eyes. "Oh, yes. I know of its historical significance. I grew up nearby in Emmett, and I've probably had as much, if not more, schooling than you." She placed both her hands on her narrow Aoife hips and looked down at Teine, who was still seated. Even seated, he was nearly as tall as she was. "It's amusing to be lectured on history by a, what... sixteen? A sixteen-year-old Human?"

Teine went beet red. "Fifteen, actually." He hoped fervently that he hadn't lost too much ground with Hamoni. She was fun, and he would have hated to make her angry when he was only trying to show himself as smart and worldly. "I'm sorry, I didn't mean..."

"It's all right." Like Madric, Hamoni dismissed Teine's apology with an airy wave. "I know how you meant it. I'm not angry. When you're done with His Majesty, there, I'll show you something *really* interesting. Something you won't find in any history book."

Unable to keep from rushing, Teine stuffed his face with one section of orange after another, dying to see what Hamoni had to show him.

Chapter 17: All the Brothers Blue

Hamoni escorted Teine to the second-floor guest rooms first. He had to watch his footing all the way, trying to decide if he should take two steps at a time or three. Since the tower was originally designed for the Krunal, the stairs had been constructed to match their shorter legs. Built steeply to accommodate the fifteen-foot ceilings on each level, staircases spiraled around the inside of the perimeter wall of the tower.

Teine thought the design quite elegant and easy on the eyes. The high ceilings gave each floor an airy yet comfortable feel, relieving the tomb-like sensation of being enclosed in solid stone. Despite the visual beauty, by the time Teine had climbed the first flight of stairs to get to the second floor, he realized that getting around Madric's Tower required physical effort, even for someone who was already fit.

On the second floor a long hallway with doors on either side split the floor into two halves. Shaking Teine out of his thoughts, Hamoni stated, "I bet you like blue." She chose the first room to the left. Throwing open a set of double doors, the Aoife girl popped the button on the wall that turned on the electric lights, then held her arms wide to display the lavishly decorated suite spread out before them. Teine could only stare.

The bed itself was a curtained four-poster, the kind most of the thin-skinned Aoife preferred, as they could draw the curtains against any drafty night. Velvet outer curtains in deep blue and the rich, dark turquoise color of the twilight sky draped around the bed, tied back with golden rope ties. The innermost layer of curtains was made of a fine lace. He'd never seen such an attractive way to keep the flies away. Luxurious tapestries adorned the walls, depicting scenes of boats at war or boats at play, and a solitary oil painting hung on the wall opposite the bed. There were also several windows, shuttered now against the storm's fury.

Teine drifted over to the painting, dropping his battered satchel on the bench at the foot of the bed without even stopping. He halted about a foot away, staring in astonishment. The portrait was an informal scene of two young Aoife boys playing in the sand of a beautiful beach. A half-constructed sand castle was in the foreground, and the turquoise of a clear sky over the azure of the ocean filled the background. The older boy was bent over laughing with his hands on his knees, while the younger, barely a toddler, had a very serious face as he scooped sand into a bucket.

"I know this painting," Teine whispered, trying for the life of him to place it before looking at the brass plate screwed into the wooden frame.

"You should," Hamoni said. "It's been in every art history book for the last two hundred years. It's..."

"*The Brothers Blue*," Teine finished. He could hear the rain pounding against the shutters, but the sounds of the storm receded into the realm of "pleasant background noise." It gave his discovery a dreamy, surreal feeling. "It's of the Solmurrians, isn't it?" he asked. Now that he'd met them and gotten a good look at the two lords of Solmurry, he could see that these two children—their poses, their faces—had been captured as surely as if Teine were travelling through time to see Madric and his younger brother as children.

"I never thought I'd see an original DesMarte," Teine whispered as reverently as if he were viewing a holy relic. "Much less this one."

"I thought you'd like it," Hamoni smiled. "Personally, I think Madric does this picture a great injustice, keeping it locked away in a guest room like this. It's one of the most famous paintings of its century. It should be down in the drawing room."

"But it does very well here with the decor," Teine countered, testing his wings as "devil's advocate." He agreed with the Aoife girl, but he was curious to see how she'd react to a contrary point of view. As far as he was concerned, she was at least as much a mystery as the painting. Why was she locked away in this tower, wearing the clothes of a servant? Madric ordered her around as though she were a Human, even though her Aoife blood was enough to give her rank over Teine and his ilk. In spite of that, she seemed companionable rather than authoritarian. It was curious.

Hamoni shrugged as artlessly as any Human scullery maid. "I don't know. I suppose. But anywhere up here where no one sees it... it seems like such a waste to keep it where no one can see it."

Teine grinned, leaning in close to the painting to examine the brushstrokes on the boys' faces. "Believe me, it's no waste. I could be up all night looking at this and still not absorb it all. DesMarte was a god."

"DesMarte was old, crabby, and flatulent." Hamoni giggled, breaking into full-on laughter at the look of horrified astonishment on Teine's face. "To hear Madric tell it, anyway," she amended. "He always says that having talent at anything is no excuse for being an egotistical bore."

Teine blinked, then laughed along with her. Truthfully, he didn't know what else he could do. Hamoni surely was nothing like what he'd expect of an Aoife.

"Come on, then," she said, catching his sleeve. "You can moan over that painting all night if you want, but there are far more interesting things upstairs."

Teine allowed himself to be dragged along. Although he was curious to see everything Hamoni wanted to show him about the tower, a part of him was longing to curl up in that lavish bed, read his letter from Vosh, and write him a reply thick with the day's adventures. Another part of him didn't want to sleep at all, he was so convinced that he'd wake up at home in his bunk at Mastiff Cohort. He wished he could kiss Leis on the cheek and tell her she'd been right. This was his life and he was going to make the most of it.

Hamoni led him back to the stairway where they climbed several more floors. "Madric's personal quarters are on the fifth floor," she whispered as they passed the landing but didn't stop. "He's probably dead asleep, but we don't want to be loud."

"What's above?" Teine asked, trying not to let her hear him panting from exertion. Those steps were awfully steep! He could have run to the Demesne and back twice with the same amount of effort.

"His magical workshop," Hamoni replied. Her voice was as full of reverence as if she had said "the tomb of a long-dead saint" or "the place where God hangs his coat."

Teine was amused. Although she was an Aoife, Hamoni was not all that different from other girls he knew, and was turning out to be not that hard to read. She positively adored Madric in the manner of a schoolgirl with her first passionate crush. Teasing her about it would ever remain out of bounds, as she was an Aoife and it was never prudent to speak to them in matters of love, but her transparency was kind of endearing and made her seem somehow more approachable. As Teine contemplated Hamoni's infatuation, the Aoife girl pulled out a ring of keys as they approached the last door at the top of the stairs.

"Here we are," she said, jingling the keys to select the right one, which she fitted directly into the lock. The door swung open, and she reached in to pop on the light switch. "Our workshop."

"Our workshop?" Teine repeated. The way Hamoni spoke, it was as though she had some claim to the complicated spread of beakers, tubes, cauldrons, and shelves of ancient-looking dusty tomes.

"Oh, I just call it 'ours' like I'd call another room 'our kitchen' or 'our billiards room,'" she hastily amended. "Not like it's *my* workshop or anything."

"You have a billiards room?" Teine asked, hopefully.

"Yes!" she beamed. "Third floor." Then, her expression turned dead serious. "Don't *ever* play Marne for money."

Teine couldn't help but chuckle, even though the mention of his child-master was like taking a cold glass of water in the face. Since he'd been at Madric's Tower, it had been easy to lose himself in the congenial company and forget his real duties. But he supposed he'd be used to the idea before long.

"Don't make such a face," Hamoni scolded, striding confidently into the room. She walked up to what looked like a giant, reinforced glass aquarium without fish and began turning a knob on the side. A pipe ran from the aquarium up through the ceiling. "Did I say something wrong?"

"No, no," Teine waved off the suggestion, coming over to watch. "I've only met Marne once, and I think he's said maybe twenty words total to me. I just don't know him at all, yet. What are you doing, anyway?"

Twisting the knob as far as it would go, Hamoni grunted with the effort. "Just changing over the tanks. Every time it rains we collect rainwater for drinking and washing. But these magical storms are something different. I'm changing which tank the collected water goes into. The magically charged water goes into this tank." She patted the large glass structure next to her. "We use it for spells and the like."

Just then, a swirling form coalesced inside the water tank, shaping itself to look like a hand, which pounded on the glass where Hamoni stood. She jumped and squeaked, and Teine yelped in surprise, tripping over his feet and falling backwards over a stool. "What is *that*?" he shouted over the splashing sound coming from the other corner of the room.

"Oh, you startled me!" Hamoni scolded, waving an angry finger at the form in the glass. It changed to something resembling a humanoid head and torso, but with a relatively featureless face. Then, she turned to Teine, "It's just a water elemental. No need to go all buggy."

"It looks furious."

"It probably is," she agreed. "He's been all full of spite since Madric extracted another one and put it in a bucket to study last week. They've all been cranky since then—so much so that we had to take the one we hoped would run our plumbing system and store him out in the fountain where he can't cause any trouble."

"You put one in a bucket?" Teine set the stool upright and went toward the splashing he'd heard earlier. "That one, on the floor over there?"

"Yes. Look, but don't touch."

That sounded like a pretty sensible plan to Teine. Just thinking of water that could move by itself was a little scary, but touching it seemed like an obviously bad idea. He padded cautiously across the room, eyes fixed on the bucket sitting next to a big desk strewn with papers. As nothing leapt out to drown him, he looked directly down into the bucket for several seconds.

Nothing happened. "I think it wore itself out," he told Hamoni, looking around at the puddles.

"Not surprising," she countered. "It's the smallest one of the bunch. It's probably not as hardy as the others." She'd drifted over and was sitting behind the other desk in the room, idly flipping the pages of a book, while reaching into her apron pocket and setting the golden bracelet out on the desk. While Teine watched, she grabbed a quill and jotted a few quick notes, then rose and came over to join Teine at his bucket vigil.

"It's probably hungry," she sighed, looking down into the vessel of still water. "I'd probably better feed it."

"What does a water elemental eat?" Teine asked, fascinated. "Water?"

"Well, that's what we've been feeding it," she replied, snatching a watering can off one of the benches. A good-sized flowering houseplant with white blooms sat next to watering can on the bench. It reached toward Hamoni with several tendrils as she took the can and looked into it.

"Ah, good, still full enough. We've been refreshing it with water from the last storm when it seems listless. So far, it seems to be working, but we're just at the beginning of elemental studies. No one's been able to capture and hold one without it expiring within a day or two until just this past year."

Teine was impressed, both by the elementals and by the amazing plant's movement. Either Hamoni didn't see, or the sight of a moving plant was commonplace enough to not be worthy of comment. Until then, Teine hadn't understood much of anything about what Madric did. He'd had no idea Madric was not only so accomplished, but also that he was paving new ground for other magicians. "And this branch of study is called conjuring? Summoning? Elem…"

"Elementalism?" Hamoni asked, sprinkling water from the watering can into the bucket. Teine watched the surface of the water closely. It looked like the ripples the added water made were out of proportion to the amount of water being poured.

Hamoni looked pleased. "Conjuring is creating something that didn't exist before. Summoning is fetching and bringing something to you that existed somewhere else." She turned and walked back to where the watering can had rested, then noticed the plant's antics.

"Oh, hungry, are we?" she crooned, reaching into a jar. She pulled out a live white mouse and casually tossed it into the thickest network of the plant's branches. The mouse was instantly entwined in vines. Teine watched as the hapless rodent emitted a loud squeak of pain and alarm before it was engulfed completely. The white blooms on the plant began to blush pink. Hamoni poured some of the magical water on the plant, then regarded it with a skeptic's eye.

"Oh, all right," she muttered, and tossed it another mouse. Within another few moments the plant's flowers had deepened in color to a brilliant red, like fresh blood, and a soft, delicate fragrance perfumed the air.

"They're called 'blood roses,'" she told Teine. "The old texts mentioned them constantly but we assumed they were extinct. That is, until they started Awakening last year," she explained, looking triumphant. "We'll be studying this one, taking cuttings and trying to get it to seed. The old records from the last Age mentioned these can get big enough to dispose of an adult's corpse."

Teine blinked, unable to get that image out of his mind. The next thing he knew, Hamoni was at his side, steering him by the arm. "Come on, then," she said, leading him from the room. She paused only to turn out the light and lock the door. "You look as though you've had quite enough for one day. Let's get you settled in for the night."

Gratefully Teine nodded and allowed himself to be led. "I think the plant tripped my breaker," he chuckled weakly. "It's been a..." he trailed off, because the day had really defied all description.

"It's all right, don't worry," Hamoni told him. Within minutes, she'd deposited him in his room and left him to his own thoughts. Teine glanced around the room as he changed into his nightshirt. He wished the storm were over so he could look out the window and determine which direction he was facing. He was certain the view would be worth the wait. After a minute, though, he was forced to give up guessing and admit that the multiple corkscrew laps around the inside of the tower wall were affecting his sense of direction.

Then Teine discovered that the magnificent suite had its own bathroom. He marveled at the size of the tub, but only got as far as imagining the running water before memories of the angry water elemental stopped him cold.

When he climbed into bed, Teine groaned with pleasure at the thick softness of the mattress and the silken feel of the sheets. His bunk in the barracks of Mastiff Cohort held a feather mattress set onto a steel spring frame. It offered good support and was comfortable enough, but this—this was *heavenly*.

Reaching for his satchel, he emptied everything onto the bed. He stared dumbly at the jumbled pile of clothes, sketchbook, journal, and mail, trying to decide what he'd do first. He knew he should read Vosh's letter right away, but a small, childish part of him wanted to toss the letter aside and write to Vosh first. Teine envisioned scribbling a long, fat, newsy letter that began with the words, *"You'll never guess where I am!"*

He laid his head on a luxurious pillow to consider his letter to Vosh. But consideration was as far as he got before he fell asleep with his cheek resting on the wire spine of his writing journal.

Chapter 18: Dreams and Dust

April 10th, 3131

Teine awoke with a start at a crack of lightning so bright he could see it through both the closed shutters *and* his eyelids. As if that weren't bad enough, the answering peal of thunder was so loud it reverberated in his chest. Somewhere else in the tower, he heard a woman shriek and the clatter of breaking flatware. Needless to say, Teine scrambled to his feet, disoriented and startled, sending his journal, letters, and art supplies flying every which way. Fortunately, his bottle of ink hit the thick rug by the bed instead of falling a couple inches away and shattering on the flagstone floor.

"Did that *hit* us?" he heard someone, probably a Human man, ask.

"I don't know how Madric could sleep through *that*," someone else replied.

Unsure of the time and feeling vaguely guilty for sleeping so long no matter *what* time it was, Teine headed into his bathroom to freshen up. When he looked into the mirror, he could see the impression of his spiral-bound notebook pressed into his cheek from where he'd slept on it.

"Oh, great," he muttered sarcastically. "That really looks classy." Taking a minute, he looked himself over, wondering if he should shave. But, as badly as he wanted a reason, the coppery stubble that grew in patches on his chin and cheeks hadn't come in enough to warrant it. He decided to postpone a bath, as well, since Madric had mentioned he'd be cleaning, sorting, and carrying furniture downstairs all day. He knew he'd have an excuse to use the lavishly-appointed bath later. Simply getting dressed and getting to work would probably be the best way to go.

Teine was just hopping on one leg, pulling on his trousers, when there was a rap on the door. "You awake?" Hamoni asked.

"Yes!" Teine called in reply, "Just getting dressed." He quickly checked himself over in the mirror, relieved to see that the impression on his cheek had faded a little. His hair was more or less in order, given that he was a few days overdue for a trim. His clothes, wadded up from their trip in the bag, were adequate for a day of labor. But he found himself wishing he could wear one of the outfits that had come with his trunk.

"Hurry up!" the Aoife girl prompted, "C'mon! There's something I want to show you!"

"Does it eat people?" Teine countered, trying to stall for time. He rubbed the mark on his face, hoping it would go away faster if he helped the blood circulate. Then, he cupped his hand to smell his own breath.

"No, silly!" she laughed. "Really, *you're* not the one on the menu. It's breakfast."

Breakfast! Now she's playing my tune, Teine thought. He swung open the door to look down at the girl, with his best and most charming smile.

"What's wrong with your face?" she asked, tilting her head quizzically to eye him. With a sigh, Teine turned his back to Hamoni and began tidying up.

"Don't bother," she said. "Really, we just heard the forecast, and this storm's going to be here until at least tomorrow morning. You'll be overnighting it in here again, as sure as you're born."

Teine liked the sound of that almost as much as he liked the sound of breakfast. Now that he was in the hall, he could smell the eggs, the bacon, and... hot chocolate?

"These people live like kings," he whispered to Hamoni, falling into step with the girl as they headed down the stairs. "I've never dreamed there were beds so comfortable, or bathrooms so luxurious, or hot chocolate at every meal."

"Ah, Madric keeps it around for the boy," she nodded. "At least that's what he says. But, I think he drinks more of it than Marne does. So, how did you sleep?"

"On my notebook." Teine pointed to the impression on his face, which he hoped was fading. "I didn't even stay awake long enough to read my mail. What time is it, anyway?"

"Oh, it's eight already," she chirped, "Though it's hard to tell when you look outside. It looks like the sun's barely up. See?" She paused, pointing up at one of the small windows they were passing. Teine made a face. It did look *very* early. He'd have guessed it for closer to five-thirty.

The table was groaning under all the dishes and plates, and an elderly Human woman with her hair done up in curlers and a scarf padded around the kitchen in her slippers. She dished up an attractive plate of food, arranging small quantities of everything on the table, then adding the loaded plate to a tray with a decanter of tea. Without a word, she headed toward the basement stairs.

"Is Marne up?" Teine asked. It felt odd to know that the one person he was responsible to was the person he'd seen the least since this whole adventure started. "Should I be...? I don't know... *reporting* to him, or something?"

Hamoni waved his concerns away. "He's probably still asleep. He was in the infirmary just yesterday, and he always sleeps a lot after he's been ill."

The rest of the household was equally informal. Kenneth and his "louts," a pair of young men a couple years older than Teine, were shoveling in their breakfast as if cornbread pancakes, eggs, and bacon were going out of style. They grinned with their elbows propped casually on the table, chewing with their mouths open. When Teine entered, they made grunts that could have been interpreted as some sort of greeting.

Sitting down on the bench next to the larger of the two boys, Hamoni shoved and elbowed him playfully until she had enough room. "Best be careful when reaching for anything," Hamoni warned Teine in an exaggerated whisper. "It's like feeding time at the Zoo this morning." The boys and Kenneth laughed, and so did Teine. Reaching for the tongs, Hamoni tossed a couple pieces of bacon onto her plate, then looked around for the cornbread. Teine followed suit.

"So, what's on the table for today, Pop?" asked one of the boys, around a mouthful of crumbs. "As much as I'd like to finish pounding fence posts in while the ground's soft, there's no way I want to try it today. Don't fancy being a lightning rod."

Kenneth sighed contentedly, smacking his lips and pushing back a bit from the table. Small jewels of amber-colored honey clung to his ginger whiskers.

"Forget the fence posts. We've got a busy day ahead of us cleaning harness." Both boys groaned, but Kenneth just grinned and rested his hands on his belly. "What about you, Teine? You planning to tackle that room of furniture?"

Teine nodded crisply while cutting one of the pancakes with a knife. "Yes, sir. Until either of the masters assign me to something else." He didn't mean to feel smug, but he could definitely tell the difference between himself, and Kenneth and his boys. The green diamond tattooed on each of their left hands and their lack of table manners were just the tip of the iceberg. Since neither of the boys had offered their names, and no formal introductions were made, Teine assumed that these people simply didn't put the emphasis on etiquette that he was accustomed to. *Madric runs a very lax ship, compared to Solmurry proper,* he thought. *But if that's the way he likes it, who am I to expect otherwise?*

Groaning with the effort, the older Human woman was slowly making her way back up the stairs from the basement. "Poor little thing," she muttered. "Still sleeping like a stone. I expect he'll be out for a few more hours."

"Maybe I can be done with the furniture by then," Teine speculated, thinking what a fine, industrious worker he'd be if he accomplished the task before Madric even woke. He had a strong desire to prove himself capable and useful. Perhaps the older brother's positive opinion of him would help him win over Lord Solmurrian.

It was just then he realized that they were all laughing at him. "Oh, don't tell me! He hasn't actually seen the room yet, has he?" asked the old woman.

Teine felt his ears start to burn as Hamoni replied, "No, no. Not yet." Her laugh, dainty and musical, danced above the chuckles and guffaws of the Humans, but managed to sting Teine just as much. "He hasn't a clue."

Grinning, the old woman in curlers waddled over and dropped two more pancakes on Teine's plate. Both the other boys made noises of protest, but she silenced them. "Last two," she said, patting Teine on the shoulder. "Eat up, son. You're going to need them."

Now bent on fortifying himself for his apparently Herculean task, Teine set to putting as much breakfast away as quickly and tidily as possible, while trying to ignore the chuckles of the working lads. He did fine until they got up to leave and one of them muttered to Kenneth, "He's so dandified, he hardly passes as Human. What, does he think he's an Aoife?"

Kenneth, to his credit, scolded the boy, but not before Teine heard the exchange. He tried to remind himself that mockery usually concealed some kind of jealousy, but it didn't stop him from being a bit angry.

"What a couple of blockheads," Hamoni grumbled, once Kenneth and the boys left the room. "I swear, I've seen inanimate objects with more personality." She glanced at Teine out of the corner of her eye.

Teine shrugged, trying to feign a cool indifference he didn't feel. "To be honest, I was kind of surprised." He dangled this statement, like bait on a hook, to see if she'd strike.

"Surprised? By what?"

Teine took a sip of his tea, blotted his lips carefully with a napkin, and turned to face her. "I've never had much to do with Humans other than the ones raised at Solmurry," he said. "I expected... more, somehow. Tell me, are they even literate?"

She snorted a little huff of derision, "Barely. Much less so than they *could* be, given their opportunities."

Trying to sound mature and worldly, Teine sighed, "I feel for them, I suppose. Not everyone is fortunate enough to be born at Solmurry."

"You do make it sound nice. But tell me, how much schooling do they make you take?"

Teine had a good laugh at that. His friend Vosh was the only other person he'd ever known who treated schooling like an unhappy obligation.

"You make it sound so... dull," he chuckled. "No, all of us get at least ten years. Then when we're fifteen or so, we become adults and get assigned to our apprenticeships, get sold, or go on for more specialized training. Sometimes all three."

"What did you want to study?" Hamoni asked. Like the boys before her, she leaned both elbows on the table and looked up at Teine, but with a dreamy expression in her eyes. "I mean, did you get any choice in what you studied before now? Did you always know you'd end up belonging to Marne?"

Under normal circumstances, any beautiful female looking at him in that way, all sweet and attentive, would have sent Teine into a flurry of dialog in an attempt to be charming. But she'd mentioned Marne, and not just in context with Teine's newfound position, either. She was *really* asking what he'd given up. Broaching that subject sent a wave of sudden anger and sadness coursing through him, dashing up against his thoughts like the storm that still battered the outside of the tower. It took him a second to realize that she was still waiting for a reply.

"No, it was a complete surprise," he admitted. "Although, if I'd been paying better attention, I would have realized that Marne seems to like my line. Four generations of amagis have worked as his nanny. My own Amagi just retired, and my full sibling Leis just took up the apron."

Hamoni whistled her appreciation. "Yes, I do think that you might have suspected."

"But I guess I didn't want to think about it," he replied. "I had plans of my own. My best friend Vosh went to play fabal. He's eligible for the draft this year and he's only a year older than me. He could be playing pro by next spring. He said he'd had a few scouts asking around and he'd always mentioned me." He could tell he'd hit home by the surprised expression on her face. "Of course I'd love to play pro 'ball! Who wouldn't? But I had a backup plan, too."

"What?" Hamoni asked.

"I've already taken the first two ships' design drafting courses by correspondence," he said. "And I got good marks. I always thought I'd be there. Not just building the ships, but designing them too."

As the words tumbled out, Teine suddenly felt what seemed like a great weight lifting off his shoulders, a cloud of tension just breaking up and floating away. Then, realization suddenly struck him. He'd *really* wanted to build ships. It wasn't his "fall-back" plan, like he'd told all his Cohort. It wasn't a "just-in-case." It had been his big dream, his one lifelong goal.

Now it was gone. And for what?

A Display Human traded on their looks alone. His brain could be packed in mothballs like an outgrown sweater, and it wouldn't affect much of anything. To parade down a walkway, his body on show like goods for sale—it was almost like prostitution!

"Are you all right?" Hamoni asked when he didn't speak for a moment. "You look like you've been slapped across the face with a rotting fish."

Teine blinked, "Rotting fish?"

"Yes," Hamoni nodded solemnly. "And I think I see the impressions from some of the scales..." Grinning wickedly, she pointed towards his cheek where he'd laid on his notebook earlier.

Teine jumped up, pulling the pitcher closer to see his reflection. "Faugh! Is that still there?"

"No!" Hamoni roared, her laughter infecting the old woman in the corner scrubbing pans. "But I made you look!"

Teine, still not ready to give in to joviality, smiled his amusement. Then he dabbed at his face one more time before folding the napkin across his empty plate. "You know, I should probably get to work. But thank you for the pleasant conversation."

"My pleasure as well," Hamoni replied. "Come on, then. I'll show you the furniture room and get you some supplies."

A few minutes later the two of them were standing in front of a set of double doors. Teine was loaded to the eyes with cleaning supplies, with an extendable feather duster tucked under one arm that kept poking Hamoni in the back of the head.

"Ow!" she said, pushing it away for the fifth time. "You know, before I open this, I think I'd better mention that Madric does *not* expect you to finish this project today. He said he thought it would take one person about a week to do right."

"Just open the door," Teine urged. "Put me in, Coach. I'm ready to play!"

She giggled, ducked the feather duster once more and swung both doors wide. "Ta da!"

Teine's eyes widened. The rooms, from what he could see of them, were packed nearly floor to high, lofty ceiling with dusty, cobwebby furniture of all kinds. Even the chandelier had been raised. Someone had had the good sense to cover the upholstered goods with canvas sheeting, but still, the sight was enough to make Teine wince. Reluctantly, he was forced to agree with Madric's assessment. "Where in the world did all of this come from?" he asked.

"Well, fashions come and go," Hamoni supplied, as if that explained everything. "I'd expect that this is the last hundred-plus years of everything that's been discarded from Solmurry's Demesne and the other..."

"Hey!" Teine interrupted, dropping the supplies in his enthusiasm. "I *know* those desks!" He shouldered his way into the room, pushing past a heavy oaken wardrobe and entangling himself in a standing coat rack. Finally he settled on a pile of carelessly stacked, child-size desks. "These were in our nursery school, before they remodeled it."

"Happy hunting," Hamoni said, pulling the doors closed behind her.

"Wait, wait!" Teine called, retracing his steps as best as he could. "Anything in particular I'm supposed to do?"

"Clean them up. Carry them down. If you see furnishings you think you might like for these three rooms for you and Marne, set them aside. Now, I have to go, or I'll start..." Hamoni sneezed so hard she nearly knocked herself off her own feet.

Teine saluted, "Yes, ma'am. I'll get it done."

"Oh, Teine... because I like you..." she added, sniffling onto her sleeve."I'll haul up a console radio to keep you company and drown out the storm."

Grinning, Teine nodded, then turned back to the enormous task ahead of him. He didn't mind the weather at all now, even though it was loud. Instead of feeling burdened by the assignment, it was kind of comforting. It was a job, with a beginning, middle, and end. No sitting around waiting for orders, no guessing what he was supposed to do. In the absence of a master or chore boss to guide him, he'd get to do the task his own way. He found himself kind of liking the idea.

"All right, you," he said, pointing his finger at the coat rack. "You're about to be put in your place. And here's a hint: it's not here." He grabbed the waxy, lime-scented block of furniture polish and the first clean rag off the pile, and descended upon his hapless victim with an evil laugh.

Chapter 19: Tested

True to her word, Hamoni had the two lads carry up a console radio. Teine immediately cleared a space for it near an outlet and plugged it in. There was only the one station, of course, but it played its share of music interspersed with news, sports reports, and updates on the storm. Though things were bad all along the seaboard, Teine felt pretty safe in the tower. Some towns inland were reporting damage, including a railroad bridge destabilized by flooding that put a halt to all train travel along that route.

Aside from the predictable weather-related damage from a storm of this magnitude, the reports of magical activity had been pouring in as well. The news was increasingly peppered with sensational reports of supernatural and magical phenomena, including a formerly docile carriage horse at a private girls' school suddenly speaking telepathically with as much skill as an average Holidocrith.

"But there's no need for concern, folks," Teine thought the announcer's tone sounded forced. "You won't have to worry about a dangerous animal pulling your daughter to school. The poor beast was immediately put down as a danger to the public good."

Teine couldn't help but cringe and wonder why carnivorous, intelligent Holidocrith were deemed perfectly safe, while a grass-eating, intelligent horse was suddenly a matter of public safety. It didn't make much sense to him, but he shrugged it off to listen to the advertisements.

Teine enjoyed the radio for the music, which in his opinion was well worth the wait through all the commercials and alarming news updates. It made his solitary task pass quickly. When the regular broadcast resumed, he hummed along with the Empyrea City Orchestra as the station played a recording of the previous night's Eoaster Ball at the Palace. Lively and made for dancing, the music was a pleasant distraction. He dusted and examined the furniture, setting aside a few choice pieces he thought might be useful in the suite he and Marne would share. The whole operation made him feel important. As Leis had said, he was on the tracks to a grand adventure. Perhaps this time next year, he and Marne would be *attending* the festivities at the Palace, rather than listening to the broadcast.

Teine's daydreaming and the work made the time pass quickly. By the time Madric appeared shortly before lunch, he'd cleaned and carried down the entire assembly of old school desks, plus over a dozen other pieces.

"Look at that!" Madric exclaimed as he came around the bend at the base of the tower stairs. He considered the clean furniture piling up in the main floor great room with an appraising eye. "You've gotten a lot accomplished. I'll send someone when lunch is ready."

As Teine continued his way back up, he couldn't help but be pleased by the praise. Still basking in the warm glow of the magician's approval, he went back into the storage room, trying to decide what to do next.

As he surveyed the mountain of furniture, something caught his eye. Even though the dust on the furniture ranged in depth from light to a years-old deep layer, it was still obvious when anything had been disturbed. And something *had* been disturbed. There was a fresh path where someone had pushed their way between a couple of bureaus and past an end table. These were clearly tracks *he* had not made.

"Huh?" Teine muttered under his breath. Curious, he followed the clean trail, wondering what the mysterious visitor had been looking for.

The trail ended at what looked like an ancient but beautifully made nightstand. Covered in handprints, the piece of furniture had obviously been handled recently. It looked as though someone had rested a hand on the top, and also touched the face of the drawer and the drawer pull. Eying the handprint as if it would betray some hint of its owner, Teine made a print of his own hand next to it for comparison. While the handprint was nearly as long as his, it was much more slender. There was no mistaking it—the mystery prints belonged to an Aoife.

Teine idly pulled the drawer open. His eyes widened in surprise as a few senta coins fell out, jingling as they hit the floor. But what was odd was that the coins fell *not* from the drawer itself, but from where they must have been shoved underneath the drawer, to fall when the drawer was disturbed.

"That's strange," Teine thought out loud. Crouching to examine the setup, he tried to see if the coins had been hidden where he'd guessed. They fit perfectly where he thought they should go, and fell out easily at not only the pull of the drawer, but even if the nightstand were disturbed at all. Standing up, he cupped the coins in his hands, contemplating them while he considered their odd placement. A glance over his shoulder confirmed that whoever had hidden the coins had made a straight-line incursion into dusty furniture territory to place this bait, and had left by the same trail. Nothing else had been disturbed, except for the path Teine had been clearing all morning.

Cupped in Teine's hands, the silver pieces looked like a healthy pile. Keeping them would have more than doubled his personal savings. And he knew that to an Aoife, they represented mere pocket change, a sum that would normally never be missed.

But this seemed like such an obvious test. Feeling oddly disappointed, Teine pocketed the money. He'd give it to Madric, of course. He'd have given it to Madric even if it hadn't been such an obvious test. And he'd do it at lunch, during the normal course of things, as such business should be handled. To run down and disturb the Aoife magician over a trifling sum would have painted Teine as petty and insecure. Teine was very secure. He was secure enough to wish that he'd found money that *hadn't* been planted, so he could show Madric he'd do the right thing even when it wasn't expected of him.

Despise his disappointment in the clumsiness of the test, Teine wasn't disappointed that Madric had *tried* to test him. It made sense to want to know the character of a new servant in one's home. The thing that rankled was the obviousness of the ploy. Either Madric thought him to be a dullard who wouldn't catch on to the bait, or Madric himself wasn't as clever as Teine had thought. If he had his choice, Teine would rather it be the former. He liked Madric and wanted to respect him.

With a sigh, Teine went back to the edge of the furniture's ranks and began cleaning the enormous oaken wardrobe he'd been avoiding right in the center of the room. He didn't fancy trying to muscle it downstairs, but the more he examined the piece, the more he thought he might not have to. With its burled wood accents and heavy gold tone pulls, it had rather grown on him. He was just shoving it into place with a bed frame and a bureau he'd set aside when the bell rang downstairs. He assumed it meant lunch, but he only had to guess for a second before he could hear Hamoni's light steps pattering up the stairs.

Lunch turned out to be a quiet affair, with both Madric and Hamoni engaged with projects in other parts of the tower. Teine was left to himself to enjoy his creamed potato soup and stuffed pocket sandwiches with apple juice. He even had time to retrieve his letter from Vosh and the notebook he shared with Leis, and get caught up on his reading.

Vosh's letter, like most of his correspondence, had been written a paragraph at a time over the course of several days. True to form, his handwriting was dreadful. Teine smiled, remembering how Vosh could pass him notes in class with utter brazenness because no one could read his writing except Teine. Vosh had been at spring training, and from the way he told the tale it was a wonder he'd had the strength to lift a pen at night after they were done with him. He'd been in training for a year, and after a summer of scrimmage play, he would be offered up on lease as a draft candidate for some of the lower-level professional teams when the season restarted in fall.

Vosh spent a page and a half moaning about his indecision over which position he preferred, and then shared a lively retelling of the dressing down he'd gotten from Driller Incladius for his waffling. According to Vosh, Incladius (or "Inky," as Vosh called him) made Solmurry's own Driller Goran look like "a toothless old huggy-hound."

Teine couldn't help but chuckle out loud at that one, for the instant he'd read Vosh's words he'd immediately pictured Marne's hound, Stinky. It was an apt comparison on two fronts. Both the dog and the coach had a perpetually sad expression, especially around the eyes. Both also sported some particularly vile breath. Teine didn't care what bravado Vosh might try to put on during a letter, Driller Goran was very intimidating, especially when surrounded by his gang of ill-tempered physical fitness enthusiasts.

Now, if he could get Vosh to share his sentiments with Driller Goran when he came home next, *that* would be a sight to see.

Leis's addition to their ongoing joint storytelling effort had been good, but unexpected. Miriam had been planning to steal one of the foreign raider's horses and ride it home to get help in saving her friend Davy, but Leis had decided that Miriam didn't have enough horse skill to pull that off. Knowing Miriam was not its master, and sensing her inexperience, the horse bucked her off and ran away.

Miriam, now injured and discouraged by her spill, needed a new plan, and it was up to Teine to give her a good one. Many interesting options raced through Teine's head, and it was a thrilling feeling to be on the receiving end of such a huge burst of creativity. Miriam, like Teine himself, had a world of possibilities available to her that Teine would not have even considered a mere two days ago.

He longed to pour out the details of his last day and a half to Vosh, or narrow down some of the choices for Miriam, but he thought he might be better off if he waited. He could spend the rest of the day coming up with *just* the right way to say what he wanted to say in his next correspondence. Leis once compared a good story to a good stew—it gets better if you leave it sit. It was a sentiment that was time-tested for the two amateur writers and one Teine agreed with heartily.

Besides, it would give him something interesting to mull over when the news broadcasts interrupted his music.

Just as he was folding up Vosh's letter and using it as a bookmark in the story journal, Hamoni came dancing into the kitchen, humming to music that Teine recognized from the radio earlier that day. "La dee dah, dum, ta da!" she warbled, twirling as if she were dancing in the arms of some invisible partner. "Come on, Teine! Dance with me!" she urged.

Teine's mouth went dry, and suddenly he felt like his hands were twice the size they should be. "Um, I..." he stammered, trying to figure out what to do. Were she a Human girl, he could just spin her up into his arms and play along. "I can't... dance," he started to fib.

"Oh, bother!" the Aoife girl laughed. "No one knows how to dance around here but Madric, and he's too serious."

Teine had a hard time applying that description to the Aoife magician, from what little he'd seen, but he didn't want to risk correcting the girl. Instead, he tucked the journal back under his arm and stood.

"Besides, Hamoni-my-dear," he continued playfully, trying to make it clear that he did like her. "It's time for me to get some more of that furniture cleaned. I've had more than enough time for lunch." To emphasize his consideration, he carried his plate and cup to the sink and spent a moment washing them before leaving them on the rack to dry.

"Well, that's what I came down to tell you," Hamoni said, sitting down on the bench to watch. "Madric said he's ready when you are. I'll meet you up there." Then, with a twirl of thick skirts and coil of plaited hair, she was gone.

Presumably, "up there" meant Madric's workshop. Heading up the staircase, Teine paused briefly to toss the journal and letter on the bed of his borrowed room before trekking up the stairs to the top floor. He'd hoped to overtake Hamoni, but conceded it wasn't likely. Like most Aoife, she was swift and light on her feet. He'd have as much luck trying to catch her as he'd have playing tag with a barn-swallow. The effort left him embarrassingly winded and, even though the door was open, he paused outside on the landing to catch his breath. A radio played in the background and Teine assumed they were continuing the broadcast from earlier.

"Damn this rotten, stinking *besom* of a thing!" Hamoni colorfully. From where he stood, Teine couldn't see her, but he sure heard that! "He really did it this time!" she groaned. "This cursed thing will *not* hold a charge today, no matter what I do to it!"

"Might have to wait till after the storm," Madric suggested mildly. He sounded preoccupied.

Teine blinked. Then he awkwardly knocked once on the door frame before walking in. He didn't want to give them the chance to say something he shouldn't hear. "Here I am," he announced, holding his arms wide. "Test me!"

"Right then," Madric said, shutting the book he was reading and setting it on his desk. "Take off your clothes and sit on the stool by the window."

"What?" asked both Teine and Hamoni in unison, identical expressions of shock on their faces. Madric bent over with peals of unabashed laughter, reminding Teine of the little boy he'd once been, preserved forever on canvas and paint in the guest bedroom. Teine crossed his arms and gave the magician a knowing smile. "You really had me going there."

Shrugging, Madric wiped one eye, his grin crooked yet friendly. "Ah, sometimes the cheap entertainments are the best. Forgive me my odd sense of humor."

"Forgive you?" Teine asked, figuring now was as good a time as any. "I'll do more than forgive you. I'll *pay* you." He sauntered over and dropped the bait money into the Aoife's slender hands.

"Hmm. My humor pays well," Madric muttered, eying the silver coins. "What would a good dance routine get me? Perhaps I can end this life of drudgery and go on to a career as a performer?"

"Very funny," huffed Hamoni from her perch. She had her elbows on the desk opposite Madric's, her dainty chin resting on her hands and her features arranged in what could only be described as a pout. Marne's golden bracelet was in front of her, suspended in thin air above a glowing stand.

"I found those sentas in with the furniture," Teine explained, trying not to stare at what Hamoni was doing to Marne's bracelet. He'd decided it was best to keep up the ruse about the money he'd been meant to find. Letting Madric know that he knew it had been placed there would not gain him anything, and it might peeve the Aoife if he made it sound like his plan had been too transparent. When dealing with Aoife, sometimes it was smarter to simply play dumb.

Pocketing all of the coins but one, Madric tossed him the spare. "Thanks, Teine. I appreciate your honesty. Now, hop up on that stool. You can keep your clothes on, I promise."

Comforted by the blandness and propriety of the exchange, Teine did as he was told, and when he thanked Madric for the finder's fee, he truly meant it. Madric's gift was still generous, no matter what his original intent had been.

As for the magical test, Madric spent a few minutes looking Teine over for any obvious distinguishing marks, asking him a handful of odd questions and passing a clear stone around different parts of his body. As nothing was painful, and the process was more amusing than alarming, Teine found his attention wandering. He listened to the continual din of the storm still raging outside and the soft music in the background, allowing himself to be lulled into a pleasant trance. So, when Madric passed the stone close by his forehead and it suddenly began to glow, Teine yelped and jerked away, shielding his eyes.

"I think we have a winner," Madric commented drily. Hamoni immediately perked up and came in closer to watch.

Madric continued to pass the stone around, concentrating more on the area around Teine's head. The glow continued, dimming and brightening in different places and distances. "Very interesting." Madric muttered. "Hamoni, fetch me my journal. From my desk."

"Am I magic?" Teine asked. He was embarrassed to admit that the mere thought that he could develop any mystical abilities left him as breathlessly excited as he would have been as a nursling. It was easy to imagine himself wearing Inquisitor's robes like Prior Vihah or summoning Elementals like the ones he'd seen from the night before. He waited, literally on the edge of his seat, for Madric's verdict.

It did not come right away. As soon as Hamoni brought Madric's journal, the mage began thumbing through back pages, apparently looking for something.

"What happens if I'm magic?" Teine persisted.

"We'd have no choice but to report you," Madric intoned. To Teine, he sounded as though he were reporting the news of a loved one's demise. Something about the way he said it suddenly chilled Teine as much as the thought had thrilled him only a moment ago.

"What happens then?" Although he wasn't sure he was ready to know, Teine had to ask.

Shutting the book with a snap, Madric looked directly at Teine and smiled warmly. "Let's not get ahead of ourselves." He picked up the stone again and it continued to glow when it was near Teine's head. "Have you ever had the feeling that a moment you were experiencing had happened before?"

Teine shrugged, "Yes, but honestly, who hasn't? Even my Amagor-"

"Have you ever had a dream that came true?"

Teine tapped his finger thoughtfully against his front teeth as he grimaced. "Good or bad?"

Madric grinned, "Doesn't matter. Either."

He was about to say no and make a joke about all the 'showing up for class naked' dreams he'd had, when something jostled loose in his memory. He drew his breath in sharply and all the hair on his arms stood up.

"What is it you're remembering?" the Aoife magician coaxed. "I can tell you remember something. Don't doubt it, just share. It might not mean anything."

"My Amagorra," Teine blurted out. "I had a dream she got sick and she was dying. She was lying in bed and looking me in the eye. It was as though she was trying to tell me something that seemed very important, more important than anything, but she couldn't talk, and I couldn't hear her."

Embarrassed, he blinked quickly, unsure where the moisture and burning sensation in his eyes had come from. He'd never been particularly close to his Amagorra, at least not like Leis was, but he remembered waking from the dream and feeling waves of regret and concern for her well-being. "The next morning, when I woke up," he continued. "I asked my sister how she was doing, if everything was fine, and she said yes."

"So, it turned out to be nothing?" Madric asked, the glowing stone poised over Teine's right ear.

Teine shook his head, his mouth soundlessly mouthing the word "no." "Later that day, she collapsed on the way to the Commons for dinner. Clinician Nocdoramus had to do a surgery on her heart."

"Ohhhh," Hamoni breathed.

Madric shot her a stern look. "Let's not get ahead of ourselves," he repeated. "Now, have you ever..."

He didn't get to finish his question, because suddenly there was the sound of a sharp rap on the window nearest them. Then another, and then several all at once, like the popcorn they sometimes cooked over the fire in the Commons.

"Is that *hail?*" Madric shouted, his question thick with incredulity. The crystal in Madric's hand brightened, then shattered violently, peppering both the Aoife and Teine with small bits of rock shards and dust. Nearly simultaneously, the device on Hamoni's desk that suspended the golden bracelet made a loud popping sound and was suddenly consumed with little flashes like miniature lightning. The bracelet fell to the desk, bounced once, and rolled off onto the floor.

"Get out of here!" Madric commanded, pushing both Teine and Hamoni firmly toward the door. "Now! I'll be right behind you. I just want to shut off the collector." He said something else that was lost to the sound of pounding hail as a gust of wind tore one of the shutters free and slammed it through the window. Glass scattered everywhere, along with hailstones the size of an infant's fist.

Teine, accustomed from birth to doing exactly what he was told, when he was told, headed for the door. He sensibly covered his head as best he could with his sleeve. As he passed the bucket where the captive water Elemental was stored, he almost tripped over himself when he saw a translucent, bluish humanoid form rising out of the bucket. One glance toward the larger holding tank confirmed his fears. Instead of just one barely-formed watery fist, the clear vessel seemed to be swarming with the vague outlines of a mob of angry, watery captives.

"Madric, be careful!" Teine yelled. When Hamoni stopped to stare, he swept the girl up and fled the room, despite her howling protest.

An instant later, Madric was on their heels, drenched from head to toe. He slammed the door to the office shut behind him, mopping the water from his brow. Instead of fear in his eyes, Teine could see his wild excitement. "Go!" Madric directed Teine and Hamoni. "Get everyone to the main floor and away from the windows!"

He didn't have to tell Teine twice. Bellowing at the top of his lungs to be sure that everyone heard him on every floor, Teine began the evacuation.

Chapter 20: Refugees and Orders

As Teine carried the still-protesting Hamoni down the stairs, he could hear glass breaking and accompanying exclamations and screams from other rooms of the tower. "Get downstairs!" he told Hamoni as he set her down, mustering as much authority into his voice as he could.

"Right behind you!" Madric assured. Teine didn't know whether to be encouraged or annoyed by the magician's cheerful expression. Madric looked as though he were having the time of his life. "Don't worry lad, the whole tower won't be coming down around our ears. We're just losing some glass. It happens periodically."

"But this..." Hamoni started.

"Is no worse than some of the others we've had," Madric insisted, raising his voice to be heard above the gale. "A little glass. That's all."

Other residents of the tower were gathering in the main floor greathall, milling around like frightened cattle in a pen. Teine recognized the old woman from the kitchen whose name he hadn't caught, one of the lads from the stable and a handful of other servants he hadn't met.

"Madric, sir," the stable boy began, nervously glancing toward the windows. "My dad's bringing in some of the neighbors. They've lost their roof."

"Fine, fine," Madric waved dismissively. Then, raising his voice to include everyone in the room, he continued. "Any refugees who want to come in from the storm are welcome. No need to check with me. Let's keep everyone on the main floor, though. No wandering about in the basement or the bedrooms."

Looking as delighted as a person planning an impromptu party, Madric clapped his hands together. "Right, then! Break out the box of board games! Let's get that good console radio in here, and build up a roaring fire in the fireplace. If we're going to have company, we'll be hospitable."

Teine was about to ask what Madric wanted him to do when the thought of his first responsibility leapt unbidden to his mind. "Marne!" he exclaimed. "Is he all right? Should I check on him?"

Madric and Hamoni exchanged a glance that Teine couldn't read, but it left an uneasy feeling in his stomach. "Likely, he's sleeping through all of this." Hamoni assured Teine. "The poor little fellow sleeps a lot after he's been ill. We're really *not* neglecting him." At a nod from Madric, she snagged Teine's arm and began to walk him back toward the stairway.

"We're just making sure he gets the rest he needs." She fixed Teine with a winning smile, which helped ease some of his concern. "I'll tell you what, if you will go bring down the radio for me, I'll run down right now to check on him."

"It's good of you to think of him," Madric remarked as he was walking away. "Your compassion speaks well of you, Teine. The more I see, the more I think Marne made a far better choice for himself than his father would have made for him."

"Thank you, sir," Teine responded, but the magician was already out of earshot.

"He really does like you," Hamoni whispered. "Now go get that radio, and it wouldn't hurt for you to grab your books and other diversions. Today will probably end up being a rest day. Madric won't want to risk any more of your pretty face to all that potential windblown glass upstairs. Oh, and thanks, by the way!" Reaching up, she blotted a couple places on Teine's face with her sleeve, and when she pulled back, the fabric was flecked with red. "If you hadn't grabbed me when you did, that would have gotten me."

Teine tried not to blush and failed. Instead, he picked a piece of glass out of her hair and offered it to her. "You're welcome. You might want to go shake off somewhere. I think you're probably still wearing parts of that window."

"Go on then," she grinned. "You're so sweet. Has anyone ever told you that?"

"Knock it off, Hamoni!" the old woman shrilled from the kitchen. "Leave the poor boy alone. I need you to get in here and help me peel potatoes, if we're going to have company."

Teine decided it was as good a time as any to make himself scarce. Still glowing from the unexpected praise and harmless flirtation, Teine headed for the furniture storage room. He planned to get the console radio and carry it downstairs to the main room, but the draft in the corridor at the top of the stairs changed his mind. If there were open windows and broken glass, he could possibly forestall any more damage in those rooms by refastening the shutters, if he could. Rolling up his sleeves, he began his investigation.

It didn't take much to check which rooms had broken windows, but fortunately, some still had intact shutters. Although he was sopping wet and his skin was stinging from being pelted by ice balls, Teine left his little side project with a strong feeling of satisfaction. Of the four broken windows he'd found, he shuttered three of them, and he was able to drag the furniture well out of harm's way in the one room he couldn't secure. Certainly a worthwhile payoff for a few minutes' effort.

Teine took a moment to retrieve his bag with his journals and art supplies and sling it over his shoulder while he carried the console radio down the stairs. He could hear doors slamming on the main level, hearty laughter and loud voices that heralded visitors. The radio was heavy for one person to carry, and Teine grunted with the effort, but he managed to get it down the stairs without any mishap. Blinking in surprise, he realized he was suddenly surrounded by a crowd.

There were several Aoife dressed in riding leathers with heraldry and armor. One of the armored men was shepherding in a large family of common farmers. The four Aoife children each carried a bundle of belongings and seemed frightened, like fawns caught in the glare of carriage lights. Blinking and shivering, they looked much like Teine had felt only the day before when all that was familiar had been yanked out from under him. He couldn't help but feel for them, noticing the steam rising from their dirty and patched garments in the warmth of the room.

Teine set the radio down, remembering his physical education classes that had drilled the phrase "lift with your legs, not with your back" into his brain with a startling permanence. It turned out to be good advice for setting down a heavy burden, too. As soon as he plugged the unit in and the music began playing, Hamoni popped her head out of the kitchen with further instructions.

"Teine, can you help these people get their things inside?"

"Sure," Teine agreed, turning to one of the Aoife in armor. "Point me at them!"

"Their barrow is in the stable," the Ranger replied, nodding pleasantly. "Aren't you the plucky one? Madric said they can camp out here in the great room till it's over."

"Right, then," Teine headed toward the stable with a playful grin at the wide-eyed Aoife children as he passed. "Hopefully there will be someone to play cards with when I get back," he added over his shoulder as he walked away.

"Momma, can we play cards with the Human boy?" Teine smiled as the child's pleas were ripped away by the wind when he stepped outside.

When Teine arrived in the stable he could do nothing but stare open-mouthed like a child at the Zoo. The staid, uninteresting cobs of the farmer Aoife were quartered in the stalls closest to the doors. Beyond the farmers' steeds, in the stalls near the back of the stable were the most magnificent mounts Teine had ever seen. There was no question—these were the mounts of the Royal Rangers.

By sheer quantity, Teine noticed the horses first, the likes of which he'd never seen in his life. They were broad across the chest and as powerfully built as the draft horses that worked the fields, but with clean legs and shapely heads with large, alert eyes. They seemed a far cry from the sleepy carting horses Teine was most familiar with.

In stalls of their own were a couple of riding deer. As soon as she saw Teine, the doe leaned her broad, wedge-shaped head out over her stall front. She lipped the sleeve of Teine's tunic when he reached out to touch her. Teine had never had the opportunity to be that close to a living deer before and couldn't help but compare them to other animals he knew. The doe's russet coat was soft and her nose was black and leathery like a dog's. The deer didn't seem to have any upper front teeth for biting like the horses did. More aloof than the doe, the stag stood at the back of his stall, his impressive rack of antlers heavy on his head like the crown of a king. Teine thought it gave him a regal bearing.

The end stall held a shiny black mule, who leaned its head over the stall gate, yawned, and waggled its long ears in a shameless bid for attention. Teine never thought he'd describe a mule as "beautiful" but this one certainly qualified. Teine allowed his feet to carry him down the aisle way.

"Aren't you a character?" he whispered to the mule. But, as he leaned in to stroke the mule's soft nose, a large wolfhound in the same stall jumped up on its hind legs and barked a warning inches from his face. Teine let out a strangled cry of alarm, stumbled backwards over his own feet, and landed painfully on his rear. "Serves me right for being nosy, I guess," he grumbled. The wolfhound grumbled back, barking a couple more times before settling back in the straw.

After everyone was safely inside the tower, and the burdens unloaded from the cart in the stable, the gathering took on festive undertones as introductions were made all around. By the time Teine returned from the stable and settled in, all the travelers were mingling and sharing their adventures of the day.

The Aoife commoners, Nardo and Davora Bobwhite, were merchant vegetable farmers from just beyond Solmurry's border. They and their family had travelled for the better part of two hours in the screaming winds to arrive at Madric's Tower after the roof had blown off their house earlier that day. The couple had three of their own children, and the fourth was a nephew staying with them for the holiday while his parents had out of town business. Also travelling with them were Davora's mother and aunt, and Nardo's mother.

Although old, the Aoife elders were all strong and healthy. They thanked Madric and his people profusely for the hospitality. In return, the Bobwhites received many compliments on their large, flourishing family from the Rangers and Madric's staff. It was highly unusual to see more than two children in an Aoife household. Two was a blessing, and three was practically a miracle.

Teine had heard that commoners had an easier time breeding, while the nobles were not just less prolific, but less hardy overall. Certainly these four youngsters, or even their grandparents, were none the worse for wear after their forced march. The memory of Marne hiding behind couch cushions, heavy golden bracelet clunking around on his frail wrist, painted a stark contrast to these hardy folk, emphasizing the differences between nobles and commoners.

The contingent of Rangers proved to be nearly as intriguing as their mounts and far more interesting than the prolific farmers. It took Teine only a few minutes of watching them interact with Madric before a stunning realization came to him: these rough-looking, battle-hardened Aoife men were at least as well-bred as the courtiers who slavishly followed the Doyen Prince and availed themselves of the hospitality at Solmurry's Demesne. In fact, now that he looked at the heraldry, some of these Rangers might have been their siblings. Some of the bluest blood in the Empyrean lounged in Madric's great room that evening. Teine couldn't help but wonder what offense these lads had committed to earn themselves a post in the forested wilds of the coastlands. Who had they displeased to be banished so? The Prince? Or did they come to their posts by choice?

Teine could tell that, as host, Madric was in his element. He was comfortable with these people and it showed. From his seat in the kitchen, Teine occasionally stole glances at Madric and his guests as they lounged in front of the fireplace in the great room.

The youngest Bobwhite child tugged at Teine's sleeve. He was a towheaded boy who seemed to be about Marne's age. "What are you doing?" he asked, looking up at Teine with big curious eyes and pointing at his sketchbook.

Teine would have thought that the sketchbook itself would have made the question unnecessary. Then realization struck. This Aoife child had next to nothing in common with his young master. Marne was a hundred years old, and for all his youthful appearance had at least forty more years and a lifetime of study over this common Aoife child. Once again, the strangeness of Marne's situation—the secrecy, his frequent illness and the mystery of his retarded aging— leapt to the forefront of Teine's mind. But he squelched his uneasiness to answer the dirty-faced farm urchin in front of him.

"Drawing pictures," he answered. He'd chosen to draw because working on his project with Leis took up too much of his thought process, and he wanted to be able to enjoy himself and socialize at the same time. "Do you want me to draw something for you?"

Suddenly, as if by magic, Teine was surrounded by Aoife children, all squealing in glee.

"Now you've done it," chuckled Mr. Bobwhite. "Looks like you get to be the entertainment for the evening."

Teine shrugged, "Really, I don't mind."

He drew many pictures for the four children, burning through the pages of his sketchbook with abandon. The adults chatted amiably around the kitchen table with the Human residents of the tower. Having just reached Human adulthood, he fell neatly between the ages of the adults and the children, but he gravitated naturally toward the children.

Teine enjoyed working with an audience and a time limit. He did some of his best drawing under pressure, and happily took request after request. Madric even managed to produce a pack of wax colors, and soon the children were busy at work coloring the masterpieces Teine drew for them. The gathering, even with the howling winds and sleet hissing against the windows, had taken on the festive air of a party. Madric and some of the Rangers drifted in and out of the kitchen, mingling and visiting. But, even though Teine looked, he didn't see Hamoni anywhere.

Just as the kitchen staff were about to serve dinner, there was an exceptionally loud crack coupled with bright lightning, and the lights went out. "I wondered when that was going to happen," Madric said from the other room. "We can't count on it to come back on any time soon. Let's break out the oil lamps." The Human staff scrambled to comply. Moments later, Hamoni came down the stairs holding a candle.

"Lights are out," she chirped. Twirling the golden bracelet around a finger, she caught the wizard's eye. "Madric, may I speak with you for a moment?"

"Certainly." Rising to his feet, Madric excused himself from the Rangers. He and Hamoni ducked into one of the side rooms and closed the door.

Teine immediately wondered what topic would require a closed door between Madric and his friends, but he didn't have time to ponder. The elderly cook was standing over him with a ladle in one hand and a frustrated expression on her wrinkled face. "Dinner's up. Do you want to carry trays or fill oil lamps?"

Teine closed his sketchbook. "Either. Or both."

"That's a good boy," she told him, her smile revealing surprisingly good teeth for someone her age. "Fill the lamps, then, whilst I make up a tray."

Teine's next half hour was so busy that he had no time to think of anything other than pouring wine, prepping and lighting lanterns, and bringing trays of rich roast and mashed potatoes with gravy to the Rangers. The next thing he knew, Hamoni was catching his eye and beckoning him into the room where he could see Madric still waited.

Both of them looked flustered and slightly angry, as if they'd been arguing, but Teine had a hard time imagining what they could argue about. Madric was clearly the master, and therefore his word was law. Puzzled, he went into the room, hoping he hadn't inadvertently done something wrong.

"Teine, we..."

"After a momen..."

Both Madric and Hamoni spoke in unison, then stopped. Madric glared purposefully at the girl. "Sorry," she whispered. "You go."

"Teine," Madric repeated. "We've discussed it and think you should spend a little time with Marne this evening."

From the intent stares he was getting from them both, Teine couldn't help but feel a little apprehensive. Why would his spending time with his rightful master require such an intense debate?

His confusion must have shown on his face, because Hamoni spoke next. "You can bring him his dinner and a lantern. Perhaps if he feels well you could play a game of cards or something. But, the bottom line is that we think you're ready."

"Ready?" Teine asked, growing even more puzzled. "What's to be ready for?" He looked to Madric for reassurance, but the Aoife seemingly had none to give. His lips were a thin line of worry.

"We think it's time," Madric told him, his features giving nothing further away.

"You've proven you can be trusted," Hamoni added, examining the bracelet she still carried. "And really, we don't have any choice, at least not for the moment."

Blinking, Teine nodded. "You can trust me, though I don't see why you're so concerned. I'm good with children," he assured them, hoping he could make them feel better. "I've gotten good marks on my nursery studies and am rated to care for both Human and Aoife infants on up. I've gotten my mark. See?" He pulled the neck of his shirt down, trying to expose the sigil markings on his chest that showed he'd indeed passed the class and gotten his rating.

Madric and Hamoni only glanced at each other and then back at Teine.

Unable to control his curiosity and his growing concern, Teine couldn't help himself. He broke training. "Exactly what is going on here?" he demanded, stepping in closer and lowering his voice to a whispering hiss.

"Don't be afraid," Hamoni consoled, placing her slender hand on his arm. "You don't have to be afraid at all. It's just Marne. He's just..."

Madric interrupted, cutting her off with a scowl. "Teine, please take him his dinner now. And behave with some discretion when you return. If you need to speak to either of us at that time, we'll answer any questions you have privately."

"Any we have answers to, that is..." Hamoni added. Her smile was placating and apologetic as she ignored Madric's glare.

Teine did the only thing that seemed reasonable. Bowing formally at the waist, he turned to face Madric. "Yes, sir. I'll see to it right away."

Chapter 21: Secrets by Candlelight

Teine's mind turned and turned on itself as he sat on the bed in the blue room and carefully packed his belongings into the satchel. Frustrated and more than a little frightened by the strange conversation with Madric and Hamoni, Teine took comfort in doing what he'd been raised to do: follow orders. He'd been ordered to go to Marne, and that was what he was going to do. He found himself wondering if he'd be able to get some answers from the boy. Unable to stop himself, Teine sighed out loud. It seemed like a cruel joke that someone as small as a six-year-old Human child could suddenly become the undisputed master of Teine's fate.

Teine stared blankly at the portrait on the wall. Brothers playing on the beach, a moment of sunshine, sand, and smiles forever frozen in time. It made him very cognizant of how badly he missed Leis. He was absolutely certain she'd be able to make sense of all this strange behavior from the Aoife. In fact, Leis might already know why people at Solmurry tended to tiptoe around the topic of Marne. It was as though Teine had landed in the middle of some strange cult.

If she knew, she'd tell me, Teine tried to reassure himself. But somehow, after everything he'd seen that day, he wasn't too sure.

It didn't take him long to pack his few belongings and leave the blue room. Humans normally didn't get full guest privileges in any of the Aoife homes, no matter who they belonged to. Teine took fleeting comfort in knowing he'd probably always be furnished in somewhat lavish quarters as long as he was traveling with Marne.

All the same, he glanced over his shoulder to once more appreciate the luxury of the furnishings and the famous portrait of the "Brothers Blue."

It was too good to last, anyway, he thought, trying not to feel sorry for himself. *It's not like I'm being evicted from Paradise.* Trying, in fact, not to feel anything at all, Teine threw his bag over his shoulder and headed back down to the kitchen.

While he had been upstairs packing, the matronly old Bess had made up a tray for him to take to the basement. "There's a good boy," she chirped, handing it to him. The dishes clanked and rattled together as he clumsily seized it, then rattled again as she patted his cheek with one wrinkled, age spotted hand. "Careful there." She lit a candlestick with a taper from the stove, then placed it on the tray so he'd have something to see by. "We can't spare a lantern, so mind the stairs, now. They take a sharp turn at the bottom, and then you're there."

The sweet scent of beeswax mingled with the meaty aroma from covered bowls on the tray, and Teine found himself inhaling for the sheer pleasure of it. "I'll be careful," he answered, giving her a pleasant nod as she held the basement door open for him. He tried hard not to jostle the tray or bump her with his satchel as he began his descent down the narrow, bricked stairway.

The candle lit a very limited radius, and Teine could barely see two steps down from his position. Within a few steps, a dank, mildew smell overpowered even the fragrant candle and hearty meal, and he found himself thinking more of a dungeon than a basement. Just as he glanced upward, hoping for some reassurance from the kitchen Bess, she closed the door, leaving Teine to navigate the steep descent by candlelight alone.

"Great," he muttered, suppressing a nervous laugh. He listened for a moment to the howling of the wind outside, trying not to imagine the tower coming down around him. *They'll probably discover my bones in a thousand years when someone excavates the ruins.*

About halfway down, Teine's feet nearly slid out from under him on the mossy flagstones. *Were those stairs original construction?* It was interesting to imagine all the thousands of sets of feet that had gone before him over the centuries. Lost in his daydream, he narrowly escaped upsetting the tray and tumbling the rest of the way down. After that, he took to peering cautiously at each step before placing his weight on it. Although standing water didn't pool on the steps, he could hear a steady dripping further down in the basement. Teine wrinkled his nose at the strengthening smell of mildew, wondering how the extreme humidity in this basement could possibly be healthy for anyone recovering from an illness, much less for a frail child who took cold easily.

After the sharp turn that had been described to him, Teine reached the bottom of the stairs. The low ceiling of the stairwell opened up into a room that looked to be used mostly to store casks and preserves. The walls were lined with jars of shelving for pickled goods, as well as many waxed rounds of cheese and other sundries protected from the dank atmosphere by their packaging. But there was no sign of Teine's young master. Glancing around and holding the tray high to maximize the effect of the candle, Teine whispered, "Marne?"

Three drips of water plunked into a bucket catching a leak before Teine heard a muffled answer. "I'm in here."

Treading cautiously toward the sound of Marne's voice, Teine inched his way across the floor. After a score of steps, he could make out the faint outline of a door with a table sitting next to it. He could see the light switch by the door and sighed; this whole uncomfortable trek into the underbelly of Madric's Tower would have been a lot less stressful if lighted with good electric lights.

Imagining the room lit brightly, it suddenly seemed much less menacing, and Teine found himself smiling at how silly he'd been to feel afraid at all.

"I have your dinner," he told the boy. "Hang on, I'll be right there."

Setting the tray on the table, Teine reached for the latch on the door and gave it a turn. The latch cooperated, but the door didn't budge. With a frown, Teine pushed harder, feeling the tell-tale stubbornness of cellar-damp wood. He bit down his momentary panic at the thought of Marne trapped. "Uh... don't worry," he called to the boy. "The door's stuck. It sure is humid down here." With a twist, helped along by a shove from his shoulder, the solid oak door burst open. Teine grabbed the candle off the tray and thrust it ahead of him to scout for Marne.

In the shadows beyond the light of his candle, a dark form rustled, rising up from the indistinct features of the poorly lit room. Two bright, electric blue orbs reflected back the light of Teine's candle, tracking him with eerie luminescence.

Eyes.

Teine was only able to squeak "wraith!" in alarm, before dropping the candle on the ground and knocking himself nearly brainless on the door behind him. The candle guttered for a second, lying broken in a pool of its own hot wax like a dying soldier, before the flame went out completely.

"Don't be a fool. Stand still," Marne's sharp command sliced through both the womb-like darkness and Teine's fog of terror like a scalpel. His words halted Teine in his tracks, an effective barrier to the blind panicked flight he was about to take.

Teine tensed at the patter of small feet coming across the flagstones toward him. "It's only me," the creature whispered. In the close space Teine realized with some relief that the small form next to him was warm and alive and had that scent he'd come to associate with Marne—like cinnamon and cloves. Then the truth struck him. Marne was certainly not a wraith—but he wasn't an Aoife, either.

The next thing Teine knew Marne's fingers were brushing against his, pushing something into his hands. "Here, take this," he said. Out of the habit of obedience, Teine opened his hands to receive the candle-holder. Before he could gather his wits about him the candle burst into flame, whole and brilliant in the darkness.

Puzzled and alarmed but strangely thrilled by the trick, Teine couldn't help knitting this last occurrence to the other mysteries that he'd witnessed since meeting his young master. Theory after theory began vying for space in his suddenly overstuffed brain. Eager for more information, he immediately turned his gaze to search for his young master's face. But Marne had turned away, retreating out of easy candle range. Uncertain how to proceed, he stayed in his spot by the door, listening to the muted and eerie wail of the storm outside while waiting for his Human eyes to adjust to the candlelight. As though reading his confusion, Marne threw him a resigned, furtive glance. Once again, Marne's eyes caught the candlelight and reflected it back.

Instead of terror, Teine was surprised at his blooming sense of wonder. Holding the candle in front of him to get a better look, he advanced a few steps closer and was able to make out a raised, child-sized bed with heavy but shabby looking drapes, a bedside table, and a stand with one of the amazing moving picture boxes he'd seen in the playroom at the Demesne. A wooden rocking horse guarded the foot of the bed like a faithful pet. This room, unlike the others beyond the door, was completely windowless. Cocooned in a blanket, a corner of it wrapped over his head, Marne lay, now averting his gaze.

"Please bring me my supper," Marne whispered, "Then, please go."

Gone was the tone of command, the certainty and confidence that had rooted Teine in place earlier. Instead, the voice was that of a young child, resigned to remaining alone in the dark.

"Yes, sir," Teine replied, out of habit. He was getting a headache from all the questions stampeding around in his head but propriety demanded they go unasked. He closed the distance to Marne's bedside and set the candle on the little bedside table, frowning at the two other empty candle-holders. Marne had been in the dark for some time.

"Please?" Marne answered, sounding even more tentative. Teine hesitated, the oddness of the plea catching and holding him there. Marne was heir to Solmurry, son of the Lord of the realm, and he held life-or-death sway over hundreds of Human lives. He owed no one a "please" except his own kin. Even though Teine had been trying to catch a glimpse of the boy's face to better discern what the child wanted, Marne's next words caught Teine completely off guard.

"Please, don't call me that."

Teine blinked, uncertain what was being asked of him. "Sir?"

"Don't call me sir. Or master, either." As if gathering courage, Marne took a deep breath, then turned his head to face Teine directly. Up close, the child's eyes were even more spectacular. His eyes reflected the candlelight like orbs of blue fire. "I believe it demeans both of us."

Teine barely heard Marne's words, he was so caught up in what he was seeing. The Marne he was looking at didn't look much like the Marne he'd been introduced to, except in the most base of generalities. The face he showed the world must be some sort of illusion, perhaps some of that experimental magic that Madric had mentioned? Aoife, even their children, generally had sharper features than Humans, with long, oblique set almond-shaped eyes, high cheekbones, narrow noses, and prominent chin and jaw lines. Marne's face, at least the one Teine was viewing right that moment, had many similar qualities, yet managed to be as unlike the face of an Aoife child as horses were to deer.

This was no deformed Aoife he was seeing. Teine was increasingly convinced that Marne was an entirely different creature. The pupils of Marne's eyes were distinctly diamond-shaped, unlike the round pupils of both Aoife and Humans, and even the irises of his eyes were an odd shade resting somewhere between blue and grey. Instead of the rich golden locks of his father and uncle, Marne's hair was variegated shades covering the entire spectrum of blonde, from sunny bright all the way to platinum. His hands, pale against the heavy woolen blanket, were even more slender and appeared to be jointed somewhat differently from the Aoife.

The child simply looked otherworldly.

And Teine could do nothing but stare dumbly at his young master with the oddest feeling coursing through him. It wasn't timidity or fear but a strange sense of purpose, as though somehow his life, his *real* life, had only just begun.

Marne sighed, struggling to sit up in the bed. His thin lips twisted into a slightly self-deprecating smile. Teine had seen that same expression before, but on Marne's other face. "Of course you realize it's rude to stare," Marne admonished him, his voice surprisingly mild. "But since I've certainly given you cause we can overlook it. Just this once."

Teine blinked, realizing that he hadn't for several seconds. He opened his mouth to speak, but could get nothing out but a couple syllables of unintelligible grunting, an utter failure for one usually so articulate.

"Go ahead," Marne encouraged. "I know you feel you must ask. You have my permission."

Teine opened his mouth again, willing himself to form words. Finally, he blurted, "What *are* you?"

Teine, Marne and the rest of the folks at Solmurry will return in Tested, Book 2 *of* The Gilded Shackle *series, scheduled for December 2015.*

Chapter 1: Chosen

Marne drew a deep, ragged breath, his voice soft but rich with sad, childish longing. "I wish I knew," he answered, resting his sharp chin in his hand, his elbow on his knee. "All I know for sure is that I'm no more an Aoife than you are."

Teine couldn't help but nod his agreement, wordless with wonder. But Marne's response only multiplied Teine's questions. He was dying to know how Marne managed to hide his true appearance so effectively. Why had he spent the ride to the tower bundled up in a duffel bag like some kind of luggage? And how did Marne light and repair the candle? Was it magic? Teine was so tangled in his own thoughts, it took him several awkward seconds to realize he was still standing there, mouth agape like a simpleton.

"Would you mind bringing the tray in?" Marne asked gently. "I'd get it myself, but I'm really supposed to stay in bed."

"Oh, yes. Sorry." Teine shook his head, then hustled to bring in the tray. Once he realized the tiny dank bedroom was several degrees warmer than the rest of the storage cellar, he closed the door behind him.

Marne had cleared the bedside table of the spare candle holders and a model glider to make room for their food. "There's a chair over by the table you can use," he told Teine, pointing into one of the dimly lit recesses of the room. "It should be big enough for you. We can both just eat here. I see no reason for formality."

Teine fetched the chair, wondering at the incredible oddity of the situation. How many Humans had ever dined at the same table as their master, even if it was only at a bedside? Masters and servants eating together from plates and bowls and utensils was unthinkable. Was it only Marne's unique situation that made it possible or would it be a regular part of the life he was going to lead? Should he pick up crisps out of the bowl with his hands or should he simply try to pour them onto a plate? Was he supposed to be serving Marne his dinner, and if so, how was that to be done properly? Brow furrowed with worry, Teine sat in the chair, folded his hands in his lap and waited for direction.

Marne raised an eyebrow, then gave a quiet chuckle that sounded far more sympathetic than mocking. "You really are out of your element, aren't you. Don't worry, be at ease. When there's no one around to impress, there's no need for the show," Marne assured him, stretching to reach the cover on one of the bowls. Setting it aside, he poured them both tea from the steaming earthenware pot. With surprise, Teine watched as Marne filled his own tea last, as though Teine were a guest. He also noted that, despite Marne's focused look of concentration, his frail arms were shaking from the exertion by the time he'd topped off the second cup.

"Here, master, let me," Teine offered, emboldened by the strange boy's kindness and apparent physical weakness. "Please instruct me if what I do is not to your liking. I've only learned the basics of setting a table, but I would welcome the opportunity to broaden my horizons."

Marne chuckled, "I'm not easy to offend. And please, Teine, no formalities. I haven't the energy for them." With a sigh, Marne settled himself back on the pillows, his cup of tea steaming near at hand.

Somewhat perplexed, Teine decided the best course of action was to simply wing it. Marne had made it clear that it would be fine for Teine to do as he liked, within reason. Hoping he looked somewhat skilled, he uncovered the small basin that held the damp, citrus-scented towels for washing before their meal. He started to reach in and take out towel for Marne before he realized that would be unsanitary, and offered the whole basin instead. Nodding his approval, Marne selected a cloth and began to diligently wipe his face and hands. Teine did the same, the ritual words of formal evening prayer on his tongue. But from the way the young master was eying the consumables, he suspected it would be fine to dispense with the prayer as well and get directly to the food. Using a wooden ladle on the tray, he filled a bowl with savory beef stew, heaping it high with chunks of seasoned meat and tender vegetables. With a flourish, he then offered it to Marne.

Eyes wide, Marne shook his head, warding the bowl off with both hands. "I wish," he sighed. "It looks heavenly. But perhaps I'd better just try the broth, first." Nodding, Teine set the first bowl aside, thinking about how good it would taste once he got to it. Mindful of the young master's wishes, he filled the second bowl with a generous amount of broth, then, as an afterthought, added a couple pieces of carrot and potato, mashing them flat with the ladle. Marne accepted the bowl as offered, taking it in both hands and giving it a long, anticipatory sniff before reaching for his spoon.

More items remained on the tray and Teine was determined to make a good impression. Deciding to play butler, he carved up one of the red pears in the bowl, thoughtfully removing both the core and the skin, and placed it on a plate. He then added a couple of slices of buttery farmer's cheese, and on a whim decided to shake a few crisps onto the plate for good measure. But his shaking was a little overzealous, and he ended up completely covering the entire plate with the tasty little lemony cookies.

"Oh rats," he muttered, trying to shake some of the excess crisps off onto a second plate. He looked up to see Marne watching him, his odd eyes sparkling with humor over his bowl of broth.

"It's perfectly acceptable to use your hands on the crisps, if you've just washed," Marne told him. "But, I was hoping for dinner and a show..."

Teine snorted, embarrassed but amused at his own discomfiture. "You don't want to see what I do for my next act, believe me," he countered, vividly imagining himself flinging crisps everywhere while trying to shake them back where they belonged. Leis was right: although Marne was physically frail and the strangest-looking creature Teine had ever seen, but he was a fair-minded, witty little fellow.

"I hope it involves making a lot of that food disappear." Marne sipped a spoonful of broth, then nodded in satisfaction. "Honestly, this is excellent, but I don't think I'll make much of a dent in what she gave us. I hope you're hungry."

"I'm always hungry." Sensing he had Marne's approval to tuck in, Teine brushed most of the crisps off onto the second plate with his hand and offered over the fruit and cheese. Marne hesitated, and Teine felt oddly elated when he took a piece of pear and immediately ate it. "Say the word if you want more."

"I will. Just focusing on one thing at a time."

The pair of them fell to dining, with Teine consuming about five times the volume in about half the time as his more finicky companion. He ate to keep his mouth busy, hoping to avoid some of the awkwardness, and praying he wasn't breaking any major rules of etiquette. Marne, for his part, seemed relaxed and serene as he nestled into his pillows, listening to the muffled sounds of the storm outside and sipping broth from his spoon. Teine was still fascinated by Marne's alien appearance, but didn't want his curiosity to offend. That, alone, was an excellent reason to remain silent. He was dying so many questions, but he didn't want to disturb the easy silence that dining together provided.

He filled the time between mouthfuls by carefully observing the room. The solo candle didn't provide much illumination, but Teine was able to make out strange markings in a glittery kind of paint on the floor and the walls. They looked similar to the ones stitched into Marne's traveling bag, but it was hard to be sure in the dim light.

Teine's mind was racing like a hound slipped from its collar, darting from conclusion to conclusion as he tried to take in everything. He wanted to sketch: the way the light from the candle fell on the rocking horse cast a shadow on the wall, giving him an idea for a new composition with soldiers and their mounts riding through a canyon, their shadows looking more fearsome than the contingent itself. He wanted to paint: only his jealously guarded oil paints would be able to capture the depth of Marne's mysterious iridescent eyes. And he wanted to write: the things he'd seen in the last few hours challenged nearly every belief he'd had about Aoife, magic, and what was possible in the world!

The core truths of the world he'd now entered were far stranger than Teine had ever imagined and his awareness of the situation was truly alarming. The ongoing need for secrecy was obvious. Even a rumor of the young master being some strange, alien, magic-wielding creature could send half the Humans at Solmurry into a panic, and it wouldn't matter how many of them had played with Marne or listened to him read them stories when they were nurselings.

Living among and educating themselves with Aoife had managed to raise Humans out of some of their baser tendencies toward superstition and xenophobia, but they were still only Human. Not even the avalanche of books Teine had read, packed full of tales of fairies, adventure, and magical creatures had truly prepared him for this, and he was more open-minded than the average Human. Most likely, Marne would be reviled as a demon, rendered helpless by any means possible, and then either killed outright or given over to the Church. Even Lord Solmurrian being home at the time would not guarantee Marne's safety.

The situation begs one burning question, Teine thought. *Who knows about Marne? Does Leis? Does Lord Solmurrian himself know that this creature is not his own flesh and blood, but perhaps a changeling of some sort? Maybe Lord Solmurrian's real son is locked away in a faerie realm while an impostor lives in his place.* The thought gave Teine a shiver of dread, but he found it hard to sustain any feeling of fear when he looked at the child across from him struggling to thrive on thin broth and peeled pear slices. Teine had always trusted his instincts and nothing about Marne seemed particularly dangerous, other than the power he had over the course of Teine's life.

He was about to refill his bowl when Marne spoke. "I want to ask your opinion on something rather important." The boy set down his bowl and reached for his tea.

Teine blinked twice. *His opinion? The day was getting stranger and stranger.* Wordlessly, he nodded and continued dipping out his second bowl of soup as though his betters asked his opinion every day.

Encouraged, Marne regarded Teine over the lip of his steaming cup, his strange reflective eyes serious. "Now that you've seen how deep this rabbit hole goes," the boy began. "Did I make the right choice?"

Teine smiled at the "Alice in Wonderland" reference, before he realized that Marne was talking about *him*.

"After all," Marne continued. "While most noble families have their secrets, we at Solmurry have more than our fair share."

Unwilling to answer hastily, Teine considered the question. Out of all the boys who were his age-mates, he could think of no one at Solmurry who had the right combination of interests, temperament, and abilities to be the guardian of such terrible secrets.

Only Marcus stood out as even a remote possibility. Marcus had a more developed physique than Teine, tending toward strength and bulk. When Teine thought "Display Model," it was types like Marcus that automatically came to mind. Additionally, his friend had a good nature, a sense of fair play, and the right temperament to enjoy the work. But he lacked...

Teine drew a blank. What *did* Marcus lack, anyway? He seemed the logical choice. Convinced that Marne wasn't trying to trap him into saying the wrong thing, Teine decided it was best to answer his question with another question.

"Why did you defy your father on this?" he blurted out, unable to contain himself any longer. After his meeting with Lord Solmurrian, Teine couldn't imagine anyone willfully defying the hot-tempered Aoife lord on anything. He was truly frightening. "Marcus would have been a more logical choice. Why not him?"

Marne didn't answer for several long seconds, and Teine began to wonder if Marne was beginning to have doubts. As much as Teine would have jumped at the opportunity to return to his old life and the chance to see which of his carefully-laid plans would come to fruition, he now found himself torn.

Could it be that he actually *wanted* this life, now that he knew it would be an adventure beyond his wildest imaginings?

"Marcus never would have asked that question," Marne answered. "That's why I selected you."

In the dim candlelight, Teine could see the boy was visibly fatigued, exhaustion showing in every line of his young, frail body. Marne set down his cup, pushed the food away, and sank back into the cushions.

"Marcus never would have asked that question." Teine supposed that was probably true. Marcus was content knowing what was, without ever questioning *why* it was. Suddenly, Teine couldn't help but feel very special. Chosen, even. All his life, Teine had watched the world around him and tried to learn from it. Apparently, someone had noticed. He was about to express his gratitude when he realized Marne had fallen asleep. Rising, he pulled the heavy wool blanket up around his frail charge's shoulder and whispered, "Thank you."

Dictionary/Pronunciation Guide

Age of Majority: 140 years of age, when a young Aoife is considered a full adult.

Alemis (Al-LAY-mus): Ersan goddess of nature, "Mother Nature." Also called the "All-Mother."

Amagi (Ah-MAHDG-ee): Honorific for "mother."

Amagorra (Ah-Mah-GORE-uh): Honorific for "grandmother" in the Empyrean.

Aoife (EE-fuh): Slender, petite, "elf-like" humanoids with pointed ears, oblique-set eyes, and angular features. The dominant species in the Empyrean.

AM: Abbreviation for "Altered Male." A Human male who has received a vasectomy.

Awakened: An item or animal that has become either sentient or magically active.

Besom (BESS-um): A low-born, trashy woman.

Bess: A positive slang term for a working woman, i.e., "She's a hardworking Bess."

Capite (Cap-EET): A grant of land from the Emperor that can never be divided or sold.

Centennial: An Aoife's 100th birthday signifying their entry into adulthood, at which time they are allowed to marry.

Closehold: The lands immediately surrounding a Demesne or Estate.

Cohort (CO-hort): A group of young Humans of the same age. Name of the barracks-style living arrangement of young

Humans grouped by age, usually given a mascot name like Mastiff or Falcon.

The Cut: A rite of passage that marks the start of adulthood for young Human males within the Empyrean. They are evaluated, and then circumcised. If not needed for breeding, they also are given a vasectomy and become AMs. Intact receive a circumcision only and are referred to as IMs.

Demesne (duh-MAIN): The main Manor house of an Estate.

Display: A beauty pageant for Human slaves where breeding stock is evaluated and judged.

Doyen Prince (DOY-un): A prince who is the acknowledged heir of a kingdom/empire and who will inherit the duties of the Emperor.

Driller: A coach and/or certified physical fitness specialist in charge of making exercise assignments and goals for Humans.

Eaoster (EE-stir): Spring equinox holiday, sometimes celebrated with fertility rites in some Ersan cultures and as the resurrection of a deity in others.

Elementals: Extraplanar creatures stuck on Ersa that can be forced to perform services through the use of magic.

Elf: An insulting slang word used by Humans from outside the Empyrean to describe Aoife.

Emmett: The closest small borough to Solmurry lands. Population about 1500.

Empyrea (im-PEER-ee-uh): Capital City of the Empyrean, also referred to as Capital City.

Empyrean (im-PEER-ee-un): The wealthy, secretive, walled Empire run by Aoife.

Empyrean Gazette: The big newspaper that covers the Empyrean's Capital City.

Eos (EE-yos): Ersa's sun.

Ersa (UR-suh): The planet/world.

Escutcheon: (Es-CUTCH-en) A shield or shield-like surface on which a coat of arms is displayed.

Fabal (FAY-ball): A rough team sport with some similarity to football or rugby, with the egg of a dragon as the ball.

Greenline Guide: A yearly manual providing base pricing guidelines for the buying and selling of Humans.

Grudge: A gladiator who answers challenges to their house.

Holidocrith (Ho-LID-oh-crith): An intelligent, psi-active, warm-blooded creature with the features of horses, dragons, and dogs.

IM: A intact Human male who has been circumcised but not given a vasectomy. Another term for Human male breeding stock.

Madric's Tower: An ancient lighthouse and watchtower on Solmurry's coast built centuries ago by Krunal stonemasons. Now houses the magician Madric Solmurrian and his workshop.

Monocular: Any enchanted single eyepiece.

Port Chandler: Coastal city in the Empyrean.

Prior (PRY-er): A priest in service of Vuaren, the Lord of Light.

Sea Dragon: A creature having both a saltwater and freshwater lifecycle. Adults can grow hundreds of feet long. They like the taste of wood and attack ships and lifeboats. Their freshwater larvae are considered a delicacy.

Sigil (SIG-ill): A magical insignia tattooed on nobles and Humans of the Empyrean, denoting identity, birthplace, ownership, pedigree, and education.

Sire and Get: A class entry Display showing a male Human and several of his offspring.

SPED: Abbreviation for Solmurry Postal Exchange Depot.

Special Reserve: A prime specimen Human slave offered for silent auction.

SS Henrietta Lacks: The starship that carried Human colonists from Earth to Ersa. The ship was named in honor of Henrietta Lacks, a 20th century woman who unknowingly provided cells from a cancerous tumor that created the first Human immortal cell line for medical research.

Syndrome: A specific set of deformities affecting some Aoife newborns, resulting in death.

Theia: Ersa's moon.

Titan: A slang word used by Humans outside the Empyrean to describe Empyrean-bred Humans.

Vuaren (VWAR-en): Empyrean God of Law, sometimes worshipped as a Saint in monotheistic cultures.

Wiydon (WHY-don): A leggy, stork-like seabird.

Wiydon Isles (WHY-don): A Theocratic Human Kingdom across the sea from the Empyrean.

The People of the Gilded Shackle

Abel of Bartheim (BARTH-heim): AM Human, sold to Solmurry by his previous master because he wanted to work at the Solmurry shipyard.

Adam of Solmurry (SAUL-meury): IM Human, about Teine's age, sold at auction as a potential stud prospect.

Adina of Solmurry (Uh-deen-uh): Female Human, Special Reserve from 2 years previous, full sister of Teine, Leis, and Samia.

Alain Solmurrian (Ah-LANE Saul-MEURY-in): Male Aiofe, younger brother of Madric, father of Marne, Lord and Master of Solmurry.

Aleric Solmurrian (Al-ERR-ic Saul-MEURY-in): Male Aiofe, historical figure who accidentally turned himself into an undead.

Alice of Mahoney (Muh-HOE-nee): Human Female, Billy of Mahoney's "rough around the edges" cousin.

Amagi/Selene of Solmurry (Ah-MODGE-ee/Si-LEEN): Female Human, mother of Adina, Teine, Leis and Samia.

Amagorra/Silvia of Solmurry (Ah-ma-GORE-uh/SIL-vee-uh): Female Human, mother to Selene, grandmother to Adina, Teine Leis and Samia.

Mr. Aylmer (AIL-mer): Male Aoife, newspaper reporter for *The Empyrean Gazette*, bought Samia as a handmaiden for his wife.

Billy of Mahoney (Muh-HOE-nee): IM Human, purchased as a stud prospect, from Peregrine Cohort, about Teine's age, is acclimated to life at Solmurry but still keeps in touch with his relatives at Mahoney.

Boric of Solmurry (BOR-ic): IM Human, celebrated stud and sire of Teine's friend Vosh, is in charge of crop rotations and work crews for the acreage near the Solmurry closehold.

Brigid Solmurrian (BRIDG-id): Female Aoife, Lord Alain Solmurrian's deceased wife, mother of Marne Solmurrian.

Clinician McIlroy (MACK-il-roy): Male Aoife, ranking physician, common born.

Clinician Nocdoramus (NOCK-door-am-us): Female Aoife, young up-and-coming physician.

Cynthia of Dinsdale: Female Human, originally purchased by Solmurry for potential breeding stock but rejected and resold at auction due to allergies.

DesMarte (Duh-MART): Male Aoife, famous landscape and portrait artist.

Driller Goran/Goran of Solmurry (GOR-un): AM Human, retired Grudge, now in service as Solmurry Driller.

Dona of Solmurry (DOAN-uh): Female Human, about Leis's age, sold at auction.

Dorian Vondereen (DOOR-ee-in VON-der-een): Aoife male, youngest son of the current Lord Vondereen, one of the Doyen Prince's retinue, tends to urinate in houseplants when drunk.

Ebric Hilliard (EB-rick HILL-yerd): Male Aoife, Lord of Hilliard, father of Nirilemi/Niri.

Earl of Broshenford (BROSH-en-ferd): Male Aoife, business associate of Lord Solmurrian, has a widowed daughter with a young son.

Edgar of Solmurry: AM Human, middle-aged master silversmith at Solmurry.

Hamoni Falshaad (Huh-MOAN-ee Fal-SHAHD): Female Aoife, apprentice to Madric Solmurrian, works in exchange for training and keeping her talents hidden.

Haneesha Falshaad (Han-EE-sha Fal-SHAHD): Female Aoife, Courtesan, professional seductress and older sister of Hamoni Falshaad.

Kenneth Blank: AM Human, Madric's groom and stable hand at the Tower.

Leis of Solmurry (LEES): Female Human, younger sister of Teine of Solmurry, granddaughter of Silvia of Solmurry, daughter of Selene of Solmurry and Lesmar of Solairn, head nanny of Marne Solmurrian.

Lesmar of Solairn (LESS-mar of SAUL-airn): IM Human, senior stud at Solmurry, Headman of Master Solmurrian, sire of Teine, Leis, Samia, Adina, Marcus and many other Solmurry Humans.

Madric Solmurrian (MAD-rick): Male Aoife, eldest brother of Lord Alain Solmurrian, talented magician, works from Madric's Tower.

Maggie of Solmurry: Female Human, known for her good nature and love of youngsters, stationed in the kitchens of the Commons at Solmurry.

Marcus of Solmurry (MAR-cuss): IM Human, half-sibling of Teine and Leis of Solmurry, son of Lesmar of Solairn.

Marne Solmurrian (MARn): Heir to Solmurry, son of Alain and Bridgid (d.) Solmurrian.

Meshamus of Adamshead (MESH-ah-miss): Deceased famous Human sculptor.

Nirilema (Niri) Hilliard (NEER-ee-lee-muh/NEER-ee): Female Aoife, daughter of Lord Ebric Hilliard, fascinated with magic, Marne Solmurrian's secret best friend.

Phoebe of Solmurry (FEE-bee): Female Human, senior housekeeper at the Solmurry Demesne, currently pregnant.

Prior Vihah (PRY-er VEE-hah): Male Aoife, High Inquisitor for the Doyen Prince, in charge of capturing, sequestering and "educating" people within the Empyrean who are found to be practicing magic in secret.

Professor Norzic (NORE-zick): Male Aoife, professor of Historical Studies for over 600 years, beloved by generations of Aoife and Human students for his lively narrative style of teaching.

Robin of Solmurry: IM Human, friend of Teine and Marcus.

Rudia of Solmurry (ROOD-ee-yuh): Female Human, distant maternal ancestor of Teine and Leis.

Salma of Solmurry (SAHL-mah): Female Human, about Leis' age, sold at auction.

Samia of Solmurry (SAM-ee-ya): Female Human, youngest full sister of Teine and Leis, sold as the Special Reserve to Mr. Aylmer of Empyrea.

Seymour of Cartierscross (SEE-more of CAR-tee-ears-cross): AM Human, friend and cohort-mate of Teine and Marcus.

Sigolier Zan (SIG-oh-leer): Female Aoife, common-born, works in Records Department of the Empyrean, is trained in the care, updating, and maintenance of the magical tattoos that identify each Human in the Empyrean.

Silpa of Cartierscross (SIL-puh): Female Human, nanny to Nirilema Hilliard.

Stinky the Wolfhound: Favorite pet of Marne Solmurrian and the staff of the Solmurry Demesne.

Sonjay Hilliard (SAWN-jay HILL-yard): Male Aoife, shirttail relative of Lord Ebric Hilliard, lives and works outside the Empyrean.

Teine of Solmurry (Tyne): IM Human, full-sibling of Leis and Samia, son of Selene of Solmurry and Lesmar of Solairn, grandson of Silvia of Solmurry, has been given as a gift, from Lord Solmurrian to his son, Marne Solmurrian, in celebration of Marne's Centennial.

Victor of Solmurry (VICK-tor): IM Human, friend of Teine and Marcus.

Vorogu and Volsney (VORE-oh-goo and VOLE-snee): Male Aoife twins, elder common-born Aoife men who have worked for Solmurry in an accountant/docent role since before Madric and Alain were born.

Vosh of Solmurry: IM Human, best friend of Teine, professional Fabal player.

Wallace of Solairn (WALL-iss): AM Human, semi-retired postmaster for the SPED at Solmurry.

Willis the True (WILL-iss): Female Holidocrith, highly decorated wartime mount for Lord Alain Solmurrian's father during the last Wiydon Isles invasion, works on the outlands of Solmurry as a shepherd.

About the Author

A long-time fan of sci-fi and fantasy, C.T. Griffith began developing the world of *The Gilded Shackle* in the 1980's as a setting to run Dungeons and Dragons games. She has a total of nine books planned for project, which will be the first of many other series set in the world. An avid tabletop roleplaying gamer and artist, she still plays and draws when she can.

Ms. Griffith lives in the Midwest with her three borzois. You can see a list of her other works and her upcoming publishing schedule at www.ctgriffith.com or find her on Facebook at www.facebook.com/author.ctgriffith.

www.ingramcontent.com/pod-product-compliance
Lightning Source LLC
Chambersburg PA
CBHW020557180626
46810CB00007B/2545